**END**

**Alan**

# Chapter 1

"Don't forget your hat," Andrius Poska warned his daughter. "It's freezing outside."

Claire took the bobble hat from its peg and jammed it on her head. "How do I look?" she asked.

"Pink," Andrius told her. It had suddenly become his daughter's favorite color, and he suspected it had something to do with a movie that had been recently released. Now, everything had to be pink, from the boots on her feet and the puffy jacket to the hat and scarf. He hoped she'd grow out of it by the time she turned seven.

"You look gorgeous," Sofija Poska said, stooping to kiss her daughter. "Like a delicious marshmallow." She made munching sounds as she buried her face in Claire's neck, causing an eruption of giggles.

"If you don't mind, I'm also starving,' Andrius smiled. "Can we go?"

He opened the front door and felt the full effect of February in Vilnius. A bitter wind bit at his exposed face, and Andrius pulled his collar up around his cheeks. It was the same every time they visited the city for Sofija's mother's birthday. Next year, he would invite her to spend her seventieth at the Poska residence in much sunnier California.

Andrius walked out into the street and waited for Claire and Sofija to leave the house before locking the front door. The plan was to go to the main shopping district to pick up some new shoes, then walk to the restaurant to meet the birthday girl.

That all changed in seconds.

The door of the van that was parked outside the house slid open, and three men wearing black balaclavas jumped out and brandished weapons. One of them grabbed Andrius by the collar and stuck a pistol in his face.

"Get in or you die right here!"

Andrius froze with shock. Even when his daughter was picked up and thrown in the van, he could not move. If he had a fight-or-flight mode, it failed to kick in. He could only watch, helpless, as his wife was dragged into the vehicle. When it was his turn, he offered no resistance. The gun at his head was enough to convince him to comply.

The door slammed shut and the vehicle sped off. Andrius was forced onto his stomach and his wrists were zip tied behind his back. The fear he felt was echoed in his daughter's eyes, but when he tried to move toward her, he was struck on the head with the butt of a pistol. He heard his daughter cry out as he fell to the floor of the vehicle, and one of his captors shouted for her to shut her mouth.

The man had spoken in Russian.

It was his third language, one he'd learned in school as well as English.

Before Andrius could ask himself what the Russians would want with him, the one-word answer flashed in his head:

Juggernaut.

His first thought was that he could never give it to them, but Andrius Poska was a smart man. It took him a matter of seconds to realize that his wife and daughter had been brought along for a reason. They would be used as leverage to ensure he gave them what they wanted.

He looked over at Sofija, his heart filled with dread. His one true love was comforting Claire, their bubbly, innocent daughter. He knew he would be forced to choose between them and the future of mankind.

Just the thought of having to do so filled him with dread.

# Chapter 2

"You sure you're gonna be okay?" Eva Driscoll asked as she handed Simon "Sonny" Baines the remote control for the wall-mounted widescreen TV.

"I'll be fine,' he assured her, arranging the sofa cushions until he was comfortable. "Tom will be here at lunchtime, and until then, I've got a series to finish on Netflix."

"Okay, but any problems, call me." She checked the time, then put on her coat and kissed him on the forehead. "I gotta go."

"Don't forget to ask them," Sonny said.

"I won't."

Eva headed out of the new apartment and took the stairs to the ground floor. She hated to leave Sonny alone in his weakened state, but at least there were no immediate threats of danger. That hadn't always been the case in recent years. Her battle with the shadowy Executive Security Office was over—for now, at least—and after she performed one last task for her former employers, she and Sonny would be able to start enjoying life again. The chest wound from the bullet he'd taken in Baton Rouge a couple of weeks earlier should have healed fully by then.

Outside, a dusting of snow carpeted the ground. More was forecast for the coming days.

Within a minute, her car arrived. The rear door opened, and Eva saw the tall figure of Richard Fernandez sitting in the back. She got in beside him.

"How's the apartment?" he asked Eva. "It's all we could find at such short notice."

"It's fine," she told him.

The deal she'd reluctantly agreed with the CIA's Richard Fernandez was for her to carry out one mission, scheduled for some time in April. In return, Eva would face no charges for her actions over the last ten days. She'd killed several men, all of whom deserved their fate, but courts rarely saw it like that. The FBI certainly hadn't. Given the choice of life without parole or putting her skills to good use one last time, Eva had chosen liberty.

According to Fernandez, President Charles Robson had disbanded the disparate black ops teams run by the CIA and other government agencies, and in turn created the National Interest Division. It was run from the White House, under the direct control of President Robson. Only he could sanction and authorize operations.

Eva was to lead the first of those missions.

"Did you make the arrangements I requested?" Eva asked.

She'd specified two actions that had to be taken before she would fully agree to participate. The first was to have her CIA file destroyed. Although a hard copy would remain in the archives, digital copies were to have been wiped. If that condition was agreed to, she wanted to be known as Nolene Daniels while working for the NID. It was the ID she'd been using for the last six months and one she had grown accustomed to.

"I told you at the time that CIA files are sacrosanct," Fernandez said. "The President agrees. However, he's agreed to transfer your file to the White House archive. They'll be sealed for the next thirty years. Is that acceptable?"

It wasn't what Eva had hoped for, but it was the next best thing. "It is," she said. "And my name?"

Fernandez handed her an ID card. "Nolene Daniels, as requested. Only myself, the President, and the Director of the CIA know otherwise."

At least it wasn't all bad news.

They rode the rest of the way in silence. Eva had no wish to engage in small talk, and she wasn't looking to make any new friends.

At the gate to the White House, Fernandez produced their IDs. The guard checked a printed list, looked at the occupants of the car, then raised the barrier.

The driver parked facing the treasury building, and Fernandez led Eva into the East Wing of the White House.

"First time?" Fernandez asked as they approached the security station.

"No, I've been pressured into killing people before."

"I meant first time at the White House."

"Oh," Eva said. "Yeah, first time."

They emptied their pockets and passed through metal detectors.

The building was as opulent as she'd imagined. A blood-red carpet trimmed with gold border covered most of the marble floor and ran the length of the hallway. She passed red-and-gold seating until they came to four columns that led to a foyer. In it sat an ornate grand piano. Busts as well as portraits of past occupants were dotted around the room.

"We're down here," Fernandez said, gesturing to a door flanked by two flags. The Seal of the President of the United States hung above the entrance. Eva followed him inside the room to an unmarked white door, and Fernandez pressed his ID against a scanner. There was a beep, and the door clicked open. Inside was a short passageway that ended at an elevator. He pressed the solitary button.

"The NID control center is located next to the President's Emergency Operations Center," Fernandez said as the car arrived and they got in. "It's a new setup, state-of-the-art."

The elevator dropped five floors, and they emerged in a hallway that branched in three directions.

"That's the EOC," Fernandez told her, pointing straight ahead. "To our right is the bunker, and we're down here."

He took Eva to the left, where there was a lone doorway. Fernandez once again scanned his ID, but he also had to undergo a retinal scan. The door buzzed and he pushed it open.

"Do I get security clearance, or will I be chaperoned every time I come here?" Eva asked.

"We've already set that up. We just need to get a scan of your retina for the database. We'll do that today."

Inside, the room looked impressive. A large screen covered the facing wall, showing a world map overlaid with wavey lines. Eva guessed they were satellite tracks. Four smaller screens surrounded it, two on either side. In the center of the room was a bank of five desks, each with an operative working from a three-screen setup. To the right were two glass-walled offices. Fernandez took her into the larger one, where two men in gray suits stood guard outside the door.

Three men sat around a large table that had seating for twelve, studying a series of photographs. There were a few more chairs up against the walls.

"Gentlemen," Fernandez said, "I give you Nolene Daniels."

President Charles Robson was the first to stand, and the other two quickly got to their feet.

"Glad to finally meet you," Robson said, offering his hand with a weary smile. He was seventy-one but didn't look a day over sixty. "Nice work on the cruise ship. Not many people could have pulled that off. You saved a lot of American lives, and for that I'm truly grateful."

Eva shook his hand, a confident grip as she would have expected from one of the most powerful people on the planet. Eva offered him a nod, nothing more. She wasn't there for the plaudits. Get in, do the job, get out.

"This is my Chief of Staff, Walter Caine," Robson said, gesturing to a man who looked to be a similar age but shorter than the President by almost a foot. "He heads up the NID and reports directly to me. You know Richard, of course." Robson said, gesturing toward Fernandez. "He's our CIA liaison. Most of our work will take place abroad, and we will utilize his assets where necessary."

The President turned to the other man in the room. He was the youngest of the group, maybe late forties, Eva guessed. Her eyes were drawn to the crescent scar, the size of a quarter, that marred his plump right cheek. "And this is Greg Sharpe, my national security advisor."

While Robson and Caine had firm handshakes, Greg Sharpe's was weak, his touch clammy.

"Pleasure to meet you," the portly man smiled. "I've assembled the finest support team available. They'll be your eyes and ears when you're out in the field."

Eva didn't share his confidence. It would be her life on the line, and it was essential that she had the utmost faith in the people watching her back. That was why she'd sounded out Farooq Naser and his girlfriend, Xi Ling, the day before. The couple had enough money to live comfortably for the rest of their days, but financial reward wasn't a factor in their decision. Eva and Farooq had been friends for a long time, and it was loyalty that swayed him. That, and his desire to prove that he was a better hacker and software developer than Xi Ling. Competition between the pair had been fierce since they'd met up the year before, and in her few brief conversations with Farooq over the last few months, it was clear that Xi Ling was still way out in front.

"I'd prefer to bring in my own people," she said.

Sharpe's pleasant demeanor evaporated. "Did you not hear what I said? These are the best people in the world. You won't find any better. Besides, there's no time to get them up to speed."

"What do you mean?" Eva asked. "I was told the mission was in eight weeks. That's plenty of time."

"That's on the back burner," the President said. "Something came in late last night that needs our urgent attention."

Eva's heart sank. The only redeeming aspect of this mission had been the amount of time available to plan it down to the last detail. Having to throw a plan together at such short notice made it all the more important to have a familiar support team backing her up. She was about to press the point when Robson abruptly left the meeting room. The others followed, and Eva had no choice but to fall in line.

"Bring up the Poska video," Robson instructed one of the techs. He turned to Eva. "This was recorded three months ago."

The large screen switched to a still image of a congressional committee. Nine senators were perched on a raised bench, and before them a man sat at a table. The video began playing.

"Ladies and gentlemen, thank you for allowing me to appear before you today."

"That's Andrius Poska," President Robson told Eva.

"Who is he?" she asked.

"Just watch and see."

\* \* \*

"Before I go any further, I should give you some background. I was born in Vilnius and moved to the United States when I was seven. I graduated MIT at the age of nineteen, and for the last two years I have been working for Camber Blair, the foremost name in cyber security. My role is to try to hack into client systems and then produce a report on any vulnerabilities that I find to help boost their security. I'm what's known as a white-hat, or ethical, hacker."

Poska poured himself a glass of water and took a sip.

"This committee was convened to assess both the benefits and risks of artificial intelligence," Poska said, "and so far, we've seen some exciting concepts that could revolutionize the way we work. I'd like to touch on a few of them, but before I continue, I'd be grateful if one of you could name an impenetrable government organization, one that has the strongest cyber security imaginable."

The senators looked at each other, all waiting for someone else to make the decision. Eventually, the representative from Houston spoke.

"NORAD."

"That's a good one," Poska said as he began typing on the laptop in front of him. "The front line of our aerospace defense." He looked up again. "And now can I have the name of a movie? Any movie. The Wizard of Oz, Top Gun, Gone with the Wind, anything."

"The Devil Wears Prada," the member for Utah offered.

"Thank you." Poska typed for a few more seconds, then sat back in his chair.

"So, the benefits of AI. Today, we've heard at length of the great potential to improve productivity and save lives, most notably in the healthcare system. AI will also help with climate modeling and the development of greener solutions to our energy needs. These could include designing jet engines that use less or no fossil fuel, or more efficient wind turbines."

Poska leaned into his computer, then looked up at the panel. "Could someone please get NORAD on the phone? Ask for the technical support team."

A senator motioned for an aide to handle Poska's request.

"As well as the benefits of AI," Poska continued, "we've also heard today about the dangers. Most of the concerns are around AI becoming too powerful, uncontrollable. Indeed, when asked to name a threat it poses, many people reference Skynet from the *Terminator* movies. At some point in the future, will AI deem humans irrelevant, or worse, an impediment? It's possible, but with safeguards we can prevent that.

"What hasn't been discussed today is what I consider the real danger of artificial intelligence, and that is the bad actor. As large language models become ever more prevalent, application programing interfaces, or APIs, allow us to tap into them and use the built-in algorithms to process our own data. Last year, the Spiez Laboratory heard from Sean Ekins at Collaborations Pharmaceuticals. He used AI to model new molecules that could be used to develop drugs to treat rare diseases. Until a few years ago, an existing molecule would have to be tweaked, then tested extensively to ensure it wasn't fatal to the recipient. Now, he can test millions of new molecules a day. When asked to give a presentation on the potential misuses of AI, he had the idea of flicking a switch in his algorithm, so that instead of creating life-saving molecules that were harmless to patients, it created the most toxic molecules possible. Within the space of a few hours, they were able to generate the blueprints for over forty thousand deadly new toxins. Some of these were more powerful, more lethal, than VX. You can all imagine the devastation that could be caused if that software fell into the wrong hands."

Poska checked his laptop again, then resumed.

"While that discovery should set alarm bells ringing, it is not the most dangerous use of AI. Senator Hall, do you have NORAD on the line?"

Hall's aide handed over a cell phone. "I do."

"Thank you. Please ask them to check the E drive on server NH34997OA. There should be a folder named Congress."

Hall spoke into the phone, then waited for a response. Eventually he declared that the folder existed.

"Ask them to open it and read out the name of the solitary file inside," Poska said.

Hall passed on the request, and his face fell as he got a response.

"Please tell us the name of the file, Senator."

Hall swallowed, then cleared his throat. "The Devil Wears Prada."

"Ladies and gentlemen, I hacked NORAD in a matter of minutes using just this laptop. I call the software Juggernaut, because once it starts rolling, it's merciless and unstoppable. In the wrong hands, you can't begin to imagine the devastation this could cause. Utility networks, financial centers, critical infrastructure such as air traffic control, all could be taken down within an hour. The country would cease to function. And it doesn't stop there. It could be aimed at our allies, too, leaving us defenseless in the face of military aggression."

Poska hit a few keys and watched a display on his screen.

"I created the software for good, just as Sean Ekins did. In this case, it was supposed to scan a vast knowledge base—a hacker's encyclopedia, if you will—and determine the best architecture to prevent a cyber attack. That could then be used as the base for future infrastructure deployments as well as recommending upgrades to existing technology, such as that used by NORAD. That software is still in its infancy, and it will be some time before we can develop a system that is a hundred percent secure, but that is the aim. When I saw Sean's testimony, I wondered if the same principle—use it for evil instead of good—could be applied to my software. Juggernaut is the answer."

"Mr. Poska," Senator Baldwin from Wyoming said, "That software should not be in civilian hands. When this session is over, I'd like you to surrender it to my aide."

"I agree on one point, Senator; it shouldn't be in civilian hands. Where we disagree is that it should be in *anyone's* hands, even yours."

"Are you refusing to hand that laptop over?" Baldwin bellowed.

Poska considered the question for a moment. "No, sir. When I've finished before you, your aide can have the laptop."

"Good," the Senator said, adjusting his jacket as a sign of victory.

Poska addressed the entire bench. "As I've said, this application of AI could bring a country to its knees in less than a day. Millions of people would be affected. In fact, potentially billions. Within hours, supermarket shelves would be stripped bare, and then the fight would be on for clean drinking water. The number of deaths would be astronomical, greater than any single event in history. I will not be a part of that."

Poska closed his laptop and pushed it to the front of the table. "Ladies and gentlemen, you asked about the dangers of AI. I've demonstrated one and told you about another. Please don't for one minute imagine that there are no more threats out there. I created Juggernaut in under nine weeks, and it would be foolish to think no one else is working on something similar as we speak. Unless AI is heavily regulated and development overseen by independent monitors, what you've seen and heard today will just be the start."

\* \* \*

Eva watched Poska stand, and the video ended.

She'd seen some things in her time, but nothing like that. If America's enemies were able to hack into one of the most secure systems on the planet in a matter of minutes, it would be more devastating than any conventional military attack. It was the worst dystopian nightmare waiting to happen.

"What's the issue?" Eva asked President Robson. "Is he trying to sell it to the highest bidder?"

Software like that would fetch billions on the open market, especially from those who wished harm upon the United States and her allies.

"No, he was true to his word," Robson replied. "He left his laptop on the table, but his last act was to wipe the hard drive using sophisticated software. Our best data-forensic people couldn't recover anything. He didn't want it falling into the wrong hands, and apparently that included ours. We enquired about backups, but he insisted he didn't have any. He said it was created to demonstrate the dangers of AI and it had served its purpose."

Eva liked Andrius Poska more by the second. "Then why are you telling me this, and what's so urgent?"

"Andrius Poska was kidnapped along with his wife and daughter two days ago," Caine said. "They were visiting the family home in Vilnius, Lithuania, when a van containing at least four suspects pulled up and they were bundled inside at gunpoint."

CCTV footage of the kidnapping appeared on the large screen. It was shot from the end of the street and images were grainy, showing little detail.

"Local police were informed when Poska and his family failed to show up for lunch with his mother-in-law. They performed a welfare check on the Airbnb house where they were staying, but it was empty. They told the mother they would have to wait two days before they could officially class them as missing, but she was persistent. She rang every ten minutes until they finally kicked into gear. Once the police checked nearby CCTV, they realized something was wrong. When they learned that Andrius Poska was an American citizen, they contacted the US Embassy and informed them of the investigation. That was when it was flagged to us. We've had Poska on a watch list since that Senate hearing."

"If the Lithuanian police are on it, why do you need me?" Eva asked.

Caine instructed one of the support team to bring up a photo.

"This is Viktor Sorotzkin," Caine said when the Slavic faced appeared on the big screen. Sorotzkin's black hair was shaved almost to the skin, and a scar ran across a nose that had been broken more than once. "The local police got a plate number from a nearby traffic camera and identified the van they were traveling in. It had been stolen the day before in Kaunas, sixty miles from the capital. Fortunately, the van's owner had CCTV at his home, and we got a good look at Sorotzkin."

"And…?" Eva asked.

"Sorotzkin is a known associate of Colonel Igor Cherenkov, who is suspected of heading up the GRU's Main Center of Special Technologies, otherwise known as GTsST, or Unit 74455."

Eva knew that the GRU was the Russian foreign military intelligence agency, but she'd never heard of this specific unit. "Will someone please get to the point?"

"Unit 74455 is their cyber warfare division," the president told her. "Now do you understand the urgency?"

Eva did indeed. If the Russians got their hands on Juggernaut, they could cripple the United States. "Are we one hundred percent sure Poska destroyed all of his copies?"

"We're working to ascertain that as we speak," Caine said. "A team is looking at every computer at Camber Blair as well as at Poska's California home. We checked the airport video, and he took a laptop with him on his trip to Vilnius. The Lithuanian police said one was recovered from the Airbnb he was staying at. A team is en route to Vilnius to check it out."

Even if all traces of Juggernaut had been destroyed, that still left the knowledge inside Poska's head. If he'd been able to create the software from scratch in nine weeks, he'd no doubt be able to replicate it a lot quicker. She shared that thought with the others.

"We came to the same conclusion," Caine said, "which is why we must move quickly."

"To be more specific," the President said, "you must move quickly."

Now that Eva knew the nature of the mission—rescue rather than assassination—she wasn't so angry about the short planning window. She was, however, more determined to get Farooq and Xi Ling on board.

"Will do, Mr. President, but first I need to bring in my own people."

"I already told you," Sharpe said, "these are the best of the best."

"They're not," Eva insisted, "and I'll prove it. Name a state."

Sharpe looked like he was going to explode, but President Robson put a calming hand on his shoulder. "Hang on, Greg. I want to see what she has."

Sharpe exhaled angrily. "Utah."

Eva took out her cell phone.

"That's a security breach," Sharpe said. "No cell phones in the NID."

"Fine," Eva said. "After I prove my point, I'll hand it over."

"It won't work," Fernandez told her. "There's a Faraday cage around the entire bunker. No signal gets in or out. Wait here a second." He went to one of the offices and brought out what looked like a cell phone, but with a wire dangling from the bottom. He plugged it in to a nearby console. "This works like a normal cell, but uses our encrypted hard line."

Eva opened the messaging app and typed a message to Farooq. "Okay, now I need a county in Utah."

"How the hell should I know?" Sharpe growled, exasperated. "I'm not *National Geographic*."

"Davis County," one of the analysts suggested. When Sharpe glared at him, he looked sheepish. "My mom grew up there."

"What's your name?" Eva asked him.

"Paul. Paul Heaton."

"Okay, Paul Heaton. Find me a website for one of the court houses in Davis County."

"Sure thing." He turned back to his computer and typed on his keyboard. Seconds later, he sat back. "Done."

"Now get me a list of cases from… Mr. President, pick a year, please."

"Twenty-oh-four," Robson said.

Eva added that information to her message. "Paul, a list of cases from two thousand and four."

It took a few seconds for Paul to get the list on the screen.

Eva asked Caine to choose one from the list.

He went to the screen and leaned in close. "Evans versus Donaghue."

Eva typed that into the message along with the information she required, then sent it to Farooq.

"Paul, please get me the social security number of the clerk who filed that case."

He looked confused. "Their social security number? What do you need that for?"

"That's the first reason my people are better," Eva told Sharpe. "They don't ask questions. They just give me what I need."

Paul took the hint. He turned to his computer and typed furiously.

"Can we agree that the selection was random, with no input from me?" Eva asked Sharpe.

He harrumphed. "I suppose."

"Good. When my guy finds the answer before Paul, I get to choose my support team."

"Not gonna happen," Sharpe said. "We've got access to just about every relevant database in the country, and more besides. There's no way Paul is going to—"

The device in Eva's hand pinged. She opened the message, then showed it to Sharpe.

He looked furious.

"Got it!" Paul shouted triumphantly.

"Is it 528-34-3768?" Eva asked him.

Paul looked deflated. "That's right."

Eva turned back to Sharpe. "Please arrange security passes for Farooq Naser and Xi Ling Xiang. They'll be here first thing tomorrow. And don't bother with background checks. You won't find anything."

"No way. We can't allow unvetted personnel access to the NID."

"Do it," President Robson said sternly. "We need the best people on this, and we can't afford to be held up by bureaucracy. Time isn't a luxury we can afford."

Sharpe looked furious, his glare directed at Eva. "Very well, Mr. President, but if this compromises our operation, I want my objections on the record."

"Duly noted," Robson said.

It was a small victory for Eva, but there was lots more work to be done. "Get everything you can on Unit 74455 for when I return," she told Caine. "I have a couple of things to take care of. I'll be back in two hours."

# Chapter 3

A pool car took Eva back to her apartment. On the way, she messaged Farooq and told him that he and Xi Ling were now seconded to the CIA. He responded by saying they'd be at Dulles on the first flight in the morning. Eva told him a car would be waiting, then turned her thoughts to Sonny.

Her plan had been to help him in his recovery from the gunshot wound, building his strength over the coming weeks in the hope that he might be able to join her on whatever mission had been planned for April. Instead, he was going to have to fend for himself for the next few days. He still didn't have full mobility in his right arm, and heavy lifting was out of the question. As long as he was capable of ordering pizza and wiping his own ass, he would be okay.

When she walked into the apartment, Tom Gray and his young daughter Melissa were already there. Gray had promised to keep Sonny company most days, and he'd found an apartment close by so that he could pop in when needed.

"You're back early," Sonny said. He was sitting at the table and playing cards with Melissa. Gray was in the kitchen, stirring a pot.

"Change of plan," Eva told him. "Something urgent came up. I'll probably have to head out this evening."

"What is it?" Gray asked. He'd scooped soup into three bowls, and he offered one to Eva.

21

She declined his offer. "A US citizen has been kidnapped in Lithuania. I have to go and bring him home."

"Sounds like a waste of your skillset," Gray said. "Can't the local police handle it?"

"It's… complicated," Eva told him, nodding her head toward Melissa.

Gray took the hint. "Darling, can you give us a few minutes?"

Melissa didn't look pleased at being excluded from the conversation. "Fine. But no looking at my cards while I'm gone," she said to Sonny.

"Scout's honor," he replied, flicking off a three-fingered salute.

When Melissa closed the bedroom door after her, Eva sat opposite Sonny. Gray joined them at the table.

"The guy I'm looking for is a hacker, and we can't allow what he's created to get into the wrong hands."

She explained the video she'd seen, as well as the evidence pointing to Russian state involvement.

"No wonder you didn't want Melissa to hear that," Sonny said. "That's gonna give *me* nightmares, never mind her."

Gray concurred. "That would be catastrophic," he said. "Modern civilizations can't cope without power and water, never mind a broken supply chain. It'll be absolute chaos."

"It'll be worse than that," Eva sighed. "You ever see people fighting over sneakers at a Black Friday sale?"

Gray nodded.

"Then imagine they're fighting for the last fresh food in the city. Or the last clean water."

"Government wouldn't be able to function without power," Sonny agreed. "They couldn't address the nation or co-ordinate law enforcement in any meaningful way. We'd be in a state of anarchy within twenty-four hours."

"The Russians wouldn't have to fire a single shot," Gray added. "They could just press a button and sit back while America tears itself apart."

"That's why I have to get Poska out of there," Eva said.

"Or kill him," Sonny offered, drawing a strange look from Gray.

"Seriously?"

"Sonny has a point," Eva said. "The objective is to make sure the Russians don't get their hands on Poska's Juggernaut software. If that means killing him, it would be his life against three hundred million others. Including yours and Melissa's," she added.

Gray had to concede that point.

"Anyway, I gotta go. I just came back for some warm clothes. Russian winters are even colder than DC's."

"Do you want me to go with you?" Gray asked.

Eva was surprised by the offer. He'd fought alongside her several times, but always reluctantly. His priority was being there for his daughter, and rightly so. "Why would you want to?" she asked.

"Because Sonny can't go in his condition."

"And Melissa?"

Gray glanced toward the bedroom door. "We can't let that software fall into Russian hands. If that happens, there won't be a future for any of us. It's not that I don't think you can handle it alone, but it's better to have me with you and not need me, than need me and I'm not there."

"Thanks," Eva said, "but I have an idea that covers both bases. You three fly out to Vilnius. If I need you, you'll be close by. If I fail to find Poska and the Russians deploy

Juggernaut against the US, you won't be caught up in the middle of it."

"That makes sense," Gray said. "You up for it, Sonny?"

"As long as you carry my suitcase, yeah."

"Then that's settled," Eva said. "Book flights and a hotel, and let me know where you're staying."

"On it," Gray said. He sat down and took out his cell phone to make the bookings.

"Take your personal tracker," Sonny told Eva, "the one the ESO put in you. That way, we'll always know where you are."

"Good idea."

Eva opened the bedroom door and told Melissa she could come out, then went inside. She emerged minutes later with a carryall. She kissed Sonny, then gave Melissa a cuddle.

Gray settled for a wave. "Best of luck," he said. "We'll message you when we get there."

"We're going somewhere?" Melissa asked her father.

"Yeah. Lithuania."

"Lithu-what?"

"Lithuania. Check it out on your phone. Consider it your geography homework for today."

While Melissa searched, Sonny asked Eva how long she'd be gone.

"No idea, but don't wait up."

# Chapter 4

When Eva returned to the White House, Fernandez was waiting by the entrance.

"You don't have to escort me in," Eva said. "I'm a big girl. I know the way."

"I just wanted to give you a heads-up," Fernandez said as they walked toward security. "Greg Sharpe isn't someone you want to get on the wrong side of. I've had dealings with him in the past, and he's a vindictive sonofabitch."

"I think he should be more worried about getting on the wrong side of me," Eva replied. "But as I'll only be in his presence for another few hours at the most, I'll try to behave."

"What do you mean?"

She wanted to press the point that she was contracted for one mission only, but now was not the time.

"You said this was time critical, so I should be heading out tonight at the latest. Unless there's an alternative solution to this problem."

"Such as?" Fernandez asked.

Eva put her bag on the conveyor belt and emptied her pockets, then walked through the detectors. The light stayed green. When Fernandez joined her, she said, "I'll tell you when we get downstairs. The others need to hear it, too."

Three minutes later, they were in the NID operations center.

"Tell me about unit 74455," Eva said to Caine. "Specifically, where are they based?"

"We call them Sandworm," he said. "It's less of a mouthful. As for their location, it's a house in Khimki, about eleven miles northwest of central Moscow."

"Can you show me?"

"Sure." Caine spoke to an analyst, and moments later, an overhead image of a rural setting appeared on the main screen.

It wasn't a densely populated area, just a few other buildings in the immediate vicinity. The location didn't appear to be fortified, so it should be relatively easy to get in and out. First, though, Eva wanted to explore two other options.

"I take it a diplomatic resolution is out of the question?"

"That's correct," President Robson said. "If Poska had been arrested in Russia, that would be different, but the fact he was kidnapped by what appears to be members of the GRU in a third country means Moscow cannot acknowledge its involvement. We don't want to raise the subject with them, as that would let them know we suspect them, and they would no doubt make it impossible to find Poska."

"Then how about a surgical strike on Sandworm's headquarters?" Eva asked. "If Poska is dead, the Russians don't get Juggernaut."

"Out of the question," Sharpe said. "We need him alive."

"Greg's right," the President said. "As Poska mentioned at the committee hearing, he was developing software that would protect us against something like Juggernaut. Even if we rescue him, the Russians, and perhaps even the Chinese or North Koreans, will no doubt try to replicate Juggernaut in some way. We have to be ready to combat that."

"As for a military response," Caine added, "that's out, too. This calls for a discreet insertion and extraction."

"Then it looks like I'm going to Khimki," Eva said.

"It's not that easy," Caine said. "Sandworm is just one of the Russian assets that we monitor closely. In this case, we have three tiny cameras hidden in the trees surrounding the building." He asked for the coverage to be shown on the screens. "As you can see, we have the whole house covered. No one gets in or out without us knowing."

"And Poska wasn't taken there," Eva guessed.

"Correct."

It was going to be much more difficult than Eva had imagined. Before she could even think of snatching Poska from the Russians' grasp, she first had to find him in the largest country on the planet. At least they had a starting point.

"You said you're monitoring Sandworm, so you must have a list of all its members."

Caine spoke, and seven images appeared on the screen.

"Which of them are known to be in Khimki right now?" Eva asked.

"All of them apart from Igor Cherenkov and Maksim Baranov were there until early this morning. They left just after sun-up."

Those two faces appeared on the screen. Cherenkov had a round, pockmarked face under light brown hair that gave him the look of a young Boris Yeltsin. A mole stood out on his right cheek. He looked more like a taxi driver than a military hacker. Baranov was much thinner, with black hair cut close to his scalp.

"Do we know where these two are?" Eva wanted to know.

"No idea," Caine said. "If we had phone numbers, we could track their cells, but we don't even have that."

"Relatives?" Eva asked. "Friends? Acquaintances?"

"That will be in their files," Caine told her.

"Then I need a laptop, coffee, and a chicken sandwich."

* * *

Eva sat alone in the smaller glass office and ate while she pored over the files belonging to Colonel Igor Cherenkov and Major Maksim Baranov. Cherenkov, the head of Sandworm, had no listed relatives. He was an only child, and his parents had died in an automobile accident seven years earlier. He did have a list of known associates, though. One of them was Viktor Sorotzkin, the man who had stolen the van used to kidnap Poska and his family.

There was no cell number for Sorotzkin, but there was an address. She wrote it down. When she had the addresses of three more associates, she went to find Fernandez.

"Have you got any assets in Moscow that can put a watch on these homes?"

He studied the list. "I can requisition three at the most. Can you prioritize them?"

Eva crossed a name off the list, and Fernandez went to make some phone calls. When he returned, he assured Eva that surveillance would be set up within the hour. "They'll be designated Oscars One, Two and Three."

"Then I just need to get to Moscow," she said.

"I'll arrange a commercial flight."

"No, better if I do it myself."

Any purchases by the CIA for clandestine purposes would be made through dummy front corporations. If the Russians had a list of those companies and they saw an airline ticket purchase from one of them, it would raise flags.

"Besides," Eva added, "I don't want a direct flight. I'll land in Riga and sneak across the border."

"That's your call," Fernandez said. "You have complete mission autonomy, just as long as you work within operational boundaries."

"Those being?"

"Don't cause an international incident, and don't get caught. If you do either, you'll be disavowed."

# Chapter 5

Robert J. Portman chewed the last morsel of eggs benedict and stared through the window at the lush garden of his seventeenth-century mansion. His property stretched far beyond the horizon, and he saw his team of grounds keepers working diligently to maintain the expansive lawn.

He pushed his plate away, and one of three lingering Filipino servers immediately removed the dirty dish.

"Coffee," Portman barked. The silver pot was well within his reach, but pouring his own drinks was beneath a man of Portman's stature. He was old money, part of a dynasty that had spawned two US presidents and countless senators. He'd never done anything as menial as preparing his own breakfast, and he never would. He'd had servants since the day he was born, and even when his wife was alive, it was always the hired help who catered to his every whim.

A second server jumped to fulfill Portman's demand, then backed away to await further instructions.

Portman took a sip of the dark Colombian roast, then took out his cell phone and unlocked the screen. He was presented with his investment portfolio, which was much the same as it had been the previous day.

That would change in the not-too-distant future.

His other cell phone vibrated in his pocket. It was highly encrypted, and he only used it for two purposes. With a wave of his hand, Portman dismissed the servants and waited until they had scurried out of the room.

He hit the Accept button. "Go ahead."

"Good afternoon, sir. I was asked to call and inform you that your accommodation at Heliopolis is ready for inspection. Would you like to arrange a visit?"

The phone began to shake in Portman's liver-spotted hand, even though he had been expecting this call for some time now.

"Of course," he said, his trembling voice brimming with excitement.

"Excellent," the female voice said. "Would tomorrow work with your current schedule?"

*Would it ever.*

"Sure," Portman told her.

"Thank you, sir. I'll ensure that a plane is waiting for you at Dulles at—"

"No need," Portman jumped in. "I have my own plane. Just have someone meet me at Harry Reid at noon tomorrow."

*Might as well use the Lear Jet while I still can*, Portman thought.

"Certainly, sir. See you tomorrow at noon."

The call ended, and Portman slowly put the cell back in his pocket.

*Heliopolis.*

Portman hadn't come up with the name, but he had been instrumental in its creation. Heliopolis, the "City of the Sun," said to have been the place chosen by the phoenix to burn its own nest and rise from the ashes.

*And rise from the ashes we shall.*

Portman returned to his investment portfolio, though it was largely irrelevant now. His paper fortune stood at a shade over thirteen billion, the majority of it invested in companies around the world. Ten years earlier, when the idea of Project Phoenix had been floated, Portman had been one of the initial investors. He'd borrowed five billion from several lenders using his stock as capital. With that money, he'd purchased a one percent stake in TNR, or Trans Nevada Rail, a fledgling company formed to build a subterranean hyper-speed railway between Las Vegas and San Francisco. On paper, it seemed an outlandish proposition: half a trillion dollars to whisk people from the coast to the gaming capital of the world in less than thirty minutes, rather than a hundred minutes on a plane. There was no way such a company would ever become profitable, unless it charged fifty grand per person.

To the outside world, it was a dumb investment. To Robert J. Portman, it was the best five billion he'd ever spent. In his mind, money meant only one thing: power. And no one had more power than the ruler of a country.

It had been his destiny since he took his first breath. Great Uncle Herbert had held the position of President of the United States in the seventies, and Herbert's son Gerald cruised into the White House twelve years later. It was always known that Robert J. Portman was being groomed to continue the legacy, but politics had changed in the last couple of decades. Where once an indiscretion could be kept from prying eyes, an errant word dismissed or denied, the arrival of the internet had made things much more difficult.

His own past had come back to bite him on the ass.

Unknown to him, a speech he'd made at a private dinner function twenty years earlier had been recorded. At one time, he could have used his money and influence to ensure no newspaper editor or TV news producer would touch the story. That was no longer possible in the age of viral videos. Once his ultra-conservative views were made known to the world, his party abandoned him, fearful of a voter backlash. It mattered not that the party's views were closely aligned with his. They had become public. The ultimate sin.

Deprived of his ride in a two-horse race, Portman had been forced to campaign as an independent in the 2012 election. It had been a disaster from the get-go. Despite hiring numerous experts to publicly dismiss the recording as a fake, the mud stuck. His poll ratings never hit higher than two percent, and the few donors he had soon backed away, tired of throwing good money after bad. Portman had thrown in the towel.

Thirteen years on from that ignominious capitulation, Portman's lust for power remained as strong as ever.

This time, no one would be able to stop him.

# Chapter 6

General Franklin Sinclair stood with his arms behind his back and looked out of the window as a squad of recruits marched double-time to a tune he was all too familiar with.

Camp Weston, his fourth—and probably last—command in the greatest army the world had ever assembled. He'd never envisaged it ending like this. He glanced over at his calendar and noted eight days to go. Not that he needed reminding. It had been all he'd ever thought of since his last meeting with Xavier.

Xavier. The man who would change his life forever. The man who had seemingly entered his life quite by accident, though Sinclair now realized it was anything but chance. Xavier had chosen him.

The fateful day had been a fresh Sunday in May, almost three years earlier. Sinclair had just left his local church with his wife when the stranger approached and introduced himself.

"Xavier Cole, pleased to meet you."

"Franklin Sinclair. My friends call me Frank. This is my wife, Diana."

"The pleasure's all mine," Xavier said. He looked up at the church spire. "Magnificent. It's one of the reasons I chose to move here."

"Oh, new to the neighborhood?" Diana asked.

"Yeah. Just arrived yesterday, still feeling my way around."

"Well, Frank and I are just going for brunch. You're most welcome to join us."

"That's most kind," Xavier said. "I'd love to."

They drove to the restaurant in Sinclair's car, and on the way, Diana asked Xavier what he did for a living.

"Human resources. And yes, it's as boring as it sounds. What about you, Frank?"

"I serve," Sinclair said simply.

"He's a general in the United States Marine Corps," Diana added proudly. "Fifth Division, out of Camp Weston.

"A general? Well, thank you for your service, sir."

The words washed over Sinclair. He'd heard them a thousand times before. It wasn't thanks that he wanted; it was power. He had some authority as a brigadier general, but he'd never reach the heights he aspired to. It was amazing that he'd climbed as high as he had, given his propensity for butting heads with his superiors.

"I think a lot more people could use some of that discipline in their lives," Xavier said. "Kids these days care more about video games and social media than the fate of their country."

"Ain't that the truth."

Sinclair had seen the deterioration firsthand. Recruitment standards had significantly declined over the past twenty years, and this was borne out by the attrition rates.

"Where do you think this country's headed, Frank?"

It was a curious question.

"Personally," Xavier added while Sinclair considered his answer, "I think we're at a turning point. Back in the day, you worked hard and you got your reward. Youngsters these days seem to want everything handed to them on a plate. I see it at work every day. Mental health days, FMLA leave, scared to death of putting in a little overtime. I bet you weren't like that when you started out in life."

Indeed he wasn't. Sinclair had been brought up the right way. Strict parents, strong work ethic, determination to succeed. Only, that hadn't quite worked out as he'd hoped. A new breed of marine had infested his beloved corps. A gaggle of sycophants who would say and do anything for a promotion. Woke warriors who flew up the ranks by embracing radical ideology such as diversity, equality, and inclusion.

"The world ain't what it used to be," Sinclair admitted.

After that initial meeting, Xavier and Sinclair had met up every week for the next few months. It was some time in the fall when Xavier had made the proposal that would change Sinclair's life.

"A change is coming," Xavier said over beers one evening. They were in Sinclair's back yard after a weekend barbeque. "A complete reset."

"What makes you say that?" Sinclair asked, curious. He followed politics and had seen nothing on the horizon.

"Because the status quo isn't sustainable. Living standards are getting worse, and not just here in the US. I'm talking about the entire planet. There will come a point when the masses rise up and scream 'enough.' When that happens, the entire order collapses. Anarchy reigns."

"Then vote for politicians who will do something for the people. Isn't that what they're for?"

"Politicians are useless," Xavier said. "They do what their masters order them to do. Not a single law is written or passed without external input. Hell, most bills are written by the lobbyists themselves. No, the uprising is coming. It's just a matter of what America looks like in the aftermath."

"I can tell you what it looks like," Sinclair said. "Chaos. Armed gangs running everything. The cruelest will rise to the top and everyone else will either serve them or suffer. Basically, a return to slavery."

"Sounds about right," Xavier said. "And where would you be in this new hierarchy?"

"Me?" Sinclair asked.

"Yeah. Let's say the apocalypse happened tomorrow. What would you do?"

"Mobilize and protect the government." The words were automatic.

"Yeah, that's what your job description says. But what would you do in reality? Let's say, for example, that a million armed citizens marched on the Capitol, intent on overthrowing Congress. The police are overwhelmed, as are the National Guard, and you're called in. Would you kill a million Americans to protect those who caused this in the first place?"

"That's one hell of a hypothetical," Sinclair said, sipping his beer.

"I guess. But think of it this way. Once you killed that first million, do you think the rest of the country will just go back to accepting things the way they are, or do you think it would descend into civil war? The people versus the establishment? And for the avoidance of doubt, you'd be part of the establishment."

"I think civil war would be a firm possibility," Sinclair admitted.

"Okay, so you have… how many men and women in the armed services?"

"Around a million in the army, including National Guard and Reserves. Not sure about the navy and air force."

"Less than a million between them, and few would be any help at ground combat. But let's say for argument's sake that you have two million active, ready-to-fight soldiers. We don't, by the way. There are only around three hundred thousand. Against how many civilians? How many would be on your side after you'd gunned down civilians?"

"There wouldn't be many," Sinclair said truthfully. "A few patriots would be willing to defend the Constitution, but it wouldn't be even numbers on both sides."

"Exactly. Even if you got ten million to sign up, you'd still be outnumbered five, maybe even ten to one. There are eighty million gun owners in the US, and between them they have over four hundred million weapons."

"But we'd have the training and the firepower."

"You would," Xavier said. "You would indeed. And so you kill a hundred and ten million American citizens, destroying towns and cities along the way. A third of the population gone, mostly working-age men. Destruction in the trillions of dollars and no one left to help with rebuilding. A collapsed economy which has reverberations worldwide. Not much of a win, is it?"

"Are you saying we should let the people take over?" Sinclair asked.

"Not at all. If that happens, we're back to the anarchy I spoke of earlier. What I'm saying is, it's a no-win situation, and it's right around the corner."

"That kinda puts a pisser on the evening," Sinclair laughed.

Xavier clinked his bottle against Sinclair's. "Sorry, didn't mean to bring you down." He took a long pull from his beer and set it on the table. "There is an alternative, though."

"There is?"

"Indeed. We've tried to run the country according to the Constitution, and look where it got us. Corrupt politicians serving their own self-interest, while the citizens increasingly struggle to survive. End-stage capitalism eating its own tail."

"Are you suggesting a coup?" Sinclair asked seriously.

"Not at all. I'm saying a revolution is coming, and I suggest we just sit it out."

"Sit it out? You mean refuse to take orders when they come?"

"No, because there would be no orders." Xavier shifted in his seat. "Imagine this. The world shuts down for a year. No power, no water, no gas, no telephones or TV or internet. Nothing works. It's like we were transported back four hundred years. What do you think would happen?"

"Smart people would try to get things working again," Sinclair said.

"What if they couldn't? What if the software that runs the power station was deleted? Water pumps wouldn't work, and supplies would quickly run out. So would food and bottled water. It would be chaos."

"Rioting would start within hours," Sinclair agreed. "The army would be called in."

"Who would call them?" Xavier asked. "No phones, cell phones, internet, radio. No way to communicate with satellites. Do we have men on horses delivering notes to camp commanders? No. Everyone would be left to fend for themselves. Except, a few people were able to sit it out in their own little city that had everything they needed. Food, power, entertainment, medical facilities, everything we take for granted now. Of the two groups of people, which one would you choose to be with? The ones struggling to survive, or those waiting it out?"

"The question is, waiting for what?" Sinclair asked.

"For nature to take its course. Survival of the fittest. Which group would you want to be part of?"

"Hypothetically?" Sinclair asked.

"Hypothetically."

"The ones who were safe in their city. Only, they wouldn't be. Once someone discovered it, they would come under attack. Everyone would want their resources."

"What if the city was hidden and no one could find it?"

"Impossible," Sinclair scoffed. "It would have to be a completely new city, and no one could know it was under construction even while it was being built. Where is this hypothetical city? On top of a mountain? On a secret island?"

"Let's say, for argument's sake, that it's underground. A vast city with enough room for a hundred thousand people. Would you want to be a part of that, or take your chances on the surface? Again, hypothetically."

"First instinct is the hidden city, but I'd want to know the end game. What happens after most of the population dies off? Who runs the country then? How do they maintain law and order among the survivors?"

"Well, we've tried the three branches of government and that isn't working out well for most people. The rich are doing fine, but the other ninety-nine-and-a-bit percent are seeing their buying power eroded day after day, pushing us toward revolution. Maybe it's time for a new model. A single ruler. An emperor."

"You mean a king," Sinclair said.

"If you prefer that term. One man, with an army at his side. They round up any survivors and get them to work rebuilding the country. Some will join the army, while the rest will work for the common good. Tend crops, build houses, run childcare, staff the hospitals. Everything we do now."

"Sounds idyllic, but something tells me there's a catch. The currency will have crashed, for one. What do we pay these people?"

"Nothing," Xavier smiled. "Everything will be provided. Those who live out the year in the city will get the best housing, free childcare and medical, free food and drink, free entertainment, free vehicles. Everything the middle class could want, all for free."

"And everyone else? The survivors?"

"They'd get free food and housing, too," Xavier said. He finished off his beer and fished another from the cooler.

"Sounds familiar," Sinclair said. "Four hundred years ago we had a certain group of people who worked all day, and in return they got free food and housing. Back then it was called slavery."

"I prefer to call it contributing to society. Those who choose not to would be free to go out on their own. There could be a small parcel of land just for them. Maybe one of the Carolinas. Perhaps even Florida."

Sinclair chuckled and popped open another beer. "It's all fanciful stuff. Thankfully, the American people are a lot more resilient than you give them credit for. It'll take a lot more than a bit of inflation to start a revolution."

Looking back on that conversation from two years earlier, Sinclair could see that the seed had been planted. Over the next few weeks, Xavier hadn't brought up the subject again, but he had asked some very strange questions about choices Sinclair would make. Always hypothetical. He now knew that Xavier had been testing him, trying to decipher his true character. That was what led to their final conversation.

"So how come you stayed a brigadier general for so long?" Xavier asked during one of their regular Sunday get-togethers. "Why no second star?"

"Oh, I wanted it, all right, but these days, the only way to get on in the Marine Corps is kissing ass. It's not who you know, it's who you blow. When I got bullshit directives, I pushed back. Others just swallowed the shit they were shoveling. Those others got the second and third and fourth stars. I wasn't going to compromise my morals or my values."

"A man of integrity," Xavier smiled. "I like that. But let me ask you something. Remember we spoke about an apocalypse a few weeks ago?"

Sinclair had thought about little else. "I do."

"What would you say if you were offered a fifth star to run the entire army in the new world?"

"I'd jump at it," Sinclair said without hesitation.

"You'd let tens of millions of Americans die?"

"I've done my research. In the next twenty years, roughly sixty million are going to die, anyway. Through old age, lack of healthcare, poor diet. We currently lose three million a year from these things, and they're only going to get worse. As the public cuts back on luxuries, businesses earn less and therefore send less in taxes to the treasury. This inevitably means cuts to social programs or higher taxes, both of which impacts the poorest hardest. If the elderly don't have enough to eat or stay warm, more of them will die. If young couples can't afford to have kids, they'll grow old with no one to support them in their retirement. I think you're right about a revolution coming. I'd say we have another ten to fifteen years at the most."

"Four," Xavier said.

That was a strangely specific response. "What makes you say that?"

"It's the timeline we set," Xavier said flatly. "In four years, a state of emergency will be called by a president of our choosing. He will do something so egregious that millions will take to the street to protest it. The president will invoke martial law and curfews and order all communications cut to prevent the spread of disinformation. Once that's in place, federal agents will go into every power station and utility company and destroy the equipment that runs them. Once the power goes out and the water stops flowing, panic will set in. By that time, you and I—and your family, of course—will be in the new city that's now under construction."

"You mean… this is real?"

"Real as I'm sitting here," Xavier confirmed.

"But I thought we were just spitballing."

"You might have been, but I've been gauging what kind of man you are. To see if you're the right fit, as it were. And you are. You're just the man we need."

"And if I was to say I was lying all this time?" Sinclair demanded.

"You weren't. I know you. It's my job to know you, and I'm very good at what I do. If I had any doubts, we would have stopped talking a long time ago, but you fit every criterion." Xavier began counting off on his fingers. "You crave power, you love your country and want the best for its people, you want the best for your family. Do I need to go on?"

"You forgot my oath to the Constitution," Sinclair reminded him.

"A document written over two hundred years ago, one so flawed that it had to be amended twenty-seven times. How does it begin? 'We the people'? And how exactly are the people doing under the Constitution? Not great, as we've established over recent weeks. It's time for change, Frank, and we want you guiding the way."

"What you're suggesting is treason," he said, not even convincing himself.

"It'll only be treason if there's anyone left to prosecute you. You think a soft-handed city lawyer is going to last two minutes once the lights go out? Anyway, treason is a matter of law, but laws aren't always right. The people who hid Anne Frank were breaking the law. The people who found her and sent her to die in Bergen-Belsen were following the law. Which of them was right, hmm?"

Sinclair couldn't argue with that.

"I don't need to sell it to you," Xavier continued. "You're either in or out. I know you'll make the right choice."

"And if I don't choose to join you?" Sinclair asked. "If I choose to take this to the authorities, what then?"

"This is the last time you see me. If you go to the authorities, they'll either think you've gone insane, in which case you lose your commission, or they believe you. They'll do their digging and find that I don't exist. *Then* they'll think you're insane. Either way, you're out on your ass, and in four years' time you have to explain to your family that you could have made them safe but chose pride over them. As I said, your choice, but I know what you're going to say."

Sinclair was furious that Xavier knew him so intimately. Of course, he wasn't going to refuse such an offer. To keep his family safe from a dystopian nightmare? To command an entire army when his career looked to have stalled? It was a no-brainer.

"So what do you need me to do?"

Xavier smiled. "Find four thousand men that you can trust. Men who will follow your orders unquestioningly."

Sinclair wasn't sure he heard him correctly. "Did you say four *thousand?*"

"I did indeed. We're looking for thirty thousand in total, but the rest will come from other bases dotted around the country. Ideally, we want single men with no immediate family. Space is limited."

# Chapter 7

Andrius Poska had no idea how long it had been since he and his family had been snatched from outside his home, but he guessed it was at least a couple of days. In that time, his captors had barely spoken to him. In fact, the only time they had was when the van stopped in the middle of the countryside. Everyone had been ordered to get out, and Poska saw two other cars parked close by. Sofija and Claire had been taken to one of them, but when Poska tried to join them, a gun was thrust in his face.

"Not you."

Poska ignored the threat and tried to run after his wife and daughter, but felt a vicious blow to the back of his head. He collapsed and everything went black.

When he woke, he realized he was in the back seat of the second car, rolling down a narrow country road. Just Andrius, the man who had hit him, and the driver.

They soon reached a border crossing. Poska thought this might be his salvation, especially when a border guard poked his head inside the window and looked him in the eye.

It wasn't to be.

The guard accepted the roll of notes offered by the driver, and the car rolled into Belarus, leaving Poska in even deeper despair. Now that they were no longer in Lithuania, it would be much harder for the police to track him down. There was no love lost between the two countries, so he couldn't rely on any cross-border cooperation.

Things got worse eight hours later. They'd stopped for gas and sandwiches outside Minsk, then continued east until they hit the border with Russia. Leaving Belarus was even easier than entering it. The four-lane highway took them from one country to another without so much as a checkpoint. It was at this point that Poska lost all hope.

It wasn't long after entering Russia that the hood had been placed over Poska's head. It made the air stifling, and it played havoc with his claustrophobia. Worse, it remained on for around an hour, until the car stopped and rough hands dragged him out of the vehicle. He tried listening for sounds that might give him an indication as to where he was, but there was nothing but the howl of a biting wind. That faded as Poska was pulled inside a cavernous building. He knew this because of the echoing footsteps. He further surmised that if it had a roof, it was leaking, because every now and again his feet would squelch in shallow puddles. The pervasive smell of damp and rust assaulted him. The place was huge, judging by the amount of time it took to reach the stairs. Ominously, they went down.

Poska hated basements.

His claustrophobia went into overdrive, weakening his legs and causing him to stumble. His captors effortlessly held him upright as they took him further underground. When they reached the bottom, Poska heard a lock turn and a door click open. He was moved forward a few more steps, then the hood was finally removed as the door slammed shut behind him.

He blinked as his eyes adjusted to the light, then again as he tried to comprehend what he was seeing. He'd imagined squalor, with moldy walls and puddles on the floor. Instead, it was surprisingly dry and fresh, probably because of the dehumidifier in the corner. In the middle of the room was a desk set up with three screens connected to what looked like a high-spec laptop.

Poska felt the zip ties being cut, and he rubbed his wrists.

"Sit," a man said in Russian, and pushed Poska toward the desk.

He turned. This was someone he hadn't seen before. If Poska had come across him in a supermarket, he wouldn't have considered him a threat in any way. The man looked like he spent a lot of time at a desk, his skin pale, his belly straining under his T-shirt. Poska felt his eyes drawn to the large mole on the man's cheek.

"What do you—"

Poska didn't see the punch coming. The fist was a blur before it struck him high on the cheek, and Poska's head snapped sideways as he stumbled into the wall and collapsed to the floor.

"Lesson one," the newcomer said in Russian, "I speak, you obey. Instantly."

So much for first impressions.

The two men who had brought Poska into the facility picked him up and dropped him in the chair.

"I saw the demonstration you did for the American senators," his attacker said. "I want Juggernaut. Log into your server and give me access."

Poska's fears were confirmed. If the man with the mole didn't get what he wanted, Poska could expect more violence. If Poska did as Mole Man demanded, then Western world would be in mortal danger.

There was worse to come.

"Do as I say if you ever want to see your family again."

That was the threat Poska had been dreading. Deep down, he knew he couldn't do anything that caused harm to his wife and daughter. On the flip side, he couldn't give Mole Man what he wanted.

For one simple reason.

"It doesn't exist," Poska said, and flinched in anticipation of another beating.

"What do you mean? I saw it with my own eyes."

"I destroyed it," Poska told him. "I didn't trust anyone with the software, not even the Americans."

Mole Man took out his cell phone. "You lie." He hit a preset number and waited for the call to connect.

"*Da*," a gruff voice answered.

"Break the little girl's finger," Mole Man said.

"Which one?" the voice asked.

"Any."

"No!" Poska shouted. "Wait!"

Mole Man spoke into the phone and said to hold off. "What?" he asked Poska.

"I… I can recreate it," Poska replied. Whether he could or not was a moot point—he would never give it to this man. All he could do was hope to stall his captor and find a way to alert his friends back in the United States that he was in dire trouble.

If he failed, he really would be.

"I don't believe you destroyed it," Mole Man said, and put the phone back to his ear.

"I did!" Poska screamed. "I told the senators that no one should have it, and I meant it. The only copy was on that laptop, and I wiped it before I gave it to them."

Mole Man considered this for a moment, then spoke into the phone. "I'll call you back."

Poska felt a weight lift off his chest, but his ordeal was far from over. He'd bought himself some time, but that was all.

"You have one week."

Poska looked at the Russian incredulous. "That's impossible!"

"Nothing is impossible. You just need motivation. The men watching your wife and daughter have voracious sexual appetites. Dmitri in particular likes them young. Think about that as you work."

The man turned and walked to the door.

"One week," he said over his shoulder. "I suggest you get started."

Andrius Poska watched the three men leave, then stared at the door that had closed behind them.

One week was, as he'd said, impossible. When he'd created Juggernaut, he'd had a vast library of ready-made components that he could tweak and plug in. Now, he would have to create them from scratch.

Unless…

He opened the laptop, praying for an internet connection. There was none. He checked for local signals that he could piggyback onto, but again came up empty.

*Think!*

The surest way out of this mess was to alert his people back home what had happened to him and where he was, but without a connection to the outside world, that plan was a non-starter.

*So get one*, he told himself.

That was easier said than done. It wasn't as if he could just ask for one…

… or could he? He would need to remote into his company servers to access the libraries he needed. Surely they would grant him access on that basis alone.

*Put yourself in their shoes. What steps would they take to stop you contacting the outside world?*

It was a good question, and Andrius Poska focused on answering it.

\* \* \*

Igor Cherenkov waited until the door closed behind him, then cursed. This was supposed to be a simple operation: get Poska to remote into his server and download the software, then kill him and his family. Now it looked like stretching out to a week at the very least, and the facility wasn't set up for that.

"Get four cot beds in here," he told Pyotr, one of the men who had kidnapped Poska and his family. "Also, some heaters, cooking facilities, and two chemical toilets. Put one in his closet. Vasili, we'll need food and water for seven days."

"How do I pay for them, sir?" Pyotr asked.

Cherenkov handed him an untraceable prepaid credit card. "Use that."

There was more to do. Lots more. If Poska was going to recreate the software, he would need to test it, and that would require internet access, which was akin to handing him a phone and inviting him to call for help. He would have to put measures in place to prevent that happening. He couldn't stand over Poska for a straight week, so he would need to install software to monitor what the man was doing. The only time he would stand over him was when granting internet access to make sure Poska didn't try to contact anyone.

Cherenkov didn't like it one bit.

Still, there was no point complaining. His boss was already going to be displeased with developments. Cherenkov's griping wasn't going to make the situation any better.

He took out his burner cell phone and initiated a secure video call to the first deputy director of the GRU.

"General, there has been a development."

"A positive one, I hope," General Vasili Turgenev replied in his usual no-nonsense manner.

"Unfortunately, no."

Cherenkov explained what Poska had told him and his planned workaround, then awaited the general's wrath. He was surprised when it didn't materialize.

"That is unfortunate," Turgenev said calmly. "I will report to the joint chiefs and get back to you. In the meantime, ensure Poska gets to work."

"Yes, sir."

Cherenkov ended the call, feeling something was amiss. General Turgenev was the hardest of hard asses. To meekly consent to giving Poska time to replicate the software was out of character.

It was almost as if he'd been expecting that scenario.

Cherenkov cast the thought aside. What the General did or didn't know was way above his pay grade. He should just be thankful that he hadn't received a dressing down.

As long as there were no more surprises, Juggernaut would soon be in his hands.

# Chapter 8

General Vasili Turgenev ended the call and instructed his driver to take him to the office of the Chief of the General Staff. The detour would mean he would have to rush to get ready for the opera later that evening, but matters of state security came before his wife's wishes.

When they arrived at the general staff headquarters on Znamenka Ulitsa, the driver took them through the security checkpoint and pulled up at the entrance to the building.

"Wait here," the General said. "I won't be long."

He walked inside and placed his pass on the scanner. The turnstile clicked, and Turgenev stepped through. Three minutes later, he emerged from the elevator and strode to Admiral Yevgeny Komarov's office.

"Is the Admiral free?" Turgenev asked Komarov's secretary.

Getting an affirmative reply, Turgenev knocked on the door and walked in.

"Vasili," Komarov said, rising from his chair. The fifty-year-old's tunic was unbuttoned, the left side festooned with medal ribbons. Everything else about him was immaculate, from his short gray hair to his manicured fingernails. "I was just about to call you."

"You were?"

"Yes. A troubling development. Please, sit."

Komarov gestured to the sofa that faced an oak coffee table, and Turgenev took a seat. The Admiral slumped into his favored armchair opposite. It was slightly higher so that he sat above his visitors. A well-known dominance technique that Turgenev also employed.

"The Americans know we have Poska," Komarov said.

That was indeed a troubling development. "I'm sure the President will be able to stall them long enough for us to achieve our objective," Turgenev said. "As we suspected, Poska destroyed his only copy, but I've been assured he can replicate it within a week. If we can hold the Americans off that long—"

"It's too late. They already sent someone."

Turgenev frowned. "They didn't go through diplomatic channels?"

"We never expected them to, but then we never envisaged being in this situation, either. If your men had covered their tracks, we wouldn't be."

The meaning was clear: if this went badly, the blame would rest squarely on Turgenev's shoulders.

"Who did they send?"

"A woman," Komarov said. "Nolene Daniels. She lands in Riga in the next hour, and has asked that a motorcycle be readied in preparation for crossing the border shortly afterward."

"A woman? Then they can't be serious about getting Poska back."

"I was told not to underestimate her. I think it would be wise for you to take the same approach."

Despite the Admiral's warning, Turgenev doubted a lone female would put a dent in their plans. "I have people in the area. They will make sure she never reaches the Motherland."

"As I said, don't underestimate her."

"I won't," Turgenev lied. He would send three men. That would be more than enough.

"The Americans also suspect Colonel Cherenkov of being behind the kidnapping. It seems one of his men was careless and was identified when he stole the getaway vehicle. That is despite your assurances that the kidnapping couldn't be traced back to us."

While Komarov appeared concerned at this development, Turgenev was downright angry. Cherenkov had assured him that all precautions would be taken. Instead, the fool had left a trail for the Americans to follow.

"Do they know where Poska is being held?"

"No," Komarov said. "I've been told that Daniels will be looking for known associates of Cherenkov and Maksim Baranov as her starting point."

"As I said, she won't make it into Russia."

"That may be the case," Komarov said, "but if she is eliminated, the Americans will not just give up. They will send someone else to follow the trail. It is better to sever any links to Cherenkov and Baranov."

"You want them killed?" Turgenev asked.

"No. That would alert the Americans. Hide them. Round them up and take them to a secure location, but don't make it obvious."

"That sounds more like a job for the FSB," Turgenev argued.

"Indeed, but the fewer people involved in this operation, the better."

That made a lot of sense. "Then consider it done," Turgenev said.

Komarov sipped his tea then placed the cup back on the table. "Will Poska be able to deliver in so short a time?" he asked.

"The thought of losing his family will spur him on," Turgenev said, "but even if he goes over by a few days, it is of no consequence. Once I take the steps you outlined, there will be no way to find him."

"Yes, you assured me of that when we first discussed this idea, but I am still concerned that the Americans might be able to trace the attack back. After all, they have rightly pointed the finger at us for several ransomware episodes in the past."

"Those were from static installations," Turgenev pointed out. "This time we will use satellite phones as Wi-Fi hotspots, and Poska will only access the internet for short periods. Cherenkov will drive him many miles from the facility to enable Poska to test the software before a full deployment, and no one will be able to trace it back to a pinpoint location."

Admiral Komarov chewed that over for a moment. "Very well. Deal with Daniels and round up anyone who might be associated with Cherenkov and Baranov. Keep me updated."

Turgenev rose, knowing the meeting was over. "Yes, sir."

He left the building and returned to his car. He instructed his driver to take him home, then closed the partition between himself and the front seats before taking out his cell phone. He selected the number for Colonel Roman Galkin, who ran a covert electronic intelligence unit in Riga.

"Galkin."

"It's General Turgenev."

He could almost hear the Colonel snap to attention.

"Yes, sir! How can I assist you?"

"An American woman will be landing in Riga within the hour. Her name is Nolene Daniels. I want her eliminated as soon as possible."

There was silence for a moment. "But… General, that's not what we do—"

"You are an officer in the Russian army!" Turgenev bellowed. "Do I really need to spell out the punishment for disobeying a direct order?"

"No, sir! I was just pointing out that—"

"I know what you were going to say, Galkin, but this is a matter of urgent national security, and there simply isn't time to get other assets in place. This has come from the very top. Do you understand?"

"Yes, sir."

"Good. Take two men with you, and try to make it look like an accident."

Turgenev ended the call before Galkin could raise any further objections. His next call was to his deputy. He would have preferred the FSB to round up the associates of Cherenkov and Baranov, but the Admiral was right: better to keep this in-house.

"Alexey. Meet me at my house in forty minutes."

# Chapter 9

At just after four in the afternoon local time, Eva passed through immigration and customs without issue. She had been issued a genuine passport in the name of Nolene Daniels, and it had raised no suspicions.

She wheeled her small suitcase out into the cold. The luggage contained two changes of clothes, her backpack, and the now useless tablet she'd been given in NID. It had contained the digital files for Andrius Poska, as well as the Russians accused of kidnapping him. Nothing she read offered much help. Eva had clicked an icon at the top of the screen, and the sanitization software had worked its magic, erasing the files and overwriting the hard drive a thousand times to make it impossible to retrieve the information.

It was her first time in Riga, but the Latvian airport was much like any she'd visited. A row of taxis waited to overcharge unsuspecting foreigners, but Eva had other arrangements. She crossed the road and took the stairs down to the lower level, where more taxis and buses waited. Beyond them, a car park was half full.

Eva checked her phone. There was a message from Farooq on Shield, the encrypted app he'd created and which only a handful of people had access to.

*Hope you had a safe flight. Heading into the WH now. Be on comms once we're set up.*

It had been sent an hour ago, which made it just after eight in the morning DC time.

"Nolene?"

The woman who was asking was blonde, her hair tied in a ponytail. Eva guessed her age at about thirty. Richard Fernandez had told Eva to expect her.

"Yeah," Eva said. "You must be Sandra."

"Actually, it's Julia."

That was the response Eva was hoping for. If the woman hadn't corrected her, Eva would have known the mission was already compromised. It was highly unlikely that the Russians knew about her visit, but little details like this could save her life.

Eva couldn't quite place the accent, but she was definitely American.

"Sorry," Eva said to the CIA asset. "Long flight."

Julia led Eva to her car, a modest sedan that looked a couple of years old and wouldn't attract attention.

Eva approved.

"I got everything on your shopping list," Julia said as they drove out of the airport. "The bike is legitimate, as you specified, and there's a spare set of Russian plates for when you cross the border."

That was good news. The last thing Eva wanted was to be pulled over for riding a stolen motorcycle. "And the other items?"

"There's a knife, three concussion grenades, the night vision glasses, plus the Sig Sauer P226 with SWR Trident suppressor you asked for. I've given you four spare twelve-round mags and sixty rounds of nine-millimeter. Let me know if you want anymore."

"That's fine," Eva told her. If she ever got in a situation that required more ammunition, she'd probably already be dead. "The weather forecast for the next couple of days says freezing temperatures."

"That sounds right. Clear skies, but daytime temperatures around zero Celsius. Tonight, it's forecast to be minus eight. With windchill and riding a bike at speed, it'll feel more like minus twenty to minus thirty. I got you a set of black leathers. Hopefully that'll help with the cold."

"Thanks." Eva had anticipated inclement weather and had purchased a set of electric heated thermal underwear on the way to the airport. The leathers were a welcome touch, though.

It didn't take long to reach the industrial area just outside the Latvian capital. As they approached a garage, Julia hit a button and the metal shutters began to rise. She drove inside, and the shutters closed once more.

Eva got out and found a light switch. A fluorescent strip flicked into life. Before her sat the motorbike, a KTM 450 SX-F. Capable of reaching over a hundred and twenty on a flat road, it was equally comfortable offroad. Julia had already used black tape to cover up the bike's standard orange fairing and seat. On a nearby workbench Eva saw the other items she'd requested.

"There's a cot in the back if you want to grab a few hours before you set off," Julia told her.

Eva took the thermal underwear from her suitcase, attached the USB connector, and plugged it into a wall socket. While it charged, she put her spare clothes in her backpack.

"Thanks, but I slept on the plane. Coffee would be good, though. White, no sugar."

"Coming up."

Julia left the garage through a side door, and Eva got to work checking the equipment the CIA handler had provided. She wiped each of the 9mm rounds of ammunition so that the shell casings couldn't be tracked back to her if she got in a firefight and didn't have to time to retrieve them. Eva then filled the five magazines before stripping the pistol. She was pleased to see that it was clean and well maintained. The NVGs were fully charged, and when she removed the knife from its scabbard, she found it sharp enough to split hairs.

Julia returned ten minutes later with two Styrofoam cups and a brown paper bag. She offered it to Eva, who opened it and found three sticky cinnamon swirls.

"Thought you might need some energy," Julia said.

"Thanks." Eva took a sip of her coffee to test the temperature, then gulped down half of it. She swallowed the first pastry in two bites, suddenly realizing how hungry she was. The other two disappeared just as quickly.

"Can I get you anything else?" Julia asked.

Eva licked her fingers clean, then started to squeeze herself into the leather one-piece. "Thanks, but I need to make a start." She zipped up the leathers, threw her bag onto her back, then jammed the helmet on her head.

Julia pressed a button to raise the shutters, and Eva kicked the engine into life.

"Best of luck."

Eva flicked a salute in reply, put the bike in first, and eased out the clutch.

* * *

Roman Galkin gripped the steering wheel as he stared at the garage that Daniels and the other woman had disappeared into. He'd made a quick phone call to the team back in Moscow, and they'd hacked into the airport security system to get a copy of Daniels' passport photograph.

She was easy to spot as she left the terminal, as her stunning looks and shoulder-length, jet-black hair made her stand out in the crowd.

Daniels had met the other woman, a blonde, and they'd driven to the garage. Now all Galkin and his two colleagues could do was wait.

"How the hell do we make it look like an accident?" Lieutenant Sergey Kurbatov asked.

It was a question Galkin also wanted an answer to. Their job was ELINT—electronic intelligence—not murder. "We'll have to wait for her to come out," he replied. "Run her down, or if she drives away, we force her off the road."

"We could make it look like a street robbery," Lieutenant Vladimir Larin suggested. "Happens all the time in Riga."

"Too risky," Galkin said. "If she cries for help, it'll attract witnesses. No, we take her on the road."

"And if she's with the blonde?" Kurbatov asked.

"Then we kill them both," Galkin said angrily. Why the General couldn't have given the task to Unit 29155 was beyond him. They specialized in this kind of thing. But no, Turgenev wanted it done immediately, and now his subordinates were also expecting him to have all the answers.

Galkin saw the blonde return from a coffee run, and he suddenly felt thirsty.

"Larin, get some coffees."

"Sandwiches, too," Kurbatov added. "Chicken for me."

Larin took Galkin's order, then got out.

"What if they don't leave this evening?" Kurbatov asked.

It was a good question. General Turgenev had said he wanted Daniels dead as soon as possible. Knowing his superior, that meant in hours rather than days. If he didn't report the kill this evening, Turgenev was going to be pissed, and that was never good for anyone's career.

"Sir, look!"

Galkin followed Kurbatov's finger and saw the garage shutters rise. He looked around to see if he could spot Larin, but he was nowhere to be seen.

*Shit!*

They would have to leave him behind. Galkin fired up the engine and shifted into first, ready to move. He just hoped Daniels was alone. It was bad enough that he had been ordered to kill the American, but two deaths…

Instead of the car they'd seen enter the garage, a lone motorcyclist left. The black hair flowing from the back of the helmet told Galkin it was Daniels. He checked once more for Larin, but there was no sign of him.

Galkin couldn't wait for him. If he lost Daniels, there was more than his career at stake. He gunned the engine and sped to catch the bike.

\* \* \*

Eva pulled out of the garage and turned right to head east. She'd already decided on a route to the Russian border that would take her most of the way down the E22 until she saw the sign for Zilupe. From there, she would take the back roads to the border and cross in the dead of night.

Rush hour traffic was in full swing, and Eva noted that other bike riders were not lane splitting, riding the white line between the lanes of traffic. Perhaps the practice was frowned upon, in which case Eva decided not to do it. She could do without incurring the wrath of the local police.

As she waited at a set of red traffic lights, Eva checked her mirror. Most of the drivers around her seemed resigned to their evening commute, either looking bored or frustrated. The driver of the car behind her was different. His eyes were fixed on her, his stare intense.

Eva sensed trouble.

It was probably nothing, but better to be safe than sorry. When the lights changed, she indicated and moved into the right-hand lane, then took a right turn. The gray Toyota followed her. It wasn't proof that she'd picked up a tail, but it was enough to concern her.

Eva weighed up her options as she continued down the road. She could easily lose them in traffic, but then she wouldn't know for sure that they were really following her. If it turned out that they were, then she wanted to know who had sent them. More importantly, how did they know she was coming to Riga?

That was all moot if they turned out to be genuine commuters. In order to find out, Eva signaled early and turned left at the next junction. Sure enough, the Toyota remained behind her. Three more turns confirmed her suspicions.

*Let's see what you want.*

Eva swerved and zipped between the line of traffic and the gutter, then took a right turn. She checked both sides of the street until she found what she was looking for: an alley filled with dumpsters and bags of garbage. She swung the bike into the narrow lane and screeched to a stop halfway down.

* * *

"She's seen us!"

Galkin thought so, too. Which wasn't surprising. They dealt in ones and zeros, not advanced surveillance techniques. "Perhaps she's just trying to avoid the traffic," he replied.

They'd soon find out.

After what seemed an age, he reached the turn Daniels had taken.

She was gone.

Kurbatov released the expletive that was on Galkin's lips. *Now what?*

Galkin slowed the car while he chewed over his options. There weren't many. Find her, or suffer the General's wrath.

"There!"

Galkin looked down the alley that Kurbatov was pointing to. The bike was there, but no sign of Daniels. Galkin pulled up near the entrance to the alley and turned the engine off.

"Looks like we do it Larin's way," he said, checking his Makarov pistol. "We'll make it look like a street robbery."

He put the gun in his waistband and got out of the car. Kurbatov followed him into the alley.

"Where the hell did she go?" Kurbatov asked as they reached the motorcycle.

"She must be in one of these buildings," Galkin replied. "We'll wait for her to come out—"

There was a grunt, and Galkin turned to see Kurbatov slump to the ground next to a dumpster. Standing over him was Daniels.

"Who are you," she demanded, "and who sent you?"

Galkin reached for his pistol, but before he could reach the grip, she lashed out with her foot, catching him in the sternum. The breath was knocked out of him, and as he staggered backward, she continued her assault, landing a roundhouse kick to his temple. Galkin fell, his eyes glazing over. He felt the Makarov being tugged from his trousers, and as his eyes started to focus, he could just make out a suppressed pistol aimed at his head.

"I'll ask you again, who are you and who sent you?"

There was no way Galkin was going to answer those questions. He feared General Turgenev more than he feared the woman before him.

That changed when she altered her aim and shot the unconscious Kurbatov in the head. The sound was more a loud pop than a regular gunshot.

She swung her gun back to Galkin. "Now you know how serious I am. Start talking and you might just live."

Galkin doubted it, but it was the one hope he had left. She was standing three yards from him, too far for him to make a move against her.

"Three seconds, or you join your friend."

Galkin barely had time to process her words when the countdown reached one, and he saw her finger tense on the trigger.

"GRU!"

She lowered the gun slightly, and her face hardened.

"How did you know I was in Riga?" she asked.

"I don't know. I was just told to follow you off the plane."

"And?"

Galkin swallowed. "And kill you."

"When did you receive your orders, and how?"

"About an hour before you landed. I got a call from my superior."

"Whose name is?"

Galkin knew he might as well tell her. The head of the GRU had his own listing on Wikipedia, so it wasn't as if he was sharing state secrets. "General Vasili Turgenev."

She gestured to his trousers. "Give me your phone. Slowly."

Galkin slid it from his pocket using just his thumb and forefinger, then placed it on the ground next to him.

"Get up," she said.

Galkin eased himself to his feet.

"Give me your friend's phone, too."

As Galkin leaned over Kurbatov's body, he wondered how to explain his failure to carry out his orders. Naturally, he would frame his report so that he wouldn't be apportioned any blame. It would be Kurbatov's fault. That was it. Kurbatov had disobeyed his instructions, and his impetuousness had compromised the mission.

As Galkin imagined the alternate version of events, he never heard the shot that ended his life.

* * *

Eva pulled the bodies to the side of the dumpster and covered them with sacks of refuse, then collected the spent cartridge shells and jumped on the bike.

As she left the alley and joined traffic, Eva cursed her decision to accept the assignment. Regrets could wait, though. The crucial decision was whether to continue or not. The GRU wouldn't have followed her unless they knew the reason for her arrival in Riga, which meant someone in NID had told them.

Eva decided that giving up wasn't an option. If they sent someone else in her place, the Russians would know about it. No, it was better to carry on and not let anyone know of her suspicions. Anyone except Farooq and Xi Ling. Neither of them would have leaked the information to the Russians, so it must be someone in NID.

Her money was on Greg Sharpe. When she'd secured roles for Farooq and Xi Ling, he'd been humiliated. Perhaps this was his revenge.

Eva concentrated on getting out of Riga. She zipped between traffic until she reached the freeway, then headed southeast. After an hour on the road, she pulled into a service station and took out her phone. She'd come up with a plan, and needed Farooq's help to execute it. She composed a message on Shield. The secure comms was only used by the small circle of friends that comprised herself, Farooq, Xi Ling, Gray and Sonny.

*GRU were waiting for me, so someone inside NID is leaking to the Russians. If I contact you on Shield, it's eyes only. Anything that comes from me through NID comms, play along. Don't let anyone know that I know.*

# Chapter 10

"I can't believe we're doing this," Xi Ling said to Farooq as they approached the gate to the White House.

"Well, we are," he replied, "so get your A-game on. I don't want to have to pick up the slack for you."

"Yeah, like that'll ever happen."

For the entire journey to Washington DC, Xi Ling had complained that they were walking into some sort of trap. Farooq had assured her that Eva wouldn't have asked for their help if she'd thought there was anything sinister going on. It seemed his words hadn't provided the reassurance she needed.

They reached the guard house, and Farooq gave their names. After checking a clipboard, the uniformed guard asked them to step aside and wait. Minutes later, a tall African American in a dark suit approached them from the direction of the main building.

"Farooq, Xi Ling. I'm Richard Fernandez." He shook their hands. "Please, follow me."

He seemed decent enough, but Farooq had been around CIA types long enough to know that first impressions were not to be relied upon.

Fernandez led them through the White House and down to the NID control center.

"Did Nolene tell you what to expect?" Fernandez asked them as he swiped his security card.

"She did," Farooq answered. "Russia, Juggernaut, GRU, the whole thing."

Fernandez frowned. "She shouldn't have shared that much detail with you. She should have let me brief you."

"If she hadn't, we wouldn't be here. We're the only people who trust the government less than Nolene, so it took a lot to convince us to help. Don't worry, we didn't tell anyone."

"Yeah," Xi Ling added. Cheerfully. "Your secrets are safe with us."

Fernandez looked dubious. He pushed the door open and took them inside.

"Wow! Nice setup," Xi Ling said as she took in the layout of the room.

"These must be her people," a new voice said. He didn't sound pleased to see them.

"This is Greg Sharpe, the president's NSA," Fernandez said. "Greg, Farooq and Xi Ling."

Sharpe didn't offer his hand. Instead, he called over one of the analysts.

"Make sure they get up to speed," Sharpe said, and walked away.

"Nice chap," Farooq said, when the National Security Advisor was out of earshot.

"Don't take it personally," Fernandez said. "He's like that with everyone. Paul, show them the ropes."

\* \* \*

Farooq Naser sipped an energy drink while he and Xi Ling listened patiently to Paul Heaton. The NID analyst was explaining the system they would be using to provide Eva with logistical support during her mission. Farooq didn't have the heart to tell Heaton that he and Xi Ling had hacked in and used it dozens of times in the past.

When the demonstration was over, Heaton told them to ask if they had any questions. Farooq promised that he would.

"Think you can handle it?" Xi Ling smirked quietly when Heaton returned to his own seat.

"I'll do my best," Farooq grinned, then logged in to the CIA server for updates from the surveillance teams. One had confirmed that a known acquaintance of Igor Cherenkov was at home and had been all day. Two others said they had seen no sign of their targets, so they were going to their places of work to check on them. The updates had been added to the system two hours earlier.

"Let's concentrate on this guy," Farooq told Xi Ling, pointing to the face on the screen. "See what they have in the files, then check Interpol. We want to give Eva as much information as we can."

Xi Ling nudged him and gave him her angry look. "It's Nolene," she said, quietly but with enough menace to ensure he wouldn't make the same mistake again.

"I know, but no one's listening." He looked around, just to be sure.

"That's not the point. Don't you think everything here is recorded?"

Farooq grimaced. "I never thought of that."

He began reading about the man whose apartment was under surveillance. He wasn't far into the file when Richard Fernandez appeared at his shoulder.

"Patch me through to Oscar Three," the CIA liaison said.

Farooq had the surveillance team member on the radio in seconds. He was one of three operatives watching the Sandworm contacts in Moscow.

"Oscar Three, this is Campus. Oscar One and Oscar Two have reported their targets missing. No sign of them at home or work. Confirm status of Whiskey Three."

"I saw him at his window three hours ago. Nothing since."

"Then I need a visual," Fernandez said. "ASAP."

"Roger that."

"Problem?" Farooq asked when comms were cut.

"Maybe," Fernandez replied. "Oscars One and Two checked on their targets, but neither of them turned up for work. For one to disappear is strange. For two… let's just say, it doesn't feel right."

"Campus, Oscar Three. He's gone. I paid a kid ten bucks to knock on his door, but there was no answer, so I checked myself. He must have gone out the back way."

Fernandez swore. "Okay, Oscar Three. Pull back and await further instructions."

"Maybe they're just being overcautious," Xi Ling suggested, "hiding everyone who can lead us to Cherenkov."

"No way," Fernandez said, staring at a map of Moscow on the big screen. "I know the Russians. They'd never go to that level of detail. No, something's wrong."

He walked away, deep in thought.

"I don't like this," Farooq whispered to Xi Ling. "I'm gonna let Eva—Nolene—know."

He took out his phone and opened Shield, but noticed that there was no signal.

"Fernandez, what the hell is this!"

Farooq looked up from his cell to see Greg Sharpe bearing down on him. He didn't look happy. Richard Fernandez rushed over to see what the emergency was.

"Why does this man have an unauthorized device in the NID?"

Fernandez looked embarrassed. "I'm sorry, sir, I forgot to check."

"Neglected to check, more like it." Sharpe turned to Farooq and Xi Ling. "You two, out. Now. Store those cell phones before you come back in."

Xi Ling and Farooq followed Fernandez to the exit, where he showed them to the staff area. It was a tiny room with a dozen lockers and a solitary chair.

"They wouldn't have worked in here anyway because of the Faraday cage surrounding the bunker," Fernandez told them, "but Sharpe has a stick up his butt about operational security."

"And we thought it was just a generic stick," Xi Ling said.

They commandeered an empty locker and put their belongings inside.

Gray would have to wait until after their shift to get the bad news.

* * *

When Farooq and Xi Ling left the building, they went straight for their phones, but before he could compose a message, one arrived.

*GRU were waiting for me, so someone inside NID is leaking to the Russians. If I contact you on Shield, it's eyes only. Anything that comes from me through NID comms, play along. Don't let anyone know that I know.*

Farooq showed Xi Ling the message.

"I guess that confirms it," she said. "Tell her about the people disappearing and ask her what her next move is."

Farooq sent the message. He also told Eva about the Faraday cage around the NID, making it impossible for them to use their cell phones. Within a minute, Eva replied.

*Damn. I forgot to tell you about that. I got my hands on two cell phones. Gonna send you some numbers. Let me know what you have on them.*

"Tell her we'll get to work on that as soon as we get home," Xi Ling said.

When they got in the car, Farooq put a hand on her arm. "What about Sonny and Tom?" he asked her. "Shouldn't we tell them?"

"Okay, but make sure they don't tell a soul."

# Chapter 11

When General Vasili Turgenev arrived at his office, he walked past his secretary without a word and unbuttoned his jacket before sitting at his desk. As ever, there was a pile of paperwork awaiting his attention, and he scanned through them to see if any related to the mission he'd given Galkin the previous evening. He'd been expecting a call from the colonel, but none had come.

There was one from Lieutenant Larin. He'd gone to get coffee as instructed, and when he returned there was no sign of Colonel Galkin. Larin had managed to find the car, and a check of the area had revealed the bodies of Galkin and Lieutenant Kurbatov. There was no sign of Daniels.

Turgenev's hands shook with rage as he took out his cell phone. He found Larin's number on the report and dialed it.

"What the hell happened!?" Turgenev bellowed before Larin could speak.

"I don't know, General. The Colonel instructed me to get coffee, and when I returned, the car was gone. I—"

"I can read a fucking report!" Turgenev screamed down the phone.

"Of course, sir."

"How were they killed, and why wasn't I informed immediately?"

"It appears they were shot, sir, and I filed my report as soon as I was able."

"Why didn't you call me directly? Didn't Galkin explain the importance of the mission?"

He heard Larin swallow. "Yes, he did, sir, but I don't have your number."

"Then you could have looked it up on Galkin's phone!" Turgenev exploded, the lieutenant's incompetence becoming too much to bear.

"I was going to, sir, but it was stolen. Kurbatov's, too."

That gave Turgenev pause. He had called Galkin on that cell phone to issue his orders, which meant there was a link back to him. If Daniels had taken it…

"Were you all carrying ID?" Turgenev asked.

"No. The Colonel told us to leave them at the office."

That was one small crumb of comfort. "Good. Lay low, and if the police come calling, tell them you have no idea what Galkin and Kurbatov were doing yesterday."

Turgenev ended the call, knowing he needed to make another.

One he was dreading.

He took a deep breath and gathered himself, then hit the saved number for Admiral Komarov.

"Vasili. I was hoping to hear from you last night."

"And I was hoping to call you, Admiral, but I only this moment heard from the men I sent to intercept the American."

"And?"

There was no way to sugarcoat it. "She killed two of my men and escaped."

The silence lasted long enough to make Turgenev uncomfortable. "Admiral?"

"I'm still here, Vasili. I'm just waiting for you to explain why you sent just two people to deal with her. Did I, or did I not, advise you not to underestimate her?"

"You did, Admiral, and I heeded your warning. That is why I sent three armed men, but unfortunately one of them got separated. The other two… well, they failed in their duty to—"

"Do not try to shift the blame to your men, Turgenev! I gave *you* the task, so it is *your* failure!"

It was unusual for Komarov to lose his temper. Turgenev had seen him angry before, but his voice had always remained calm, though heavy with fury. "Of course, Admiral. And I shall rectify the situation immediately."

"You'd better," Komarov warned him. "If anything prevents us replicating and deploying Juggernaut, I'll hold you fully responsible."

Before Turgenev could respond, the call ended. He put the cell on his desk, then slowly stroked his chin as he thought of his next steps. He knew Daniels planned to enter Russia. Given the time that had elapsed since the death of Galkin and now, she had probably already done so. She had been planning to visit the friends of Cherenkov, but that had been taken care of. So, what would she do now? What would *he* do?

Daniels had Galkin's cell phone, which worried him. The Americans were no doubt working on the content of the phone at that very moment. Not only was it proof of the GRU's involvement in Poska's kidnapping, but it contained his own phone number. He wasn't the most technically gifted, but he knew cell phones could be tracked.

He picked up his desk phone and hit the button for his secretary.

"Get me a new cell phone right away."

Once it arrived, he would transfer the contacts over, then destroy the old phone. He would have to let everyone know his new number, but he would do that after the successful launch of Juggernaut. For now, he would inform only his superiors and the relevant people in his team.

With the phone problem dealt with, he returned to Daniels' next move. Once she discovered that the links to Cherenkov had been severed, what would she do? Her objective was to find Cherenkov, and ultimately Poska, and now the best way to do that was to speak to the man who gave Cherenkov his orders.

Would Daniels really come for him, the head of the GRU? He didn't think it likely, but then he'd thought three men would have solved the problem by now. He'd failed to heed Admiral Komarov's words once; he wouldn't make the same mistake again.

He woke up his cell phone and looked up the number for the commander of Spetsnaz GRU.

# Chapter 12

Robert J. Portman walked past the smiling stewardess without so much as a thank you. When he stuck his head out of the aircraft, he saw a woman dressed in a black skirt suit waiting at the bottom of the steps.

"Welcome, Mr. Portman. If you'd like to follow me."

She waited for him to descend the stairs, then slowly led him to a nearby helicopter. Portman climbed in the back and sat in one of the two forward-facing plush seats. The woman took a seat in the opposite corner of the cabin.

"My name is Vanessa. If you have any questions, don't hesitate to ask."

She put her headphones on and adjusted the positioning of the microphone so that it sat over her cherry-red lips, then looked out of the window.

Portman appreciated that. He hated nothing more than small talk, especially with those he considered beneath him.

Which was the vast majority of the people on the planet.

Nevertheless, he looked this one over. She looked to be in her late twenties, maybe early thirties. Slim. Confident. The kind of woman he would have taken a shine to once upon a time. These days, the only thing that aroused him was the thought of Project Phoenix.

And it was almost here. The day America rose from the ashes. But like the mythical phoenix, first it had to burn.

He thought about the length of the journey that had brought him to the doorstep of Heliopolis. Over fifty years. The moment the tax rate dropped from its high of ninety-one percent had set the wheels in motion. The drive to accumulate capital had begun, and it had accelerated ever since. It was always going to be a slow process fraught with difficulties, the main one being how to convince the population to go along with it.

That had been the easy part. All that was needed was to distract the working class, to get the people fighting among themselves so that they didn't see the theft happening before their eyes. Give them someone to blame for their declining living standards, and there were plenty of scapegoats. Immigrants. Blacks. The poor. Lowering education standards in public schools made this easier. The dumber the voter, the easier it was to convince them of your narrative.

The noise of the engine intensified, and the helicopter rose smoothly into the air and pointed its nose north-west.

Portman felt a tingle of excitement, a rare occurrence these days. For one, he still couldn't believe he was living to see this moment. Project Phoenix had been a long game, designed to run for a hundred years, long enough for the point-one percent to suck just about everything out of the economy. Once they had all the money, they wouldn't simply be rich; they would be rulers. Governments would fall, to be replaced by emperors.

Kings.

The 2070 deadline had been drastically cut at the turn of the millennium with the advent of two powerful tools: a conservative-leaning news channel, and social media.

Instead of having to share their hate by word of mouth, the ignorant could now devour it daily and share it with the world. It took another ten years to really take off, but by the middle of the twenty-tens, it was clear that Project Phoenix was achievable fifty years early.

Which was just as well.

For years, intellectuals had tried to tell the world that the huge wealth inequality the US—and indeed, the rest of the world—was experiencing would lead to bad things, but their voices were drowned out by establishment figures decrying the doom-mongering, leftist nonsense. The advent of social media made it harder to silence those voices. Graphs that might once have been of interest to a few thousand economists globally could now be shared with billions of people. Thirty-second videos showing comparisons of prices and living quality now and fifty years ago were reaching a huge audience, and resonating with many. People could feel their spending power diminish year on year, and it wasn't sustainable. There was simply no way the rich and powerful could get away with it for another fifty years.

Project Phoenix needed one final push, and donors like Portman had been more than happy to oblige. They funded not only Heliopolis, but also the political action committees that would install a president sympathetic to their cause. They needed a patsy, someone who would willingly do their bidding while oblivious to the goal. They already had their man. Ty Mason, a businessman who had managed to fail upward his entire life, despite a catalog of disastrous dealings. After appearing on a reality TV dating show, Mason had become a household name. His newfound stardom led to regular appearances on right-wing media as a financial guru, which in turn resulted in his own one-hour slot. It was on one such show that a guest had praised Mason's financial acumen and suggested he might be the right man to steer the economy.

"Why don't you run for president?"

That guest had, of course, been paid to float the idea by the architects of Project Phoenix.

Delusions of adequacy not only convinced Mason that it was a logical next step in his career, but he was soon approached by several billionaires willing to fund his campaign.

The men behind the social media giants were key members of Project Phoenix. Even though the next election was two years away, Mason was already being pushed into the feeds of all users. His nomination as the party's candidate was assured, and everything was in place for when he was catapulted into the White House. All major cabinet roles would be filled by Project Phoenix staffers, from Secretary of Defense to Homeland Security and the Department of Justice. The moment Mason took his place in the oval office, his team would spring into action. The federal workforce would be slashed, making it impossible to deliver the services the majority of Americans relied upon. SNAP benefits, social security, Medicaid, Medicare, VA services, all would be decimated. While this was going on, an immigration crackdown would hit the agriculture industry as the undocumented migrant workers would either be deported or flee. Mason would start a trade war with the entire world, claiming to redress the harm America had faced for the last fifty years. This would exacerbate the food shortages. Half the country wouldn't be able to afford fresh produce. Those who could, would have to pay an exorbitant price for it. American companies would suffer, resulting in more job losses.

That was only the beginning.

Mason would fire off a barrage of executive orders, most of them unconstitutional. It didn't matter. Implementing a nationwide abortion ban; repealing laws that protected the LGBTQ+ community; legalizing segregation; identifying anyone on the autism spectrum—adults and children alike—and classifying them as "unproductive." They would then be sent to specially constructed "Patriot Camps" where, following the repeal of child labor laws, they would be set to work for giant corporations that loved to take advantage of cheap labor. The idea was to overwhelm the citizenry with a broad array of measures that affected and enraged everyone.

To get them angry.

To get them on the streets.

Only then would Project Phoenix reach the end game.

Martial law would be declared, and the military would take to the streets. The first things to be shut down would be communications and electricity. Without TVs and cell phones, people would be left in the dark. Those with generators would receive no channels as international fiber cables were cut off. Panic would set in. Ports and airports would be closed, allowing no one to leave the country or get in. No electricity also meant no water being pumped into homes. Food would spoil with no power for refrigerators. Once the bottled water supply ran out, people would start to die. Food stocks would last longer, but would eventually run out. The collapse of the US would have a ripple effect on economies around the globe. Tens of millions of

Americans would die, but that was necessary. It was far easier to control a smaller population.

All the while, Portman and the rest of the members of Project Phoenix would be safe in Heliopolis.

And now they had an even better way to bring about the collapse of the United States.

Juggernaut.

Portman had been shown the video by one of the congressmen on the committee, and the plan had been put in motion: kidnap Andrius Poska and force him to replicate the software.

Then the problems began to pile up. How to snatch him without anyone noticing that he was missing? How to ensure no one tried to launch a rescue mission?

Portman had come up with the perfect solution. What better way to avoid interference than to have another superpower do the dirty work? Portman rubbed shoulders with some of the richest people on the planet, and one of them was Yaroslav Durov. Durov had the ear of Leonid Pertsov, the Russian President, and it wasn't long before Portman was sitting in the President's box at the Bolshoi discussing the details. In return for Russia carrying out the Juggernaut attack, but otherwise not invading the US while it was vulnerable, Portman offered Pertsov a personal gift of $200 billion in gold, to be paid the following year. He added a warning that overt aggression against the US would be seen as an act of war by NATO. With Russia already bogged down in a war with Ukraine, they wouldn't have the manpower or logistics to take on the entire West. Once America was back up and running, all existing sanctions would be lifted, and trade could resume between the two countries. Russia's economy would recover from the damage inflicted over the last few years and once again become a superpower.

Portman's one concern was that Pertsov might take NATO out of the equation by targeting those countries, too. Hell, the Russian might attack every country on the planet. Portman was sure he had that covered, though. He told Pertsov that if he were to only use Juggernaut against the USA, as planned, no one would learn of his involvement. To ensure that happened, US embassies in all NATO countries would be sent a diplomatic pouch containing details of Juggernaut. They were to be opened and given to the leaders of the Western nations in the event of a massive cyber attack against any NATO country, and would detail Pertsov's involvement and culpability. The retaliation would be swift and brutal.

It was a lie. There would be no such memo, but Pertsov wasn't to know that.

In the end, it seemed the money alone had been enough to convince the Russian president to go along with the plan.

Thanks to Juggernaut, a few keystrokes could destroy everything vital to the American way of life. What would have taken almost three years, with numerous pitfalls along the way, would be done in minutes.

"We're almost here," Vanessa said over the headset. "I instructed the pilot to do a fly-by."

Portman looked out of the window and saw little but desert. It was his first time at Heliopolis. Over the years, he'd had quiet dinners with the nominal owner of TNR, who had updated him on the progress of the ten-year project. To visit the site in person would have invited unwanted scrutiny.

Vanessa unclipped her belt and moved to the seat opposite Portman.

"There it is," she said, pointing out the window.

Portman saw a speck in the distance. It didn't look like much, but that was the intention. Heliopolis was underground, with just a vast sand-colored metal building sitting atop it. Next to that was a gigantic circle with a letter H in the center.

"Do you see the airstrip?" Vanessa asked.

Portman looked, but apart from the building and landing pad, he saw nothing but sand and rocks. "I can't see anything."

"That's good," Vanessa said. "We invite all guests to try to spot it, but so far no one has. It's actually there, just to the right of the building."

Portman squinted, but could see nothing.

"It's a remarkable piece of engineering," Vanessa continued. "The runway is covered by almost a hundred and sixty thousand interlocking squares designed to mimic the original land. Before construction began, engineers mapped out every inch of the ground and fed that information into a 3D printer. That produced the numbered squares you see below us."

Portman hadn't been told about an airport. "Then why have me fly to Las Vegas if we could have flown straight here?" he asked.

"It's for departures only," Vanessa smiled.

That made no sense. "How can you depart if you're unable to arrive?"

"All will be revealed," Vanessa assured him, buckling her seatbelt.

The chopper began to descend, landing smoothly in the center of the H.

Portman reached for his belt buckle, but Vanessa put her hand on it.

"Please wait until we are inside."

Portman was confused, but sat back in his seat as the blades slowed to a stop. Suddenly, the ground beneath them seemed to give way as they sank into the earth. Only now did Portman realize how big the landing platform was. It easily measured a hundred yards across, the length of a football field. The platform fell slowly, smoothly, through a vast steel tube, then settled to a stop.

A small vehicle appeared and drove to the nose of the helicopter. Moments later, the chopper began to move forward.

Portman looked out of the front window and his heart caught in his chest.

"My God!"

"Impressive, isn't it?" Vanessa smiled.

Impressive wasn't the word. The cavern Portman was gazing into had to be at least a mile long and half as wide. It was by far the largest man-made structure he'd ever seen, a true feat of engineering. Not only that, it was filled with a myriad aircraft, from old fighter jets to commercial airliners, helicopters to military transport planes. There were also hundreds, perhaps thousands of vehicles, many stacked on shelves that ran down the entire length of the cavern.

"What are those?" Portman asked, pointing to some futuristic craft.

"Electric air vehicles," Vanessa told him. "Gasoline only lasts six months, and we expect to be down here for double that. The guys on the science level are working on extending the shelf life as we speak, but just in case they can't achieve it, we need a way to get people back to the refineries to get them up and running again. They will travel in electric cars and buses, while the EAVs can provide air cover in case the ground forces run into trouble."

Vanessa made it sound like a military mission, which seemed apt. Once society collapsed, it would be every man for himself. Anarchy and lawlessness would spread throughout the land. Few of the survivors would be friendly.

"If you follow me this way, I'll show you to your quarters."

Vanessa led Portman to an elevator. The outer door was plain steel, but as it slid open, Portman saw a plush carpet and mahogany panels.

They stepped in, and Vanessa placed her wrist over a lit panel. The door closed.

"You'll get one of these when you arrive next week," she told Portman as they began to drop. "This is the members' elevator, and it won't move without it. We want to ensure that there's no unauthorized access to your floors. The rest of the personnel have their own elevators spread around the compound."

Portman had been told about that security measure in one of his regular meetings, but didn't mention it. Better to let Vanessa give him the full tour in case she skipped anything.

The car pulled to a gentle stop and the door opened onto a grand hallway. There appeared to be more elevators off to the sides, and in the center, black leather sofas formed a square around the largest glass table Portman had ever seen. The ceiling was at least sixty feet above his head.

"This is the members' accommodation level," Vanessa said as she walked out into the foyer and headed to the right, her heels clicking on the marble flooring.

They weren't elevators, but glass doors to what looked to Portman like a subway train.

Vanessa clicked a button, and the door slid sideways. She gestured for Portman to go first, and he noticed there was enough room for ten people.

"The members' accommodation floor is built in four rows of twenty-five homes," Vanessa said as they took their seats. "Fifty on this side, fifty on the other side. Yours is number twenty-seven."

She once again used her wristband to close the doors, then selected his house number from the display. "There are seven shuttles on this line, and to go from here to the last house takes just under two minutes. It uses electromagnets, so no harmful emissions."

The car set off and quickly reached an astonishing speed. Portman saw flashes of white at regular intervals. In less than a minute, he felt it slow down again.

"Here we are," Vanessa said as it stopped. She once again used her wristband to open the shuttle's door. An outer glass door swished open, and Portman found himself at the entrance to what would be his home for the next year. The rectangle next to the large white door told him the method of entry.

"Allow me," Vanessa said.

The door clicked, and Portman stepped into the hallway.

And was blown away.

The entrance looked to be an exact replica of his home in Virginia, right down to the pictures on the wall.

"This is… how did you manage to do this?"

"That would be… me," a voice said, and Portman spun around.

"Seddon!"

Seddon Blake, the world's richest man, his fortune approaching half a trillion dollars, ambled over to Portman and clasped his hand.

"You like it?" Blake asked, casting his gaze over the hallway.

"I do. I'm just… how did you do this? You've only ever been to my house once."

"Once is enough," Blake smiled. He took off his glasses and showed them to Portman. "The latest in my AI range. They measure distances and identify materials, so I can replicate any room I've been into."

"Is the entire house the same?" Portman asked.

"Sadly, no. I could only replicate the rooms I saw, so you'll have the replica rooms downstairs. I never saw the kitchen or upstairs, so I had to take a few liberties. Come, let's explore."

Vanessa remained by the door while Blake and Portman walked through the house.

"I'm afraid the pictures are just cheap replicas. You can bring the real things with you. In fact, I think my people are scheduled to be with you in five days."

"Your people?" Portman asked.

"Yes. Obviously, you'll want to bring some of your treasures with you. I've arranged for a team to come to your house and pack everything up for you. Don't worry, they'll take great care of your possessions. Speaking of which, are you bringing any of your own staff along?"

"No. You mentioned before that I could only invite single people. No one with families, you said. All of my people are married or in relationships."

"That's correct," Blake said. "You tell one person, they want to bring their wife and kids along, and before you know it, we've got hundreds of thousands of people trying to get into Heliopolis. Better to let me make those arrangements. So, here's the living room, which you'll recognize. Let me show you the kitchen."

They went through a door to the right. The dining room was again replicated in every detail, but beyond that, the kitchen was completely new. Portman approved, though what it looked like or how it functioned was irrelevant to him. He hadn't prepared a meal in decades.

"Through there is the staff quarters," Blake said, pointing to a door. "Room for the four people I've assigned to you. I trust that will be enough?"

"Only four? I have a much bigger team at home."

"I'm sure you do," Blake said, "but here you won't need any gardeners, or a driver, or anyone to do the laundry. Obviously, you won't have a garden, and laundry is centralized. You'll have a chef, a waiter, a butler *cum* personal assistant, and a… companion. You can choose one for the entire year, or just dip into the pool whenever you feel like it. You can decide once you get settled in."

Portman gave him a sly grin. "You thought of everything."

"Didn't make this much money by skimping on the details," Blake winked.

The tour continued upstairs. After climbing the sweeping staircase, Blake showed off the master bedroom.

Portman was impressed. The room was huge, the bed enormous, the en suite luxurious. It was even better than his bedroom at home.

"Your stylist did a fantastic job, Seddon."

"Thank you. He's going to be staying with us here. Him, and a team of the world's leading architects. They will spend the next year designing our palaces for what I like to call 'the resurrection.' The day we return to the surface and fulfill our destinies."

"I've been meaning to ask you about that. Apart from Phoenix members, how many people will be in Heliopolis?"

"Roughly a hundred thousand," Blake replied.

"Uh-huh. And how can you be sure that none of them will go to the newspapers, or the FBI? I asked you this at the very beginning and you told me not to worry, that it was covered. Care to explain now?"

"That wasn't easy, let me tell you. We planned this very carefully, and recruitment began the day the first shovels were in the ground. Basically, it boils down to a trait the personnel share with Phoenix members."

"And what's that?" Portman asked.

"Narcissism."

"I beg your pardon?"

"You're a narcissist," Blake repeated. "And don't think you're not. You're a classic example." He began to count out on his fingers. "A heightened sense of self-importance; envious; a need for excessive admiration; you display arrogant behavior; a… a… a lack of empathy. Do I need to go on?"

Portman had never been so offended. And by a peer, no less. "I resent that remark. And those things alone don't make you a narcissist."

Blake laughed and threw an arm around Portman. "They do, my friend, and it's nothing to be ashamed of. Do you think we'd be where we are now if it wasn't for narcissism? And besides, a year from now, few will know what the word even means, and those who do would never dare use it to describe us."

Portman had to concede that Blake had a point. "So how does that help with recruitment?"

"Well, first we identified all of the positions we needed to fill, for both the coming year and beyond. Then my specially selected team identified the very best people in their respective fields: architects, scientists, doctors, nurses, chefs, the army special forces, engineers of all descriptions, the list goes on and on. Each person was befriended by a clinical psychologist, who through a clever series of questions got to delve into each candidate's personality. We eliminated anyone with any sign of empathy, of compassion. We were left with people whose only aim in life was self-aggrandizement. The kind of people who would let ninety percent of the world's population die for their own selfish gain."

"What about cleaners, janitors, housekeepers, people like that?"

"You don't have to be rich to want to be a narcissist," Blake said.

"But if they were to change their minds?" Portman asked.

"It's simply not in their nature. It's like a cat deciding to become a dog. But just to be sure, when we made our proposal, we had different psychologists in the room masquerading as lawyers. Not one of the candidates showed any signs of hesitancy. I mean, given the option of becoming a high net-worth individual in the new regime, or taking your chances in dystopian America, what would you choose?"

"And if just one had said no?"

"They would have died before they had time to regret their decision," Blake said casually.

Blake seemed confident in his process, which was enough to satisfy Portman. "So, what else can you amaze me with?"

"Plenty," Blake smiled. "I'll tell you all about it over lunch." He took out his cell phone and brought up an app. "I'll send you a link to this in the coming days. It's to help you get around Heliopolis. For instance, here's today's menu from one of the twelve restaurants on the fifth level. These are just for us, obviously. The other personnel have their own catering arrangements. Let's see… you like lamb, right?"

"My favorite," Portman said.

"Perfect. Our order is in. It should be ready by the time we get there."

# Chapter 13

After two long years, the big day was almost here. Less than a week to go before he and thirty thousand others would deploy for the last time.

His last time as an American soldier.

The plan was simple. Go into lockdown, and once they emerged into a new kingdom, the country he had vowed to serve would be no more. Instead of a president, congress and judiciary, there would be a single ruler. An emperor. A king. The country might still be called America, but it would be in name only.

Sinclair still had plenty of work to do. The toughest part had been finding an excuse to take four thousand men from their bases without attracting unwanted attention. Fortunately, one of the men who would be joining him in Heliopolis was Donald Killman, the Secretary of Defense. Between them, they decided that the best way to explain so many military personnel and equipment congregating in the Nevada desert was to cast it as a training exercise in rapid deployment. Killman had notified Congress in a closed meeting of the Senate Armed Services Committee that the snap exercise would be announced the following Monday. The purpose was to see how long it would take to get the men and equipment in place at short notice. This was essential to ensure first response units were prepared for war. The choice of a desert location was meant to replicate actions that would normally take place in the Middle East. Congress had approved the plan.

Seven days.

Seven days until he and his men would cross a sacred line.

Finding enough people to fulfill Xavier's demands had been a challenge in itself. He'd had to start with his immediate subordinates, a couple of colonels who were loyal to a fault. He'd given the names to Xavier, who had checked them out and declared them suitable for recruitment. Sinclair had then tasked the officers with compiling a list of active-duty personnel who were single. There weren't that many. He had then had to include married personnel with no dependents. Xavier assured him there would be room in Heliopolis for couples, but that children would be a barrier due to the limited space available. Having sent the list to Xavier, it had been nine months before Sinclair had heard anything more. Most of the men under his command had agreed to the proposal. Many of the recruits were from poor rural families, and they had only signed up because of a lack of other job prospects. Free healthcare, free food, free lodgings, all things they couldn't afford to pass up. The vast majority had decided that, having bought into the lifestyle, they wanted to maintain it, especially when they learned that such trivialities as rules of engagement and oversight would no longer apply.

There had been a spate of mysterious incidents, including automobile accidents and suicides, because not all of those approached had been willing to take part. More than two dozen saw it as treason, an affront to their oath.

Others didn't want to abandon their families.

Sinclair's parents were both dead, as were his wife's. They'd never had children. How the enlisted men could leave theirs to their own fate, he didn't know. Would he have been able to do that, to let his elderly and infirm mother and father take their chances in a world of chaos? No, he wouldn't. But Sinclair knew that he was not all men. Of the hundred thousand people who would spend a year in Heliopolis, many would have left parents behind. Sisters, brothers, perhaps even grown children.

*What have we become?*

It was far too late to have second thoughts. Backing out now would do no good, nor would blowing the whistle. For one, he couldn't stop what was coming. By the time anyone took his warning seriously, the world would have fallen apart. All that would serve to do would be to leave him and his wife on the outside.

Sinclair put his tunic on, buttoned it, and left his office. He walked out into a crisp afternoon. Clear skies, but a storm was brewing.

# Chapter 14

"You okay?" Gray asked as Sonny gingerly exited the taxi.

Sonny winced as he straightened up. "I'll be fine. It only hurts when I laugh. Or move. Or breathe."

"In other words, you want me to get the bags."

"Hey! I'm hurting here!"

"I know," Gray laughed. "You've reminded us every hour for the last two days."

"Really?"

"Really," Melissa said, winking at her father. "You're worse than me, and I'm a ten-year-old girl."

"Come on," Sonny moaned. "I'm not that bad."

"She's joking," Gray said, anxious to get going. He wheeled the cart with the suitcases into the departure lounge, going slow so that Sonny could keep up.

After checking in, they went through security, then found a restaurant.

"Remember what happened in England a few years ago?" Sonny asked when Gray returned from the counter with two coffees and an orange juice for Melissa.

"The bombings? How could I forget?"

Gray and Melissa had been caught up in one of the explosions at a London hospital, and it had been touch-and-go whether she'd survive. Thankfully, there'd been no long-term damage.

"I have a feeling things will be much worse if Juggernaut goes live," Sonny said.

Gray had to agree. While the attacks in England had been horrific, the perpetrators had been rounded up quickly, and life had returned to normal within a couple of weeks. If the Russians launched their cyber attack, there would be little the Americans could do to stop it. The effects would last a lot longer, and the death toll would be much higher.

"Then let's hope Eva does her job."

"Even if she does, do you think that'll be the end of it?" Sonny asked. "You don't think the Russians would try to build their own version?"

"It's a possibility," Gray agreed. "Hell, even the North Koreans might have a go. Maybe the Chinese, too."

It was a sobering thought. Gray had been following the news on the subject, and while much had been made of the rise in AI, governments around the world had so far been slow to recognize the dangers, focusing instead on the benefits. They'd signed the leading companies up to a voluntary code of practice, but that wasn't worth the paper it was written on. He suspected that, just like the major tech firms, AI companies would soon grow so big that regulating them would be nigh-on impossible. Even if laws were passed, it was unlikely that pariah states would pay them much heed.

"Then we better hope Eva can get Poska back so that he can come up with some kind of defense against them." Sonny rose like an old man. "Let's go find our gate."

It was a long, slow walk, and when they reached the gate, Sonny eased himself into a chair.

"Are you sure they stitched you up properly?" Gray asked quietly. "I don't think it should hurt so much after eleven days."

"It's my ribs," Sonny told him. "The bullet broke two of them, remember?"

"I know," Gray said, "but I've never broken one, so I don't know how bad it is."

"You smashed five when that building collapsed on you back in twenty-eleven."

"Yeah, but I was in a coma for two months afterwards. They would have healed by the time I woke up."

"Then let me tell you," Sonny said, "they hurt like a—" He saw Melissa riveted to the conversation. "They hurt a lot."

"Obviously."

People started filing past their seats, heading for the boarding desk.

"Come on," Gray said, standing.

Sonny got to his feet, and they stood in line. It took a couple of minutes to reach the front of the queue, and Gray handed over their boarding passes. The attendant was mid-thirties, with black hair cut in a bob. As she checked the documents, a cleaner walked past the desk carrying two large garbage bags. He bumped into Sonny, who let out a groan and clutched his chest.

"Are you okay?" the attendant asked.

Before Gray could speak, Melissa jumped in. "He was shot, here," she said, pointing to her own chest.

Gray gave his daughter an angry look, but the damage was already done.

"When did this happen?"

"A couple of weeks ago," Sonny said.

The attendant adopted the industry-standard look of sympathy. "I'm sorry, but the airline doesn't allow passengers to fly if they've had major surgery within the last four weeks."

Gray had been expecting this. In hindsight, he should have warned Melissa before they traveled. "How about if he signs a waiver?" he asked.

"I'm sorry, the airline won't allow it."

"Then what about a note from a doctor stating that he's fit to fly?"

"I'm afraid that won't make any difference. I can't even suggest another airline because they all have the same rules in place, and I'm under instructions to inform them if there is a passenger who is unfit to fly. I'm sorry."

"Can't you just not tell them?" Sonny pleaded.

She shook her head. "If I don't, and something happens to you, I'd lose my job and the airline could be sued by their competitors. I'm s—"

"Sorry," Gray finished for her. "We get it." There was no way he was going to change the attendant's mind. "Come on," he said to Sonny.

"What do we do now?"

"Not much," Gray had to admit. "We could try to charter our own plane, but I suspect we'll run into the same problem."

"Then Eva's on her own? Tom, Farooq said someone in NID is working with the Russians. She needs us."

"I know she does, but if I go to Vilnius to help her, that leaves Melissa to take care of you, and we both know that won't be enough if it all kicks off."

"True," Sonny said glumly.

"I'll text her when we get back to the apartment and let her know," Gray said. "In the meantime, draw up a list of provisions. If Eva doesn't stop Juggernaut, we're going to have to dig in."

# Chapter 15

"This is the best lamb I've ever tasted," Robert Portman told his host.

"Glad you like it," Seddon Blake replied. "The chef has three Michelin stars, you know."

"Impressive." Portman looked around. "So is the venue."

"It's a replica of my favorite restaurant in Paris," Blake said, sipping his red wine. "The other eleven are also modelled on some of the most famous restaurants in the world. Just in case people feel nostalgic."

"You thought of everything. So, tell me what else I can expect here."

"Plenty. I'm afraid I won't have time to do a full tour today, but when you arrive, your butler will be fully briefed on the entire facility and will be able to take you anywhere you want to go. Except for the personnel areas, obviously."

"Obviously." Portman had no intention of associating with the riff-raff.

"Anyway, in a nutshell, Heliopolis is built over nine levels, each one a shade over two thousand yards long and a thousand wide. Floor height differs depending on the use. On the first level, we have transport, as you saw. Below that is storage, and on level three it's personnel accommodation. Level four is member accommodation."

"A hundred thousand of them, wasn't it?"

"A shade under that. Some of those are the armed forces. Mostly army, and a few air force and navy. The rest are to service Heliopolis and get things up and running again once we resurface.

"We're on level five, the dining floor. Below us is the recreation deck. There's a cinema, library, running track and gym, tennis courts, even a small park. Again, the other ranks have their own facilities. On level seven it's the hospital and nursery, plus more storage. Level eight is tech. That's where we're working on advanced robotics, AI and green energy. Lastly, at the bottom of the facility we have agriculture. That consists of fresh fruit trees and homegrown vegetables. There's also a substantial farm with close to half a million animals. That will provide us with fresh food for the next year, plus enough animals to begin repopulating the planet."

Portman gestured to a nearby waiter and pointed to his empty plate. "I've said it before, Seddon, and I'll say it again. What you've done here is beyond impressive. It's truly remarkable. One thing puzzles me, though. How are you going to power this facility?"

Blake laughed ironically. "Solar power. I know, the very thing we've been railing against all these years. Turns out it's the best option for us, short of building our own nuclear reactor."

"You can do that? I mean, power all this with solar?"

"Sure. The infrastructure is already in place, out in the desert. The panels themselves are in storage. All we need is thirty hours advance notice of the power going out and we can clip them in place and hook them up. That will produce half a gigawatt of electricity a day. What we don't use will be stored in gigantic batteries."

"But still, is half a gigawatt enough?"

"More than enough," Blake told him, "We have half a million nine-hundred-watt panels, all self-isolating, so if one fails, the rest of the row keeps working. You could power a small city with that."

With Portman's background in politics and Blake being the tech bro, he decided not to question the man's expertise.

"Anyway, if you think this is good, wait until you see what I have planned for next year." Blake wiped his mouth and put his napkin on his plate. The waiter appeared immediately and took it away. Once they were alone again, Blake looked at Portman, and his demeanor changed in an instant. The jovial host was suddenly ominously serious. "The reason I came here today is for an update on Juggernaut."

"It's on track to be ready on Sunday. We'll perform a test run, targeting Bismarck, North Dakota. It only has a population of seventy-five thousand and most will be asleep at the time, so a temporary outage in the electricity grid and mobile communications shouldn't make the news."

"And if that goes well?" Blake asked.

"Then we launch nationwide on Thursday."

Blake stared at him for a moment, then polished off his wine. "There's a been a change of plan."

Portman didn't like the sound of that. "What do you mean?"

"We go worldwide."

"But… we can't. I mean, the Russians won't go for that."

"Correction; they *have* gone for that. You see, moments after you spoke to Pertsov at the ballet, he called me and told me everything. Me being the richest man in the world, and Pertsov being the second, we naturally have… aligned views. Seriously, a memo to US embassies? Is that all you could think of? But, yeah, when you came and floated the idea to me, I already knew all about it. In fact, it was already in motion.

Portman was stunned.

"Oh, Robert, don't pout. It doesn't become you." Blake smiled. "And there's no need to worry, I still tell everyone that this is your operation. I just wanted to enhance it, for all our benefits."

"You could have said something up front," Portman countered. "I would have been happy to fill you in on the details." That wasn't strictly true. He would have done so grudgingly at best.

Blake waved his protest away. "It's done. In the past."

This was the problem with Seddon Blake. He was undoubtedly a genius, capable of imagining the unimaginable and bringing it to life. Be it AI targeting drones for the military, or humanoid robotics, Blake was always years ahead of the rest of the field. The flip side was that he was unreliable. He had a habit of abandoning meetings at short notice, or changing agreements at the last minute.

As was the case here.

Portman was curious, though. If Blake was taking something as serious as this in a new direction at such a late stage, he must have spotted a great opportunity.

"So, now what?"

"Now," Blake said, leaning into the table, "we cripple and take over not just the good old US of A, but the entire world!" He threw his hands in the air theatrically. "Think of it! Why be the joint ruler of one US state when you can have your own country? Who wants to be Second Emperor of

Alabama when they can be the king of Australia? Or Nigeria, or… or… Qatar?"

Blake made a convincing argument, but the Russians wouldn't just hand Blake the rest of the world. If anything, they would want to split the spoils down the middle.

"What do we get, and what does Pertsov get?" Portman asked.

"Well, geographically, it made sense to give him Europe and China. They are, after all, on his borders. We get North and South America, Africa, the Middle East, and the Far East. Japan, the Philippines, Australia, all of that."

"He gets all the culture," Portman said, "and we get sand and poverty?"

"And critical minerals," Blake smiled. "Trillions and trillions of dollars' worth. Everything we need to leap ahead in the technological race. And what we don't have, we can trade with our new ally."

Portman didn't share Blake's enthusiasm. Involving Pertsov was necessary to ensure there was enough time to replicate Juggernaut. That didn't mean Portman trusted the Russian. If he could have built Juggernaut without Pertsov…

An idea formed in his mind.

"NID sent a woman to find Poska," Portman said, creating his plan on the fly. "What if we were to give her his location?"

"Why would we do that?" Blake asked, confused.

"Bear with me," Portman told him. "We give her Poska's location, and she brings him home."

"And we lose Juggernaut," Blake said.

"No, we just work on it from Heliopolis. We bring Poska *here*."

Blake sat back, and a smile spread over his face. "We wouldn't have to share with the Russians."

"Exactly!" Portman said, slamming his hands on the table triumphantly.

Blake folded his arms. "There's just one tiny problem."

"Which is?"

"What's Poska's location, hmm?"

*Fuck!* Portman hadn't thought this through. "Yes, granted, we don't know that. Yet. But I can get it."

"No need. I'll handle it. In fact, I'll handle everything from this point on." Blake stood. "Nice idea, though. I like it. Come, let me show you some more of the sights."

# Chapter 16

Andrius Poska struggled to keep his eyes open, but one look at the photograph of his wife and daughter next to the laptop spurred him to keep going. If anything happened to them, he wouldn't be able to forgive himself.

He coughed, something he'd been doing a lot recently. Even though the dehumidifier was working twenty-four-seven—probably to prevent the moisture affecting the computer—the stench of damp and mold lingered in the background. If the Russians didn't kill him, the damage the air was doing to his lungs probably would.

He'd made good progress on the Juggernaut replacement, but most importantly, he'd devised a way to send out a distress call. Having imagined what he'd do himself to prevent someone raising the alarm, he'd deduced that his captors would install a key stroke logger, enabling them to see every character he typed. That was all but confirmed the previous day when Mole Man had asked him to step out of the room for a few minutes. Working on the assumption that everything he did was being monitored, Poska had opened a plain text file and copied a large slice of code into it. He'd then deleted any unwanted characters, leaving only the plea for help.

*Call FBI. I am Andrius Poska. I was kidnapped and being held in Russia. Location unknown. Trace the data packages to find me.*

He'd then compiled the code containing that message into a component that prevented anyone seeing what he had written.

To make sure someone found it, he'd chosen to deploy it to a system he'd hacked as part of his job a couple of weeks earlier. It belonged to a video game manufacturer, and he knew the IT team responsible for it would be working feverishly to fix the flaws he'd highlighted in his report. As part of their service, Camber Blair included monitoring modules of clients' servers, and one such module looked for newly created files. Poska prayed that they'd installed it, otherwise it was unlikely that his message would be found in time.

It was now ready to be tested.

Poska considered getting some sleep first, to make sure he was refreshed for the big moment, but time wasn't on his side. The sooner he deployed the message, the greater the chance of being rescued before he was forced to let Juggernaut go live.

He drained his cold coffee and stretched, then got up and banged on the door. He heard the bolts being pulled back, and the lock turned. Poska stood back.

"What?" the guard barked.

"Tell Igor I'm almost ready to test the first module. I need an internet connection."

Poska had heard his captors use the name when talking about Mole Man.

The man slammed the door shut without a word, and Poska returned to his desk. He sat back in his chair and closed his eyes, fatigue washing over him. He must have drifted off, because he woke to find Igor shaking him. He looked at the clock in the corner of the screen and saw that it had been over twenty minutes since he'd asked for the Mole Man.

"I was told it's ready."

Poska yawned. "No, not yet. I just need to test one of the modules before I can continue. There's no point going any further until I know this works."

His captor adopted a strange look of both anger and disappointment. Poska took that as a small victory.

"Which module? What does it do?"

"It's an anti-virus detector. I need to know that it's able to identify the security measures in place."

Igor seemed to ponder his request, then he put his hands in his pocket. "Are you sure that's what it does?"

Poska swallowed. He wasn't a great liar, and deceit was well outside his comfort zone. Hell, this whole experience was. "Yes, I'm sure." He knew that the games manufacturer used well-known anti-virus software, and he'd hard-coded the name as the module's return value. That would make it appear to be a successful test.

"Does it do anything else apart from tell us that they use Norton Enterprise edition?"

Poska began to sweat. How could Igor possibly know that? He'd taken great care to extract the letters to make up that name from copied code before pasting it into his compiled file. Unless...

"For example," Igor continued, "you weren't planning to leave a message for the FBI, giving them your name and the fact that you're being held by Russians in an unknown location?"

Andrius Poska felt bile rising in his throat.

"I have a laptop which mirrors yours," Igor explained. "Every keystroke you make, every line you type, I see it on my screen. I saw the message you created, and this is what happens if you try anything like that again."

Igor took his hands from his pocket and tossed something to Poska, who caught it against his chest. When he looked down at the tiny, bloodied finger in his cupped hands, his blood froze. A howl of despair tried to leave his lips, but the only bodily function that worked was his gag reflex.

"You have five days left," Igor said, seemingly oblivious to the stench of vomit. "I suggest you get to work."

# Chapter 17

Eva Driscoll stopped near the entrance to a parking lot, just a stone's throw from the sprawling GRU building. Twilight was creeping along the streets, the day's final beams of sunlight fading into dusk. A chill embraced her, the mercury flirting with the icy grip of frost.

Farooq had been able to identify one of the numbers she'd sent him. The last person to call her attackers the night before was General Vasili Turgenev, the head of the GRU, which meant the man she'd killed had been telling the truth. It didn't take her long to find a picture of the General, and Farooq had been able to determine where he lived. He'd also tracked Turgenev's phone to the GRU headquarters a couple of hours earlier. All Eva had to do was wait at a point that he was sure to pass on his way home, and access his cell phone. She would then wait for him to contact Igor Cherenkov. Once he did so, Farooq would be able to trace Cherenkov's location, and Eva would do the rest. It irked her that she would have to wait for his reply, since Farooq wasn't allowed his cell phone inside the NID bunker.

Eva put the night vision scope to her eye to watch the vehicles leaving the GRU compound. The general would no doubt use an official car with a driver, so she discounted any vehicles with single occupants. Initially, a few cars trickled out. That soon became a stream as the working day ended. Eva spotted a few likely targets, but none of them carried

Turgenev. As the activity died down once more, she wondered if he was even in the building. Perhaps he'd left before she'd arrived, and she'd wasted the last few hours. She was about to message Farooq for an update on the General's position when a ZIL limousine left the gates. Eva checked for a rear passenger, and saw Vasili Turgenev speaking on his cell phone.

Eva put her own cell phone in the holder on the handlebars and set off in pursuit. She kept the bike a few cars behind the limo while she readied her phone. Farooq's software would allow her to access Turgenev's cell phone and give her complete control, allowing her to listen to all conversations even if there was no call in progress.

When the app was ready to connect, Eva pulled around the vehicles ahead of her and got behind the general's ZIL. She checked the screen for the number matching the one she'd memorized, but it didn't appear. That was strange. The software normally had a range of about twenty yards, and she was a lot closer than that to the target vehicle. None of the numbers in range were the one she was looking for, which meant either Turgenev had switched phones, or he had some kind of security system that masked its signal.

As she could only gain access to one cell phone at a time, Eva chose to be patient. If she stuck behind the ZIL long enough, eventually she would be able to determine which phones were on board. If there was only one, it would be easy. If there were two, one could belong to the driver, and it would be a coin toss as to which one she targeted.

After all that had happened so far, she could do with a bit of luck.

\* \* \*

"We're being followed, sir," Turgenev's driver said, looking at the general in his rear-view mirror.

Lev was widely regarded as the best driver in the GRU. If he said they'd picked up a tail, Turgenev believed him.

"Any idea who it is?"

"No, sir," Lev said. "It's a woman on a motorcycle. That's all I can tell you."

A woman on a bike? Could it be the American agent who had killed his team in Riga? Turgenev wasn't taking any chances. "Call it in. I want a team to intercept her. And notify the local police. If it's who I think it is, we'll need all the resources we can get."

Lev got on the radio, and Turgenev resisted the temptation to turn and look behind him. Doing so would alert the tail.

"They'll be with us in five," Lev said.

Turgenev said nothing. Instead, he checked that his door was locked and his seatbelt tightly fastened.

\* \* \*

It was several minutes before Eva was able to narrow it down to just two cell phone numbers. She was trying to decide which one to target when a car horn sounded behind her. She checked her mirror and saw two black-clad figures on motorcycles weaving between traffic, and they were closing on her. It could just be coincidence, but it felt more like déjà vu. Eva wasn't taking any chances. She selected the first number on her cell phone, waited a few seconds for it to connect, then shot past the ZIL and took the next right. Another glance in her mirror told her that her instincts had been spot on. The two bikes were right behind her, and gaining fast. Unlike her previous encounter in Riga, there was no way of outmaneuvering these Russians. Where she went, they could follow.

That only left one option.

Eva maintained a steady speed, allowing them to close. As they did, they split, aiming to approach either side of her. It was just what Eva had hoped for. She spotted a delivery truck coming toward her in the left lane. When it got to within ten yards, Eva stamped on the brake and jinked left. The rider approaching her had no option but to take avoiding action, which put him straight in the truck's path. Even over the roar of the engines, Eva could hear the sickening crunch as man met machine.

There was no time to congratulate herself. The other rider had pulled ahead of her, and he was reaching inside his leather jacket with his right hand. Eva kicked the bike down into second and twisted the throttle all the way open while pulling back on the handlebars. The front wheel shot up in the air, and Eva aimed it at the rider's back. He wasn't as naïve as his companion, and he countered the move by weaving to the side and hitting the brake. Eva dropped the wheel and looked behind her. Her opponent was once more reaching for a weapon, and she discounted braking to let him fly past her. It was a dance they could have performed indefinitely, and Eva was keen to end the confrontation. She saw a gap in the oncoming traffic and went for it, narrowly missing the front of a bus as she crossed the lane and mounted the expansive sidewalk. There were plenty of pedestrians, but none were foolish enough to try to stop her. Instead, they jumped aside as she passed, making progress easier. Eva sped to the corner, then rejoined the road, unzipping her leathers as she searched for a side street. She found one and dashed down it, skidding to a halt and turning to face the junction.

Her pursuer appeared seconds later, by which time Eva had her weapon drawn. She fired two shots at the moving target. The first missed, while the second pinged off the bike's handlebars. She tried a third time, but the gun jammed. Furious, she tossed it aside and reached for the throttle. The rider returned fire, but Eva was already moving, head down to reduce her profile, closing the gap in a deadly game of chicken. Her opponent blinked first, and Eva flew past him. She almost collided with a car as she made the corner and gunned the engine as she sought to flee the area.

Eva stole a glance behind her and saw that she had a healthy lead over the Russian rider, but he wasn't her only concern. The sound of sirens grew louder, and it wasn't long before she saw the first of the police cars. It was coming toward her, and fifty yards out the driver screeched to a halt and angled the car to block the highway.

Eva effortlessly slid around the back of the car before the occupants could get out, but there was more trouble ahead. Two more police vehicles were barreling toward her, and the one she'd passed was now back on her tail.

The other motorcyclist was also gaining fast.

Eva abandoned the busy main road and ducked down a side street. It was a big mistake. Vehicles lined both sides of the street, and the road was barely wide enough for both lanes of traffic. Eva was forced to slow down to match the speed of the cars ahead, and that allowed the other rider to close significantly. Eva was almost knocked from her bike when a bullet ricocheted off her helmet. A couple of inches to the right and she'd have been dead.

Spotting a gap in the oncoming traffic, Eva flicked the bike sideways, but was only able to overtake two vehicles before she was forced back into her own lane. She looked back and saw that her pursuer was now closer than ever.

Worse was to come. Up ahead, traffic was at a standstill. With no way out, and access to the sidewalk blocked by parked cars, Eva only had one option. With her heart racing, she closed on the car in front and popped a wheelie, launching the bike onto the vehicle's trunk. She was glad she'd opted for a dirt bike, as its design was optimal for such a move. Eva rode the vehicles like bumps on a motocross circuit, earning a barrage of horns and shouts of rage as she put distance between herself and her pursuer.

When confronted with a truck in front of her, Eva took to the roofs of the parked vehicles, then jumped the bike down onto the sidewalk. She powered to the junction and shot across, defying the red light.

Another mistake.

The gap she was going for closed as the lead car braked, and Eva slammed into it. She was catapulted into the air and came down hard, the wind knocked out of her. She lay there for a few seconds before her instinct told her to get up. Gingerly, she forced herself onto one knee, but that was as far as she got. Two bodies slammed into her, pinning her to the ground, while a third policeman stood over her, his pistol pointing at her face.

# Chapter 18

Gray entered the house and put a bag of groceries on the kitchen counter. The place they'd rented was an hour and a half outside of D.C., one of just a handful of homes a stone's throw from the Potomac. Gray had spent the entire morning sourcing the supplies they'd need to stay off grid if Eva failed in her mission. He and Sonny were sure she wouldn't, but it didn't hurt to be prepared. He'd purchased a second generator to act as a backup to the one that came with the property, and they had enough fuel, cans of food, and water to last them at least three months. They didn't have many weapons, just two handguns, but Gray had bought several boxes of ammunition and spare magazines. If things went south, the provisions they had would be worth a fortune. They could always source more weapons from anyone foolish enough to try to rob them.

The house was quiet, which wasn't normal.

Rather than calling out, Gray took the pistol from his waistband and held it in a two-handed grip as he moved down the hall.

Still silence.

Gray reached the bathroom and put his ear to the door. There was no sound of running water, but as he was about to move on, he heard a groan coming from inside. Gray took a couple of steps backward, pistol up and ready, then kicked the door open and rushed inside.

He'd expected to find an adversary, but instead saw Sonny struggling to put his T-shirt on. Gray lowered the weapon, relieved.

"If you want the bathroom, you just have to ask," Sonny said. "No need to shoot me."

"I thought something had happened," Gray replied.

Sonny started carefully combing his damp hair. "In my state? Fat chance."

Gray put the gun back in his waistband. "Where's Melissa?"

"In her bedroom, watching a movie with her headphones on. The soundtrack is all hip-hop, and she knows how much I hate that."

Gray sighed. The prospect of imminent nationwide anarchy had him constantly on edge. It was likely to get worse before it got better.

He walked back into the living room, followed by Sonny.

"How's Eva doing?" Gray asked.

"Last time I saw her she was outside GRU headquarters, then she started moving. That's when I took a shower."

Gray peered at the tracking software on the laptop, then clicked to zoom into her location.

"That doesn't look good," Gray said, frowning at the screen.

Sonny joined him. "It doesn't."

The green dot was stationary inside GRU headquarters. Gray checked the telemetry and saw that it hadn't moved in the last fifteen minutes.

"Something tells me she's not there for a social visit," Sonny said.

Gray didn't think so, either. In her last message, she'd said she was going to try to get access to a GRU cell phone, but

Gray didn't think her stupid enough to walk into the lion's den to do it.

"Maybe she's on the roof," Gray suggested. He switched to the 3D version, which showed that not to be the case.

"They must have captured her," Sonny said, concern etched on his face.

Gray had reached the same conclusion. He also knew what he had to do. He and Sonny had discussed the fallout of a Juggernaut attack, and it wouldn't stop at the American borders. The US dollar was the global currency, so the financial meltdown would be felt worldwide. Eva was the only one who could prevent it, so leaving her in the hands of the Russians wasn't an option.

"I'll check with Farooq, see if he knows anything."

"You'll have to wait until his shift finishes, remember?"

Gray sent a message on the encrypted Shield app anyway. He would wait for the reply.

Sonny got up and walked toward the hallway.

"Where are you going?" Gray asked him.

"To pack. I have to get her out."

"Don't be stupid. For one, they'd never let you on a plane, and even if they did, what use would you be to her? You can't even dress yourself."

"Then what?" Sonny glared. "We leave her? 'Nice try, Eva, but you're on your own'?"

"Oh, sit down, drama queen. I'll get her out."

Sonny turned. "You will? Without any persuasion?"

"Of course. She told us it's an off-the-books op, so we can't expect the Americans to do anything except wash their hands of her. And if she fails… well, we know what happens."

Sonny sat down on the sofa. "Normally you give the schpiel about having to look after Melissa. What's changed?"

"Juggernaut. If it goes live, nowhere will be safe for her."

# Chapter 19

General Vasili Turgenev peered through the grille in the cell door. After learning that the woman had been captured, he'd immediately returned to headquarters, eager to know if this was indeed Nolene Daniels.

There was no doubt about it. The picture sent by the American contact matched the woman he was looking at.

"Open it," he barked at the guard outside the cell.

The man fumbled with his keys before managing to unlock the door. He stood aside to let the head of the GRU inside.

Daniels was sitting on the solitary bunk, her wrists and ankles shackled and attached to a chain that fed through a large metal loop in the wall.

Turgenev remained by the door, out of reach.

"What to do with you?" he asked rhetorically.

"You could give me my phone call," Daniels replied.

She was confident, assured, despite her situation. Admiral Komarov had been right in saying she wasn't to be underestimated. Turgenev suspected that, as the Americans would say, this wasn't her first rodeo.

"I don't think so. But while I'm deciding on your fate, you can tell me what you know about Andrius Poska's whereabouts."

"How about you tell me where he is, and I'll tell you if it matches what I know?"

Turgenev smiled. He had to admire her spirit. "I think not. So, back to my original question: what to do with you?"

"Send me home with a stern warning not to return?" Daniels suggested.

"I was thinking more along the lines of life in prison, or death by firing squad. After all, I assume this is a black op, with complete deniability. Your American masters would be unlikely to object."

That appeared to strike a chord. Her face dropped momentarily, telling Turgenev he'd been right in his assumption. He decided to end the conversation there, giving her something to think about.

He left the cell, and the guard locked it behind him.

"No one goes in there without my permission. That includes you."

The guard nodded and Turgenev trekked back to his office. He had to report to Admiral Komarov and see what his superior wanted to do with the woman.

"General, we found something interesting on her phone."

Turgenev turned to see a member of the forensic technology team hurrying toward him.

"What is it?"

"She has some software that allows her to gain control of other cell phones. And I mean complete control. It's far superior to anything I've ever seen before."

"Analyze it, see if you can reverse-engineer it."

"Yes, sir. But I think you should know that when we discovered it, it was connected to your phone."

Turgenev took his cell from his pocket and woke it up. Nothing appeared out of the ordinary. "Are you sure?"

"Positive, sir. I heard you talking, clear as day. Your voice was picked up on your cell's microphone."

Mercifully, he'd changed phones earlier in the day, so there was very little sensitive information on his new device. Still, it was a worrying development.

"I want to know everything about that software. Where it came from, who has access to its feed, where the data is stored. I also want countermeasures, something that will block this software. Roll it out to all devices in the organization."

"Yes, sir. We also found sophisticated encrypted messaging software. It's called Shield. I've got my best men working on it."

"Very good."

Turgenev dismissed him, then hurried to his office. The question of what to do with Daniels remained, but for now at least, one of the options was off the table. He would have to keep her alive, just in case his tech team needed answers that only she could provide.

* * *

Eva watched the door slam shut, then tugged at the chain that was fastened to the wall. Her action was more out of desperation than any real hope it would yield. The chain held, but it didn't dampen her spirit. There would be other opportunities to escape.

There had to be.

If they were going to kill her, they probably wouldn't do it here in the cell. Most likely they'd take her to a remote location and shoot her before dumping her in an unmarked grave. Whatever they had in mind, Eva would be ready.

The one thing she couldn't count on was a rescue mission. The op was off the books, so President Robson wasn't

125

going to be sending a SEAL team in to bring her home. Even though she had the tracker hidden in her bra, she couldn't count on Gray. With Sonny unable to fly, there was no way he was going to leave his daughter. Even if he did, one man was never going to triumph over the entire Russian state apparatus.

No, she was on her own.

Should she have been so confident in her exchange with the General? Her training said to act submissive so that her captors would think her less of a threat. If tortured for information, it would add credence to her claims that she knew nothing. There was nothing to be gained in that respect. Turgenev already knew why she was here, and what her objective was. Regarding the threat she posed… well, she'd already demonstrated that by killing two GRU officers. Three, if the motorcyclist hadn't survived his head-on crash with the truck.

It was done, now, anyway. There was no changing the past.

Her future—and that of the Western world—was in her own hands.

# Chapter 20

Tom Gray walked into Melissa's room and stood by the side of the bed, watching her as she lay on her stomach watching a movie on her phone. The hum of a music track floated from her headphones, and her head rocked with the beat in a steady rhythm.

Melissa must have sensed him. She turned and took her headphones off, then paused the movie. "What did you get from the shops?" she asked.

"Erm… a few things. You can take a look later. First, I have to tell you something."

Melissa sat up. "Has it started?"

"Has what started?"

"That Juggernaut thing you and Uncle Sonny were talking about?"

Gray sat down next to her. "No, darling." *At least, not yet.* "No. It's about Eva."

"What about her?" Melissa asked slowly.

She looked like she didn't want to hear the answer. Gray sympathized; he didn't want to provide it.

But he had to.

"She was captured. In Russia."

Before he could elaborate, Melissa sprang to her feet.

"You have to get her out!"

"I know, but… wait… what?"

"You have to rescue her," Melissa repeated. "She saved our lives on the *Pearl of the Orient*. She also stopped you going to jail. It's the least you can do."

It hadn't been the response he'd expected. "Of course, darling. That's what I came to tell you. I just… I thought you'd be sad."

"Why would I be sad? Eva's family. So is Uncle Sonny. We have to look out for each other." She leaned in close and dropped her voice. "And if I'm honest, I don't think Uncle Sonny's up to it."

Gray suppressed a smile. "Yeah, I guess you're right."

He pulled her in for a hug, knowing that the road ahead would be difficult and fraught with danger. But he also knew that he couldn't abandon Eva, not when she needed him the most. And as he held his daughter close, he vowed to do whatever it took to bring their friend home safely, no matter the cost.

\* \* \*

Having squared things away with Melissa, Gray returned to the living room and looked up a number on his phone. He hated to ask for help, but he was wise enough to know that he couldn't take on the Russians alone. If it came to it, he would, but he much preferred to have backup.

"Hi, Travis. It's Tom Gray," he said when the call connected.

Travis Burke owned a freight company in Spring Hill, Tennessee. They had a common bond in that they'd both been screwed over by the ESO. Eva and Gray had helped Travis escape the evil organization's clutches. It was time to call in a marker.

"Hey, Tom. How's… wait. Please tell me you're in the area, just passing through, and you thought you'd catch up."

"I wish that was the case, but I need your help."

Silence greeted Gray.

"I was wondering when this call would come," Travis eventually said. "When you took down the ESO, I thought that was all behind me. I guess I was wrong."

"No, you were right," Gray said. "The ESO is gone. It's Eva. She needs our help."

As another silence fell, Gray considered reminding Travis that Eva had recently saved his life, rescuing him from the ESO compound in the New Mexico desert. He didn't need to.

"I guess I owe her," Travis eventually said.

He sounded reluctant, and Gray understood why. *Wait until he hears what the job is.*

"On one condition," Travis continued. "After this, we're square, and I'm out."

"Deal," Gray said.

"So, what kinda trouble is she in?"

"The worst kind," Gray said. "I can't give you details over the phone, but we'll rendezvous in Riga. Book yourself on the next available flight."

"Where the hell's Riga?" Travis asked.

"Latvia. I'll send you my ETA as soon as I have confirmation. See you there."

"Wait… do I need to bring anything?"

Gray thought about it for a second. "Your A-game."

He hung up. "One down, one to go."

"I was thinking," Sonny said. "Should we tell Farooq that you're going in?"

Gray considered it momentarily. "Best not to, not with a Russian mole inside the NID."

"Yeah, fair point."

Gray made his second call. This one was to Rees Colback, another man whose life Eva had saved.

"What?"

"Is that any way to speak to an old friend?" Gray asked.

"Tom! Sorry, I didn't recognize the number. How you doing, bud?"

"I'm good," Gray said. "Eva, not so much."

"Sorry to hear that."

"She needs help, Rees, and you're the only one I could turn to." Again, there was understandable hesitation. "It's not the ESO, if that's what you're thinking," Gray added.

"Then what is it?"

"She's being held by hostiles overseas. That's all I can tell you over the phone."

"You have to give me more than that," Rees said. "Are you talking about individuals, or a nation-state?"

Gray couldn't lie to him. Doing so would shatter the bond they shared. "The second one," Gray said. "I'll be honest, it's not going to be easy."

"And how many men do you have so far?" Rees asked.

"Just me and Travis," Gray admitted.

"That's it? What about Sonny?"

"He took a bullet to the chest a couple of weeks ago," Gray said. "He's fine, but he'll be out of action for some time."

Gray heard Rees pop open a can.

"Who else is on your list?"

"Just you," Gray said.

There was a slurping sound, then nothing.

"What do you say?" Gray pressed.

"When would we leave?"

"Today. As soon as possible. I'm meeting Travis in Riga."

There was a sigh. "Tom, you know better than anyone that you should never push a bad position. Three men isn't enough if you're talking about our red friends, and as Riga is just a few miles from there, I'll assume you are. I also imagine there's been no planning beyond how to get there. What about weapons? Transport? Evac?"

"We'll figure it out on the way," Gray said, already knowing that Rees was right. He'd put no thought into it besides getting Eva out. That was the surest way to ensure things went to shit.

"You'll get yourselves killed is what you'll do. Forget it, Tom. If you leave her, she dies. If you go, you die, too."

Again, Rees was right on the money. No matter how Gray looked at it, this was a suicide mission. There was one swaying factor, though.

"You might be right, Rees, but there are many more lives at stake than just me, Travis and Eva. If she doesn't complete her mission, the number of dead will be in the tens of millions. Maybe more than that. I have to go, with or without you."

"Nice try, Tom, but if it was that serious, the US government would be sending the entire Seventh Fleet."

Gray felt like he was losing the battle, and there simply wasn't time to explain the situation fully, never mind convince Rees to change his mind. "You know what? Forget it. Travis and I will go in. But be warned: something bad is coming. If you're not already a prepper, I suggest you become one, real fast."

Gray hung up.

"Not interested?" Sonny asked.

"No. And I don't blame him. He's right. I don't have a plan."

"But you will have," Sonny said. "We'll work on something while you're in the air and compare notes when you land. It won't be the first time we've thrown things together at the last minute."

"Yeah, well, for once I just wish we had a couple of weeks' notice to work through the details. Actually, scrap that. I just wish this shit would end and we could have a normal life."

"Yeah, me, too," Sonny sighed as he stood. "But it is what it is, so forget all that for now. Focus on getting Eva back, or none of us will have a life, normal or otherwise."

# Chapter 21

"Whoever it is, they're doing a great job of covering their tracks," Farooq said to Xi Ling. "I've been through the bank accounts of everyone who works in NID, and there's nothing unusual."

"Same here," Xi Ling said. She'd worked on checking other financial vehicles that could be used to launder money sent by the Russians.

"Then they must have offshored the money," Farooq decided. "It's probably being held in the Caymans or Switzerland. Either that, or they were paid in cash."

"Unlikely. I imagine it would take a lot for someone to sell out their country, and leaving that amount of money lying around is just asking for trouble. No, it's out there somewhere. We just have to find it."

Farooq yawned. "I'm beat." It was only nine in the evening, but they'd been up since five that morning and had done a ten-hour shift at the White House. Most of that time had been spent sitting around waiting to hear from Eva, and for some inexplicable reason, being inactive always sapped Farooq's energy. The working day was followed by another three hours once they got back to the apartment. They hadn't wanted to perform this task with others around, especially Greg Sharpe. The president's National Security Advisor was a micromanager, always hovering to see what the analysts were working on.

"I'm beat, too. Let's call it a night and make an early start before we go in."

"No," Farooq yawned. "Let's get a full night's sleep and forget this. They obviously know how to hide their tracks in a digital world."

Xi Ling gave him a curious look. "You don't think our skills are good enough?"

"Our skills are fine. The best," Farooq countered. "They just aren't suited to this problem." He stretched. "We can discuss a new approach in the morning. I'm gonna take a shower."

"Hey! Ladies first."

# Chapter 22

"Don't forget," Seddon Blake said, "the movers will be with you on Monday, and we expect you to be here on Tuesday. My people will be in touch for an exact time. If there's anything you want to bring from your other residences, you'll have to get them to your place before then."

"Understood," Robert Portman said. "And once again, thank you. What you've accomplished is… magnificent."

*I know*, Blake thought. "No, thank *you*, Robert. Without your generous contribution, it would never have happened."

It was a straight-out lie. Portman was seventy-seventh on the list. If he'd passed on the opportunity, there were plenty who would have willingly taken his place.

Blake helped Portman climb into the helicopter, then walked off the landing pad. Once he was clear, the huge structure began to rise on three gigantic hydraulic columns.

Blake sighed.

Poor Robert. His idea was good. Brilliant, Blake had to admit. However, Portman just wasn't the man to implement it. He might be as wealthy as the rest of the people due to arrive at Heliopolis in the coming days, but money didn't equate to intelligence, especially in the case of old money.

New money, now that was different.

Seddon Blake was truly a self-made man in every sense. His parents had been poor. Dirt poor. There was no family handout to get his first venture up and running. No inheritance money. No, Blake had started from the very bottom. And he wasn't an instant success. He made mistakes, but made damn sure he learned from them.

Blake made his first million when he was twenty-two. He had his first billion by the time he celebrated his thirtieth birthday. In the following twenty-five years, his wealth had ballooned to half a trillion.

With that kind of money, he had only one peer: Leonid Pertsov. The Russian president already ran an authoritarian regime, so there were no transparency rules to follow. People knew what he wanted them to know. Period. That enabled Pertsov to perpetrate the largest heist in history. When public services and infrastructure were sold off to the highest bidder, it was on the understanding that half of any profits were secretly sent to Pertsov's bank account on the Caribbean island of Nevis. Overall, Pertsov's fortune was probably greater than Blake's, as it was all in cash, not tied up in stocks, bonds and properties.

The similarities didn't end at their net worth. Like Blake, Pertsov understood that capitalism has its limitations. You can only force the working class to accept so much hardship before they cry, "Enough!"

America had almost reached that point, and the backlash was growing. While once Blake controlled the narrative through his social media company, his efforts were being diluted by new outlets which he had no control over. The cry to tax the rich was increasing in volume, and once on that road, there was no turning back. Sure, Blake could relocate to any country on the planet—one with a more favorable tax system—but he couldn't take all his wealth with him. A two percent wealth tax would hit him for ten billion dollars, which the US government could easily seize from his property portfolio before he liquidated it. Even if he had enough time to transfer those houses into the names of others, the IRS could still go after his companies.

Seddon Blake would rather see America crumble before he gave up his money.

The long-term plan had worked well. Too well, if he was honest. He hadn't expected the gullible masses to vote for their own demise, yet they'd done so time and time again. Promise them a better future, then cut their security net at the first opportunity. The last government had cut SNAP benefits and free school meals, resulting in hundreds of thousands of job cuts in the supply chain. They had also cut taxes on the biggest corporations. And still the people voted for it because his social media algorithm spewed out the lies and the uneducated swallowed them with a big dollop of ketchup. How long they would have believed the fantasy of pain today, glory tomorrow, was up for debate. Only, there would be no glory tomorrow. It would be pain in perpetuity.

Today, they lived paycheck to paycheck.

Tomorrow, there would be no more paychecks.

Blake would own everything. If people wanted to eat, or provide shelter for their loved ones, they would have to work for him. If they didn't want to, they would have no place in his new society.

Yes, it was slavery, but wasn't that how things had been for the last twenty years? If you work all day only to provide yourself with food and housing, isn't that the same thing? Work or starve to death? At least in Blake's new world, they would have security. A place to sleep. Free food. A day off every two weeks. Well, maybe every month. No point spoiling them.

In many ways, capitalism had spent the last fifty years preparing the population for this moment. It glorified suffering through the phrase, "pull yourselves up by your bootstraps." If you can't afford a home, it's because you don't work hard enough. Capitalism demands obedience. People have to put up with intolerable bullshit at work for fear of being fired; companies announce record profits yet refuse to give cost of living raises; they no longer offer affordable healthcare packages; slash bonuses; demand staff work sixty hours a week without paying any overtime. And people just put up with it. When they don't, they are simply replaced by someone who will.

It was slavery by any other name.

When the residents of Heliopolis returned to the surface, there would be a lot of work to do. Getting his satellites back online would be the first task. After that, the power grid. Only then could he think about ensuring his factories were operational once more. There was no telling how much damage would have been done to them. Maybe none. Maybe they would have been burned to the ground. There was simply no way of knowing. Just to be sure, he'd stored a duplicate of every single machine his companies owned on the storage level. His people would also spend the next year perfecting the robots that would power the new era in manufacturing.

As for the citizens of the new kingdom, they would once again be split into three classes. The ruling class, with himself on the throne. The middle class would be the residents of Heliopolis, who would oversee the rebuilding process. The working class would be left with the menial jobs. Crops had to be picked. Houses and businesses cleaned. Garbage hauled. Cities torn down and reconstructed.

All in Blake's image.

As for Portman's idea of cutting Pertsov out of the equation… that wasn't going to happen. The Russian President was Blake's closest friend, though they hadn't met in many years. They did, however, communicate weekly, and the only people who knew this were Blake and Pertsov.

Preparations in Russia were at the same stage as the United States. Pertsov had his own version of Heliopolis, though not quite as grand. It was built purely for his soldiers. The Russian people were more resilient than the US population, who had become reliant on technology and creature comforts like supermarkets stocked with food and clean drinking water. The Russians were by no means savages, but they had endured hardship in the past and could do so again, so it would require greater effort to enslave Pertsov's nation. One advantage Pertsov had was the relatively low number of gun owners. In America it was different, but Blake had the solution to that. His attack drones. Not the military drones that drop heavy ordnance, but smaller, more agile AI-powered machines the size of a suitcase. They carried two nine-millimeter machine guns and two hundred rounds, and could operate autonomously or be flown remotely. Once targets were identified, the machine's AI would take over. The artificial intelligence could prioritize the targets and create a plan of attack within milliseconds, then execute.

Anyone refusing to comply in Blake's new world would have no place in it.

"Sir, you have a shareholder call scheduled in eleven minutes."

Blake turned, thanked Vanessa, and headed for the elevator.

# Chapter 23

Andrius Poska was running on caffeine and adrenaline. His body craved sleep, but he couldn't afford any down time. Doing so would knock him off the exacting schedule.

It would also invite the nightmares.

He'd had a brief rest five hours earlier, but the moment he'd stopped thinking about code, his mind switched to his wife and daughter. He was suffering mental anguish, but it would be exponentially worse for them. For one, Poska still had all of his fingers.

The thought of his daughter's bloody digit again brought bile to his throat.

He tried to cast the picture from his mind, determined to produce a working version of Juggernaut before the deadline. He'd vowed never to give it to the Russians, but if he didn't, his family would be tortured to death. Even if he did deliver, they were still certain to die. What else were the Russians going to do? Let them go free to tell the world what had happened? No, they would be silenced.

All three of them.

It was a hopeless position. After much deliberation, he'd decided that all he could do was minimize the pain. Refusing to complete the task would see his wife and daughter punished, as would failing to deliver on time. It was pointless even trying to escape. Even if he managed to, it would be a death sentence for Sofija and Claire.

If he gave the Russians what they wanted, he could at least hope for a quick end for all of them.

First, he had to complete Juggernaut, and now came the first major test. He needed to copy some compiled libraries from the servers at Camber Blair, the cyber security firm he worked for. To try to replicate these files would take him months, time he didn't have. If his bosses had been informed of his kidnapping, they were sure to have worked out the reason for it. Their first step would surely be to lock the servers down tight, or even take them offline temporarily. That's what he would have done. The problem was, he didn't know for sure that anyone knew he was missing. He wasn't due back from vacation for another six days, so unless he was reported missing by Sofija's mother and his disappearance was somehow reported to Camber Blair, no one would be any the wiser.

For the first time in his ordeal, he hoped no one knew of his predicament.

Poska got up and knocked on the door, then took a couple of steps backward. When it opened, he asked to speak to Igor. He received a grunt in reply, then returned to his desk.

Igor burst into the room moments later, looking like he'd just woken up.

*It's okay for some*, Poska thought.

"What?" Igor barked.

"I need internet access so I can copy some files from my company servers."

Igor took a satellite phone from his pocket. "Move," he said, and shooed Poska aside. He sat down in front of the laptop and opened the internet settings. After entering some details, he stood.

"I'll be watching everything you do," Igor warned Poska.

It wasn't necessary. Poska knew he would never be rescued, and that even if he was, it would be counterproductive. He had no intention of raising the alarm.

He remoted onto the company servers and entered his username and password, then held his breath as he waited for it to connect. A circle appeared on the grayed-out screen, spinning slowly in contrast to Poska's racing heartbeat.

*Please. Please!*

The screen refreshed, and Poska pumped his fists as he saw the familiar file directory. Fearful that his connection might be spotted by someone at Camber Blair and terminated, he quickly copied over the files he needed. The transfer dialog calculated the time remaining as six minutes, which wasn't unusual given the size of the files and the unorthodox internet connection. It made for an anxious time. Poska sat with his fingers crossed, his butt cheeks clenched, hardly daring to breathe as he watched the seconds tick down.

It was a bittersweet moment when the last file completed its transfer. He'd cleared the main hurdle, but in doing so he'd condemned himself and his family—not to mention countless others—to death.

"It's done," he sighed.

Igor severed the connection and put his satellite phone away. "When will it be ready?"

*He's asking me to name the date of my death.* "Sunday, as instructed." Poska thought he might be able to finish sooner, but he was in no rush to facilitate his own demise.

Igor walked out of the room, speaking over his shoulder. "It better be."

# End of Times

# Chapter 24

The moment he got off the plane, Gray checked his phone. Eva's tracker showed that she was still inside GRU headquarters. He wasn't sure if that was good news or bad. Maybe she was already dead. Ignoring the cacophony of different languages and the hum of activity around him, he zoomed in as close as he could. After a few moments he was relieved to see the dot move. It only shifted a few pixels across the screen, but it suggested she was pacing the room she was in.

At least she was still alive. He only hoped it remained that way for the next few hours.

Gray passed through immigration and out into the arrivals area. Travis Burke wouldn't land for another two hours, so Gray looked around for somewhere to grab a coffee. As he did, he felt a strong hand on his shoulder.

Instinctively, he tensed, his training kicking in. He spun around, ready to confront whoever was behind him. The stranger was Gray's height, but better built, and there was a grin on his mahogany face.

"Relax, Tom," a familiar voice said.

Gray's eyes widened in surprise as he found himself face to face with the last person he expected to see here.

"Rees?"

"In the flesh."

"But… what are you doing here?" Gray asked. "You said you wouldn't help."

"I know, but I couldn't let you do this alone. Eva's one of us, and we don't abandon our own. Besides, it sounds like some bad shit is about to go down. I'd rather try to prevent it than be stuck in the middle of it."

Gray offered a stoic nod. "I appreciate it. We're going to need all the help we can get."

Rees hefted his backpack onto his shoulder. "Where's Travis?"

"His flight lands in a couple of hours," Gray told him.

"Then let's find a place to talk. We need to go over the plan."

Gray simply stared back at him.

"You do have a plan?" Rees pressed.

"Sort of," Gray admitted.

They found a quiet corner in a nearby café. Over steaming cups of coffee, Gray laid out the scant details of the operation: they would drive to Moscow, wait for Eva to be moved, then rescue her in transit.

Rees managed a laugh, though he clearly wasn't amused. "That's it?" He shook his head. "Man, I knew this was a mistake."

"Then let me tell you what happens if we don't rescue Eva and her mission fails."

Gray kept his voice low as he explained the Juggernaut situation. By the time he was done, Rees looked like he was going to throw up.

"That's some scary shit."

Gray nodded. "Tell me about it."

They sat in silence for a while. Gray pondered the logistics problem, while Rees tried to digest the indigestible.

With over an hour and a half until Travis was due to join them, Gray suggested they eat. They found a fast-food outlet and ate burgers while they waited.

"If we're gonna free Eva, we'll need hardware," Rees said, referring to weapons. "What's the plan for that?"

Gray had no connections in the area, but he spotted a couple of passing airport cops, which gave him an idea. It wasn't perfect, and they would probably only get their hands on a couple of pistols, but it was a start.

"We'll deal with that once we get to Moscow," Gray told him. "The first thing we need is wheels."

"If you find something over ten years old, I can probably hotwire it."

"No need," Gray told him. "I'll buy a couple of bikes. We don't need the local police on our backs."

"Sounds good. What about the border? We just gonna ride across like tourists?"

"No. Eva said she was going to go cross country. We'll do the same, hence the bikes."

An overnight bag landed on their table. "Hey, guys," Travis Burke said, looking around. "Where's the others?"

"This is it," Gray said as he stood. They shook hands.

Travis clapped Rees on the back. "Hey, brother. So, what's the deal?"

"I'll let Tom explain it," Rees told him. "I'm still trying to get my head around it."

Gray outlined the plan as they walked out of the terminal. With it being sparse on detail, he was done by the time they reached the taxis. Gray had already found a motorcycle dealership online, and he gave the driver the address.

An hour later, Gray had purchased two second-hand Honda dirt bikes. Travis had never ridden one, so he opted to ride pillion on Gray's machine. They stripped their luggage of non-essentials and strapped what remained to the back of Rees's bike.

"I hope you slept on the flight over," Gray said as he fired up his machine. "It's about to get intense."

# Chapter 25

After spending the night in a cheap hotel, Gray, Rees and Travis woke early and spent hours looking for the ideal spot in the center of Moscow. Eventually they found a place with a good flow of traffic on the main street and a side street off to the right which was quiet and secluded enough for their purpose. It had no CCTV, and just a handful of residential apartments. They parked one of the bikes there, and Travis and Rees waited at the other end of the street for Gray's signal. He took a position on the main street half a mile away.

All they could do now was wait.

Gray checked Eva's location once more. She still hadn't moved. He didn't know if that was good news or bad. It was great, of course, that Eva was still alive, but it would be impossible to spring her from GRU headquarters. If they didn't move her, this whole trip would have been for nothing.

It was half an hour before Gray spotted what he was looking for. The police car was a white Ford Focus with a blue stripe painted down the side and a light bar sitting atop the roof.

Gray had already prepared a text message to send to Travis: simply, "Go." He hit Send as the cop car cruised past, then pulled out of his parking space and followed it closely.

When the target vehicle was three hundred yards from the side street, Gray made his move. He hit the gas and drew level with the cop car, then swerved left and collided with it. It wasn't a huge impact, but it was enough to get the driver's attention.

Gray jerked ahead and started to weave the bike within the lane, trying to appear drunk. He checked his mirrors and saw the car's light bar illuminate, followed by the siren. Gray slowly looked behind him, then made an exasperated gesture. He signaled right, then pulled into the side road, and saw Rees and Travis approaching nonchalantly from the other end of the street.

Gray pulled over to the curb and turned the engine off. He made a couple of attempts to lower the kickstand, then he stumbled off the bike and fell to the ground. He sat up and faced the police car, a confused look on his face.

His ploy seemed to work. The two cops exited their vehicle and kept their pistols holstered, which meant they didn't see him as a threat. They stood over him, and the larger, older officer took the lead. He started berating Gray while the junior officer examined the side of the car, looking for signs of damage.

From the corner of his eye, Gray saw Travis and Rees casually walking toward the scene. He staggered to his feet and took a step to the side before steadying himself. The older cop grabbed Gray's shoulder and slapped his helmet. It was obvious that the officer wanted Gray to remove it, but that wasn't part of the plan. Thankfully, Travis and Rees were now close enough that Gray could launch into action. He took hold of the cop's wrist with his left hand and used his right to push the man's elbow upward. The cop doubled over, and Gray kneed him in the face, then swept his legs away. The cop fell hard, hitting his head and knocking himself out.

Rees was just as efficient. As the younger Russian reached for his weapon, Rees pinned his gun hand to his side and kicked his legs out from under him. The kid toppled like a bowling pin, and once on the ground Rees delivered a punch to his head that put his lights out.

"Grab his weapon, then get them in the car," Gray said, stuffing the older cop's Makarov into the back of his pants.

Travis relieved the other cop of his weapon, but instead of lifting the unconscious kid, he paused.

"If we leave them alive, they'll alert others when they come 'round."

Gray knew that Travis was right, but killing the innocent police officers wasn't something he was comfortable with. "We'll just have to take our chances," Gray told him.

"Or," Rees offered, "you could wear the big cop's uniform and put us in the back of the car, as if we're your prisoners. I mean, I ain't seen many black Moscow cops, have you? We could put these two in the trunk."

Gray liked the idea. It solved the problem of what to do with the Russians, and the clothes looked close to his size. "Okay, we'll go with that."

After stripping the larger cop, they bundled the pair in the trunk. Gray put on the uniform, and it was a reasonable fit.

"Let's buy some tape and secure these guys properly. We can't have them banging on the trunk when they wake up."

"What about the bikes?" Rees asked. "Should we park them somewhere in case we need them again?"

"Okay," Gray agreed, "but make it quick."

Rees picked up Gray's bike and rode off. He was gone for about three minutes, returning at a jog. "I left them around the corner. Should be safe there."

Gray drove the police car to a local garage, where he purchased some masking tape. They then found a quiet spot and Travis and Rees bound the prisoners tightly while Gray checked on Eva's position.

She still hadn't moved.

# Chapter 26

"Come!" Vasili Turgenev bellowed.

The door to his office opened, and in walked the head of the forensic technology department, snapping to attention in front of the general's desk.

"Sir. We've been through every byte of data on the woman's phone."

"And?"

"It appears to be new. A burner. The only time she has used it has been for the Maps app, the messaging app called Shield, and the app that managed to connect to your cell phone."

"Yes, yes, but what of those apps?" Turgenev asked, irritated.

"They were downloaded from two distinct websites. No URL, just IP addresses. I have my team dissecting the code as we speak."

"What about the woman?" the general asked. "Could she provide you with any help?"

The soldier's face momentarily suggested it was the stupidest question he'd ever heard, but he quickly remembered whom he was addressing. "No, sir. She's just the end user. She couldn't tell us anything that we don't already know."

That settled one question that had been plaguing Turgenev.

He dismissed the soldier with a wave of the hand. Once he was alone, he stood and buttoned his jacket. If Daniels was going to be of no help, there was no point delaying the inevitable.

Turgenev took the elevator down to the detention block and walked along the corridor. Several of the cells were occupied, but none contained prisoners as dangerous as Daniels. That was why three guards stood outside her cell.

"Go and tell my driver to meet us outside in three minutes." To the others, he said, "We're taking her for a long walk."

His meaning was clear.

Under normal circumstances, Turgenev would have instructed the men to drive the prisoner to a forest an hour outside of the city and put a bullet in the back of her head.

Not this time.

Daniels had proven herself to be a worthy adversary. Not only that, she was here to thwart the most important mission in Russian history. She could not be allowed to do that.

To ensure Daniels didn't escape and foil Juggernaut, Turgenev would kill her himself.

One of the guards disappeared, and Turgenev gestured for the others to open the cell door.

* * *

The deadbolt on the door screeched as it was pulled back, waking Eva from a troubled sleep. She sat upright, completely unaware of the time. There was no window in the cell, so she might have slept for ten minutes or ten hours. It felt like the former.

The door opened, and General Vasili Turgenev walked in. He was quickly flanked by two guards. They moved toward Eva, both holding cuffs. She could see that one pair was for her wrists, the other for her ankles.

They were moving her.

The question was, where? And why? It probably wasn't to a five-star hotel.

"Care to tell me where we're going?" she asked Turgenev.

He didn't reply. Didn't even look her in the eye. He focused on the restraints being placed on her.

Eva stole a glance at the two guards and saw one of them give the other a brief, malevolent grin.

She'd seen that look before. It suggested something bad was going to happen, and they were looking forward to it.

They weren't going to transfer her to a new location.

They were taking her to her final destination.

Once the new restraints were on, the guards removed the chains around her wrists and ankles, then pulled Eva to her feet. The floor was cold under her bare feet.

Turgenev was first out of the cell, and he stood back as Eva was escorted out, then followed down the corridor.

Eva knew she didn't have long. Would they kill her here, in the grounds of the GRU headquarters? Eva thought it unlikely. That meant a journey, which would give her a little time to work on her escape. Her guards were both in their thirties. One lithe, with close cropped blond hair, the other showing the beginnings of a paunch. The former would offer the most danger in a fight. The General himself was in his late fifties, maybe early sixties. That didn't make him any less formidable. He looked to be built of granite. Probably a veteran of the war in Afghanistan. Taking all three of them out wasn't going to be easy. The one factor on her side was that the guards had cuffed her hands in front of her, rather than behind.

The outlook darkened when they exited the building. A car was waiting, the driver standing by the open rear passenger door. He, too, looked like he could hold his own in a fight.

Eva's head was forced down and she was pushed into the car. The blond got in beside her, and Turgenev took the other rear seat, sandwiching Eva between them. Once the driver and front passenger got in, they set off.

\* \* \*

Gray jerked upright in his seat. "She's moving," he said.

He waited to see where the green dot marking Eva's location was heading, then handed the cell phone to Rees and started the car.

"Navigate for me."

Gray drove the car out of the rear of the industrial unit where they'd been hiding for the last three hours. His heart began to race, as it always did when a confrontation was close.

"Take a left at the end of the street," Rees said.

Gray followed the verbal directions for the next ten minutes, until eventually they were on the same road as the target vehicle.

"I'll stay behind it until we can identify which one she's in," Gray told the others.

It didn't take long. Rees noted that Eva had made a right up ahead, but Gray only saw one vehicle make the turn.

"It's the limo," he told the others, following directly behind the ZIL.

"This isn't good," Travis noted, and Gray wholeheartedly agreed. If he stayed on their tail for too long, he was sure to be spotted. Fall back too far, and Eva might be dropped at her destination before they had a chance to intercept and snatch her.

The current location wasn't the ideal place to make the stop. They were in a retail district, with busy shops all around them. Too many witnesses for Gray's liking. He eased off the gas, letting a gap build up in the hope that someone would get between them.

The gap started to fill, and soon there were five cars in front of Gray. With Rees still tracking Eva on the cell phone, that was as close as they needed to be.

Twenty minutes later, Gray's adrenaline levels were still high. Traffic had thinned once more, and only one car separated them from the limousine. They were on the outskirts of Moscow, heading northeast.

"Any idea where they're taking her?" Travis Burke asked.

"Let me take a look," Rees said, and expanded the map to see what lay ahead on the route.

Gray already knew. He'd seen enough spy movies to know how the Russians made undesirables disappear.

"They're going to shoot her," he said. "We have to move in now."

They were on a highway. Traffic was light, but what they were about to do wasn't going to go completely unnoticed. That didn't matter. Civilians were unlikely to interfere in a traffic stop, and even less likely to stick around if it escalated.

Gray identified the switches for the roof lights and siren.

"Rees, don't make a move until I give the word."

"The word being?"

"A loud bang," Gray said.

He hit the switches and waited for the limo to pull over. And waited…

And waited…

"Is that guy deaf and blind?" Travis wondered aloud.

"Maybe the GRU have immunity," Rees suggested.

Whatever it was, Gray knew he had to come up with a different plan. He was going through options when the limo's blinker came on and it started to slow down.

"Okay, here we go. Heads up."

Gray eased the car to a stop behind the ZIL. He left the engine running as he got out. Throughout the journey, he'd played a scenario out in his head. Get to the driver's window, shoot him and any front passenger, then focus on those in the rear.

That plan disintegrated even as he was walking through it.

The driver of the limo got out, angrily waving his hands as he berated Gray. Gray had no idea what he was saying, nor did he care. The plan was screwed. Time to improvise.

Gray whipped out his pistol and shot the driver twice in the chest. The man staggered backward, but didn't go down. He reached for his own weapon, but Gray was still advancing and had switched his aim to the man's head to avoid what must have been a ballistic vest. Two more rounds found their target and the driver collapsed.

* * *

Eva didn't know what the driver was saying, but he didn't sound happy. Police sirens tended to have that effect on people. He had a back and forth with Turgenev, then hit the indicator and pulled to the side of the road.

158

The traffic stop was an unwelcome distraction. Eva was preparing to launch her escape en route, because once they reached their destination, she knew her options would be limited. In the confines of the car, her adversaries had nowhere to go. Launching an attack while going seventy miles an hour had its dangers, but everyone in the vehicle would face them.

Eva just had to get lucky.

The driver got out, and Eva heard him shouting at the police officer. Her head snapped around when the sound of gunfire filled the car. She saw the driver stagger backward and reach for his weapon, but two more shots dropped him.

Eva didn't know what the hell was happening, but knew she had to act. Cops didn't shoot GRU officers for no reason, so either someone wanted to rescue her, or she was the target.

When the front passenger got out, Eva saw the blond reach for his own gun. She seized her chance. She took full advantage of having her hands in front of her and elbowed the blond guard twice in the face. She then unclipped her seatbelt and jumped onto his lap with her back to the door, pinning his arm so he couldn't draw his weapon. At the same time, she kicked out at General Turgenev, striking him in the face.

In the confined space, it was difficult to hit with real power or do much damage with her bare feet, but it took his attention away from getting his hands on a weapon.

There was another burst of gunfire from outside the car, but Eva had other problems to deal with. The blond had recovered from her lightning attack, and he grabbed Eva around the throat with his free hand. She struck him in the ribs with her elbow, but it seemed to have no effect. His grip

159

was relentless. He managed to buck and twist until his other arm was free, then threw Eva into the footwell. He drew his pistol and pointed it at Eva's head.

The next shot blew in the passenger side window and emerged from the blond's forehead, spraying Eva with blood. The shooter moved into view and aimed at Turgenev.

"No!" Eva shouted. She pushed herself back onto the seat just as the other passenger door opened and someone stuck a pistol in the General's face.

"Tom?" Eva looked around. "Please tell me you didn't bring Sonny."

"No. He's safe at home. You okay?"

Eva used her sleeve to wipe the blond guard's blood from her face. "It's not mine."

The other door was yanked open and the blond's body was pulled out. Rees Colback took its place.

"Hey," he smiled. "Mind if we tag along?"

"As long as you get me out of these," Eva said, holding up her cuffs.

Rees rifled through the dead guard's pockets and found the key. He removed her restraints, then searched the other bodies and collected their weapons. He got in beside Turgenev and handed Eva a pistol, placing the Russian in the middle seat. Gray got behind the wheel.

"Who's this guy?" Rees asked.

"The man who knows where Andrius Poska is being held." She banged on the driver's seat. "Get us out of here."

"Where to?" Gray asked.

Eva handed Turgenev the cuffs and stuck her gun in his ribs. "Somewhere remote."

# Chapter 27

Farooq Naser sat back in his chair and sighed as he rubbed his eyes.

"Still nothing?" Xi Ling asked, sipping her cold tea.

"Nada."

Farooq had been sifting through the ELINT—electronic intelligence—chatter coming out of Russia. Anything regarding an American woman, Nolene Daniels or Eva Driscoll in particular. There had been nothing.

There was no good reason for Eva to go silent, and certainly not for two full days.

Xi Ling rubbed Farooq's arm. "She's a big girl. She knows how to take care of herself."

He returned a smile, but her words didn't ease his anxiety. "I know, but—"

A message flashed up on the screen. It was from Camber Blair, the company Andrius Poska worked for, reporting an external entry to their system.

While Farooq was reading, the message disappeared.

"What the…?"

He searched for the message based on the time of delivery, but it was nowhere to be found.

Someone had deleted it.

Farooq surreptitiously cast his eyes around the room. Walter Caine, the President's chief of staff, was in a conference room with the national security advisor, Greg

Sharpe. Neither of them were on a computer. Two of the three analysts were in the glass-walled break room, which left Paul Heaton.

And he looked nervous.

"Did you see that?" Farooq asked Xi Ling quietly.

"What?"

Farooq explained what had happened. "I'm sure it was Paul. Just to be sure, can you get onto the server and check the database log files? Any instruction to delete a message will be tied to a user login."

"Sure," Xi Ling said, "but is there any reason you can't do it yourself?"

"I won't be here," Farooq told her. "I'm going to Camber Blair." He rose, doubled over, and groaned. "I shouldn't have eaten that reheated truck stop burrito," he said, a little too loudly. "I'm heading home for the day."

She watched him go, then shrugged at Heaton, who was looking at her. "What can I say? He eats like a racoon."

She got to work on the database, knowing she'd do it in half the time that Farooq could ever dream of.

\* \* \*

Farooq maintained the act all the way to his car, then made a miraculous recovery. He typed the address of the Camber Blair building into his Satnav and set off. It was a short journey, barely twenty minutes, but his first encounter with their security suggested it was going to be a long day.

The security guard at the gate asked if he had an appointment. Farooq flashed his White House pass, but that didn't have the effect he was hoping for.

"Sorry sir, but no one is permitted entry without an appointment. No exceptions."

There was little point in arguing to be let in. The guard had a job to do, and to ask him to disregard his duties could cost the man his job. He reversed, turned the car around, then parked a short distance away. He called Xi Ling on the NID direct line.

"Can you get me the name of the head honcho at Camber Blair? I can't get past the gate."

Xi Ling told him to wait, then he heard the keyboard click for a full thirty seconds. Xi Ling read off the name.

"Thanks, honey. See you later."

Farooq looked up the switchboard number for the cyber company and dialed. After going through all the automated bullshit, he asked to speak to a human.

A perky voice answered. "Camber Blair, Victoria speaking, how may I direct your call?"

"Hi, Victoria. Can I please speak to Chuck Evans?"

"May I ask who's calling?"

"Farooq Naser."

"And what is it regarding, Mr. Naser?"

"That's ears only, I'm afraid," Farooq told her, crossing his fingers.

"One moment, please."

Orchestral music filled Farooq's ears for what seemed an eternity. Eventually, the receptionist returned.

"I'm sorry, Mr. Evans is unavailable."

Farooq had feared as much. He didn't want to give too much away over the phone, but he had to speak to the man at the top. He cursed himself for not asking Xi Ling for a direct cell number for Evans.

"Please tell him it's regarding the intrusion last night and the message sent to NID within the last hour."

The music returned, but this time the intrusion was brief.

"Chuck Evans. How can I help you Mr.… Naser?"

"Hi. You sent a message to the NID recently. I'm here to investigate."

"There's no need. We have our best men on the job."

"Trust me, there's more to it than I can discuss over the phone. I need to speak to you in person."

There was silence while Evans considered the proposal.

"Let me call NID and confirm you are who you say you are."

"No!" Farooq said, with panic in his voice. He took a breath. "No," he said again. "Someone at NID is compromised. They are working with the people holding Andrius. If you speak to the wrong person, we lose our only chance to save him." Farooq felt the conversation getting away from him. All he could do was rely on logic. "Look, you sent a message to NID saying your servers were accessed last night, correct? I could only know that if I was at NID. If, as you said in your message, the credentials used belong to Andrius, then I can track him and get him out before Juggernaut goes live."

The use of the app's name seemed to shock Evans into action.

"When can you be here?" he asked.

"I'm looking at the gate right now. Tell the guard to expect me."

Farooq ended the call and waited until he saw the man in the sentry box pick up a phone, then drove to the barrier again. It rose before he had a chance to stop.

Farooq parked as close to the entrance as he could. It was a four-story rectangular building with few windows dotted at irregular intervals. Inside, the foyer was all glass and chrome. Farooq looked for the reception desk. Instead, he saw a man in his fifties wearing chinos and a faded red polo shirt.

"Mr. Naser, I'm Chuck Evans. Come with me."

Farooq followed him to a stairwell, and they climbed to the third floor. At the top, a corridor ran left and right.

"What did the intruder access?" Farooq asked.

"From what we have gathered, several digital components that Andrius created several months ago. The ones he used in the Juggernaut demonstration."

"Do you think it's him?"

"It has to be," Evans said as they reached a door marked Sensitive Area. Evans swiped a key card into a reader and the door clicked open. "After you."

Farooq walked into another hallway. This one had three doors set into the right-hand wall. Evans opened the second.

The room was a collection of workstations, and Farooq immediately noticed that there were no windows. Light was provided by LED bulbs in the ceiling. There were twelve desks in all, but only one was occupied.

The man sitting in front of a dual monitor setup was clearly expecting them.

"This is Roger," Evans said. "He'll give you whatever you need."

Roger stood and let Farooq have the seat. Evans stood back so as not to crowd him.

"Okay," Farooq said, flexing his fingers before pulling the keyboard into a comfortable position. "Which server was it?"

# Chapter 28

"This will do," Eva said, and Tom Gray pulled the car off the dirt track and turned off the engine. The forest engulfed them, the canopy overhead casting a false twilight. Gray got out and opened the rear door. Rees exited, and Eva jabbed her pistol into Turgenev's ribs.

"Go."

The General shimmied over and climbed out of the car. Eva followed, drinking in the heavy woodland scent as her bare feet landed on the cold ground.

"What you are doing is an act of war," Turgenev said. They were his first words since being captured.

"And what you're doing with Andrius Poska isn't?" Eva asked him.

"We are protecting the *Rodina*," the General said with conviction.

"Protecting your Motherland by destroying mine? Doesn't seem fair." Eva spun him around and kicked him in the base of the spine. "Move."

Rees took up position on Turgenev's left, with Travis on his right. Gray fell in step with Eva as the quintet marched deeper into the woods.

"Thanks," Eva said quietly. "For coming for me. It can't have been easy leaving Melissa."

"Actually, it was her idea."

Eva looked at him, confused.

"Yeah," Gray said. "I told her you were in trouble and her first thought was that I should get you out. Obviously, that was my plan all along, but Melissa was totally on board."

Eva was stunned. Previously, Melissa had been reticent to see her father leave her. Now she was advocating for it. The little girl was growing up fast.

"I'll thank her when we get back," Eva said. For now, there was work to do. "Stop!" she ordered.

Turgenev halted and turned to face her.

"Where is Andrius Poska?" Eva asked him.

"You know I cannot tell you that."

Eva never dreamed this was going to be easy. "Tom, you got a knife?"

"Never thought to bring one to a gun fight," Gray replied.

Rees and Travis shook their heads.

"Shame," Eva said, and shot Turgenev in the foot.

The Russian collapsed, rolling on the ground as he tried in vain to alleviate the pain. Through clenched teeth, he rattled off a diatribe in Russian.

"I don't speak the lingo, but I'm pretty sure he's not complimenting your hair," Travis said.

Eva didn't think so, either. She stepped to the General and lifted his uninjured foot so that it was level with her chest. "Where is Poska?"

"I will never—"

Eva placed the muzzle of the pistol in the crook of Turgenev's knee and pulled the trigger. Blood and bone erupted as his kneecap disintegrated.

"I can keep this up all day," Eva said, letting go of his leg. She stood back and gave Turgenev time to reflect on the situation.

A thought jumped into her head as she watched the general squirm in agony. She went over to him, pleased to see him recoil in terror. She was getting through to him. Eva went through his pockets and found the general's cell phone. It required facial recognition to open it, so she held it to Turgenev's face. The screen refreshed, and Eva removed the security settings before going to his contacts. They were written in Cyrillic. That was easily remedied.

"Tom, I need your help. Get your phone out."

Gray took his cell from his pocket and followed Eva's instructions. In settings, Gray showed her where to find the language menu. She selected English from the list. When she returned to the contact list, she immediately found what she was looking for.

The number for Igor Cherenkov, the man suspected of holding Andrius Poska.

She was about to ask Gray to contact Farooq and ask for a trace when she heard the familiar Shield notification sound.

"It's Farooq," Gray said. "He has a location for Poska and wants to know if I can go to Russia to get him out."

"He doesn't already know you're here?" Eva asked.

"No. You said there was a mole inside NID, so I didn't tell him in case the message was intercepted or Farooq inadvertently mentioned it. He doesn't even know you're safe."

That made sense. Eva hadn't had the chance to check in.

"How do we play this?" Gray asked.

Eva thought about it. NID didn't know whether she was alive or dead. Would they send someone else in? Given the criticality of the mission, that was a distinct possibility. She couldn't have that.

"I'll contact NID and tell them I managed to escape," she said. "That way they won't send a replacement to get in our way."

"Are you sure?" Gray asked her. "What if the mole tells his contact and they move Poska?"

It was a valid point.

"Besides," Rees said, "it took us a couple of days to get here. Even if they send someone direct to Moscow, it would be twenty-four hours before they were briefed and ready to go. That gives us plenty of time to grab Poska and be on our way home. Especially now that we have his location."

"He's right," Travis added. "Let them think you failed. While they're working on a plan B, we can finish the mission."

Gray nodded his agreement.

"I haven't reported in for a couple of days," Eva pointed out. "They might have already sent someone to finish the job."

"Then I suggest we get moving," Gray said. "I'll tell Farooq our current situation and warn him not to tell anyone. Let NID think you failed. That way, the Russians won't be looking for you."

"You forgot about your little rescue mission." Eva pointed her weapon at Turgenev, who was now quiet as shock kicked in. "I think they'll know when they find the bodies on the highway. And his."

His usefulness expired, she shot the General in the forehead.

"Then we make our move before word gets out," Gray said, tapping on his phone. He waited for a response, then showed the screen to Eva. "Poska's location. Let's go."

# Chapter 29

It took Xi Ling only minutes to force her way into the NID database and scan the log files. These detailed every transaction, every query to the database. The instruction to delete the message had indeed come from Paul Heaton.

It was just a matter of what to do with that information. The obvious answer would be to inform Walter Caine, the man in charge of running NID, and let him deal with it.

She was halfway to her feet when something made her pause. What if Caine was in on it? What if Heaton was just following Caine's instructions? She sat back down. Even if Heaton was working alone, all she had was a log file with his name on it. He and a half-decent lawyer would be able to explain that away.

No, she needed real proof. Irrefutable.

Cell phones were not allowed inside NID, otherwise she would have accessed Heaton's device long ago, when news of the mole first broke. She formulated a new plan.

Xi Ling kept one eye on Paul Heaton for an interminable five hours before the clock ticked over to the end of the shift. A few minutes later, he got up and stretched before heading for the exit. Xi Ling gave him a few yards' head start, then followed. He was leaving the locker room when she got there, and he offered a brief smile as he passed.

*Let's see you smile when this is over, asshole.*

XI Ling collected her phone and purse. She brought up the cell hijacking app, which displayed fourteen numbers within a twenty-yard radius. Many of those numbers would drop off the list once their owners departed. She followed Heaton out of the White House and into the car park, where the number of options fell to two.

Xi Ling looked around to see which other cell phone she could be picking up, but there was no one else within range. It didn't take her long to realize why she was picking up more than one signal.

Heaton must have a burner cell in his car.

Now she had to figure out which was which. That was easy enough.

"Paul!"

Heaton turned, and she came close to him. "Hi. Look, once this mission is wrapped up, Farooq and I will be having a barbecue at our place. We'd like to invite you over."

He smiled, but Xi Ling detected no warmth or gratitude. It seemed to mock her, like he knew something she didn't.

"Sure," he said. "Just let me know when."

"If you give me your number, I'll text you."

For an anxious moment it seemed that he was going to refuse to give her his number, but he eventually shrugged, as if to say, "Ah, what the hell." He recited his number, and Xi Ling added it to her contacts list.

"Great. I'll be in touch. Have a good one."

As she walked away, Xi Ling selected the other number from the list. She waited for it to connect, then got in her own car and began the journey home. The software would allow her to hear everything Heaton said, whether he was on a call or just mumbling to himself while sitting at traffic lights.

It didn't take long for the move to pay off.

"It's me," she heard Heaton say. "Still no mention of sending in a backup team, and they have no idea where Poska is being held."

"Do they know what happened to Daniels?" another voice asked.

"They have no idea. As far as they know, she dropped off the face of the earth."

"Okay. Let me know if there are any developments."

"There was one thing," Heaton said. "Camber Blair noticed that Poska accessed their servers. They sent a message to NID, but I managed to intercept it before anyone noticed."

"Are you sure?"

"Positive," Heaton assured the other man. "Someone would have said something by now."

"Very well. Update me again tomorrow."

"Will do. But… there's one last thing. You still haven't told me the arrangements. You know, for when it happens."

"Patience. There will be a test on Sunday, and if all goes well, we will launch on Thursday. I'll be in touch well before then."

Xi Ling heard the call end, but Heaton wasn't done talking.

"You better be in touch, you arrogant fuck. No way I'm risking my life to get left behind."

Heaton's voice was replaced by rock music, and Xi Ling turned down the volume on her cell phone.

That was all the proof she needed. She played back the recording of the conversation, then messaged Farooq on Shield.

*Definitely Heaton. Heard him talking to someone about it after work. More details when I get home.*

Farooq replied quickly.

*Nice work. I also struck gold. Twice. Found Poska, and Eva is alive and well.*

That was a huge relief. Xi Ling sent one last message.

*Wonderful! I'll get takeout and you can fill me in.*

* * *

Farooq was already home when Xi Ling returned to the apartment. He had set a bottle of red wine on the table to breathe, and lit a couple of candles. She put the bag of food next to the wine, kissed her boyfriend, then sat in front of her laptop and powered it on.

"Can you plate the food while I do some digging?"

"Sure," Farooq said. "What are you looking for?"

"The owner of a cell phone." Xi Ling gave him a breakdown of events, starting from the moment she found proof that Paul Heaton had deleted the message from Camber Blair.

"It'll be a burner cell," Farooq said as Xi Ling typed. "Whoever Heaton spoke to would have to be a special kind of stupid to use their registered phone to commit treason."

"I know, but if we didn't check it first, who'd be dumber, them or us?"

"Fair point."

Seconds later, she hit the Enter key. "Yeah, it's a burner. Okay, let's see where it is."

Farooq plated up the food while Xi Ling put a trace on the cell phone. As a plate of seafood linguini was placed in front of her, the tracking software got to work.

"What about your news?" Xi Ling asked. "Why did Eva go silent for so long?"

"She was captured by the GRU and held in a cell. Luckily, she was carrying her tracking device, so Tom was able to see where she was and got her out."

"He sprang her from GRU headquarters?"

"No," Farooq said, "he, Rees and Travis rescued her while she was in transit."

"That's good. Are they back on track?"

"Yeah," Farooq said. "I was able to track the data packages from the Camber Blair server. I sent Tom the co-ordinates." He spooned some food into his mouth. "Tom told us not to mention that Eva escaped. As far as we're concerned, she's still missing."

"Don't talk while your mouth's full. It's not polite."

Farooq chewed and swallowed. "Sorry."

"It's okay. And…" Xi Ling watched the tracker settle on a large building. "…Heaton's contact is in a country club."

"That figures. Keep an eye on it. He has to go home at some point. When he does, we'll know who's behind this."

# Chapter 30

"Are you sure that's it?" Eva asked.

The four were in the tree line, three hundred yards from the shell of what had once been a factory. Or perhaps a warehouse. It was difficult to tell under the light only of a crescent moon.

"That's what the map says," Gray replied.

"Let's take a closer look," Eva said. She edged sideways, staying within the trees until she was level with the brown hulk of an ancient truck, its bodywork long since destroyed by the elements. She dashed to it and peeked around the front of the hood. She waited for the others to catch up, then moved to the next point of cover, a mound of rubble punctuated with scraps of tarpaulin and rusted metal rods. Eva could now make out more details of the building.

Forests of weeds. Shattered windows. In one corner, a section of the roof had collapsed inward.

What stuck out most was the man smoking next to an SUV.

He was standing at the far end of the building, scrolling through a phone between puffs on his cigarette. Between his cell and his cig, his night vision would be shot.

*Advantage Eva.*

"I'll take him out," she said. "When he's down, form up on me."

Gray searched the base of the rubble pile for a suitable weapon. Guns would come later. He found a shard of glass and wrapped one end with a strip of tarpaulin, then handed it to Eva. She thanked him and ran at a crouch to the side of the building.

Eva slowly made her way to the far end, where the smoker was lighting a second cigarette with the remnants of the first. He flicked the spent cig into the air and returned his attention to his cell phone.

The target was large, someone who spent a lot of time in the gym, but brawn rarely mattered unless it was combined with brains. From what Eva saw, the target lacked the latter.

Eva, eye on the prize, focus unrelenting.

She delivered three jabs to the neck and then buried the makeshift weapon in the man's throat. The kill was swift, silent. Eva lowered the corpse to the ground, scanned the area, then waved the trio over.

While she waited, she slipped off one of the cheap sneakers she'd purchased on the way to the old factory and removed a small stone. She slipped it back on as the others reached her.

They went to the large entrance and stuck their heads around the doorway. The place was deserted.

"There must be a lower level," Eva said. There was certainly nothing above them.

She drew her pistol, a cue for the others to do the same. Eva took the lead, while Gray covered their left flank and Rees the right. Travis took the rear.

The smell of decline was everywhere, a mixture of mold and rust, damp and decay. If not for the guard she'd killed, Eva would have sworn the place was deserted.

They walked the length of the interior and saw nothing that looked like a trapdoor. That left the dark doorway up ahead. The door was off its hinges, lying against a wall. Eva pointed her gun in that direction, indicating that she was going in.

At the doorway, Eva stopped and listened. She heard nothing, but when she put her head around the door frame, she saw a faint glimmer of light below. She backed up and gathered the others closer.

"Tom and I will go ahead," she whispered. "You two stay here and cover us. If we're not out in five minutes, you're up. Try to take Poska alive, but if you can't…"

She let the sentence tail off. There was no need to state the obvious.

Rees and Travis nodded their understanding and took up defensive positions.

Eva checked she had a round in the chamber and that the safety was off. She took a deep breath, let it out slowly, then checked the stairway one last time.

Clear.

Eva moved slowly, her feet silent on the stone steps. Fourteen of them, which ended on a small landing. The next set of stairs, to the left, were better illuminated. She paused on the twelfth step, listening, but still heard nothing, so she crouched and stuck her head around the corner.

Still no sign of anyone.

Eva was halfway down the second flight of stairs when a door opened on the floor below and a man stepped out into the hallway, biting into a sandwich. When he saw Eva, he froze for a second, then dropped his food and reached into his waistband for his gun.

There was no time for Eva to close the gap and take him out silently, so she aimed at center mass and put two rounds in his chest.

All subtlety abandoned, she jumped the remaining stairs and trained her gun on the open doorway. She felt Gray's hand on her shoulder, letting her know he was right behind her. Eva flashed her head inside the room for a split second. Seeing no one, she entered and checked behind the door. The room was empty. A TV played a Russian program, and next to a sink was a dish drainer stacked with plates and cups. On a table was a laptop, its screen full of code.

A shot rang from the hallway, quickly followed by return fire. Eva rushed to the door and saw Gray with his weapon up. Then she spotted the second dead Russian lying in the hallway.

"He came around the corner," Gray said.

"That room's clear," Eva said. "You lead."

Gray went first, stopping when he reached the corner. He crouched to take a look, then stood and moved out. Eva followed and saw two doors. One on the left wall, the other at the end of the hall. They checked the nearest one first. It was a toilet, and empty.

The second door had deadbolts at the top and bottom. Only the top was closed. Eva pulled it aside, cringing as it squealed in protest. She pushed the door open and stood aside, waiting for gunfire.

None came.

Gray held up three fingers and gestured for Eva to go low. She understood, and waited for his countdown. On three, Gray sprang into the room and Eva crouched as she joined him, her weapon searching for its next target.

There were none.

There was no one in the room. A desk, computer and a bed against one wall. A dehumidifier hummed in the corner.

"Where the hell is he?" Gray asked.

Eva had no idea. The three men they'd killed would not be guarding an empty room. Were they too late?

She crouched down and checked under the camp bed. Nothing.

She felt Gray's foot tap her on the thigh. She followed where he was looking and saw the door he was pointing to with his gun. Eva straightened as Gray took up a position to fire inside the room. She took hold of the handle, twisted it and pulled the door open, making sure to stay out of Gray's line of fire.

Gray didn't shoot. Instead, he took a couple of steps backward and barked a command.

"Out! Now!"

Eva saw a pathetic figure emerge from the room, his hands raised. His hair was a mess, his face covered in stubble, but he was unmistakably Andrius Poska.

"That's him," she said to Gray. "Let's go."

She grabbed Poska to pull him to the exit, but he planted his feet.

"No! I can't leave."

Eva wondered if he had Stockholm Syndrome, where hostages develop an affinity with their captors. It was known to manifest within days in some situations.

"Andrius, we're here to take you home," she said calmly.

"No!" he repeated. "I need to stay. I need to finish it."

"You can't," Gray said. "It'll kill millions of people. Maybe billions."

Tears fell as Poska's face creased up. "I know. But they have my wife and daughter. If I go with you, they will kill them."

"If you finish it, they'll kill them anyway," Gray said.

*"You don't think I know that?!"* Poska screamed.

Poska was facing an impossible dilemma, and Eva could sympathize. He had to choose between killing his own family or millions of strangers. She wouldn't have found that easy, either.

"They already cut my daughter's finger off," Poska said through the tears. "If I leave… if I don't finish this… they'll torture them to death. I'd rather they die quickly when I'm done."

Gray raised his gun and pointed it at Poska's head. "Yeah, well I've got a daughter, too. I'd rather she didn't die at all."

Eva stood between the two men. "No, Tom. We need him alive." She forced his gun arm down. "If he can build Juggernaut, then so can someone else. Maybe not soon, but eventually we'll be facing the same threat. Who better to counter it than the man who created it?" She turned to Poska. "Can you create a program that will be able to stop something like Juggernaut?"

"Of course. That's what I was working on before I was kidnapped."

Eva took Gray aside. "We need him alive. The *world* needs him alive."

"You heard him. He won't come with us."

"I know." It was a hopeless situation. Eva could only see one way out of it. "Where are they holding your wife and daughter?" she asked Poska.

"I have no idea. We were separated in Lithuania, before I was taken across the border into Belarus."

That wasn't good.

"Did your captors ever speak to the people holding them?" she pressed.

"Yes, one of them did. Lots of times. His name is Igor. He's the one in charge here."

Eva knew he must be talking about Igor Cherenkov. The description certainly matched. Only, he wasn't one of the three Russians they'd killed.

"Does Igor leave here at night?" she asked.

"Yes. I tried to speak to him a couple of times during the night, but they said I had to wait until the morning."

"What time does he usually get back?"

"Early," Poska told her. "Around seven."

Gray checked his watch. "About three hours from now. What do you have in mind?"

It wasn't the ideal plan, but it was the only way Eva could think of to get Poska to go with them. "We wait for Cherenkov to return, get into his phone, then ask Farooq to track Poska's family. We'll get them and come back for him."

She could see that Gray didn't like the idea much.

"What if Cherenkov comes back, see's everyone dead, and decides to move Andrius?" He asked her.

Another good point, but one that she had covered. She reached into her bra and pulled out the tracker. She gave it to Poska.

"Swallow that," she said.

He took it and examined it.

"It's a tracker." Eva told him. "We're gonna go and get your family. If Igor moves you, we'll know where you are."

"And what do I tell Igor when he returns?" Poska asked.

"That you heard one loud bang and it woke you up. Nobody entered this room. You understand?"

"But—"

"But nothing. Stick to that story. We'll be back as soon as we can."

She waited for Poska to swallow the tracker, then ushered Gray out of the room.

"Wait!" Poska shouted. "You said Igor would be back in three hours?"

Eva could see his mind working, as if trying to solve a puzzle.

"Did you see a computer anywhere?" Poska asked her.

"There's one in the kitchen."

Poska ran from the room, and Eva followed him. He stopped when he saw the dead guards, then tiptoed past them and into the kitchen. He glanced at the screen, then ran back to his own room and checked his own laptop.

"The one in the kitchen, take it with you," Poska told Eva. "Take it far from here and destroy it."

"Why?" Gray asked.

"Please, just do it. I don't have time to explain. I have to get to work."

Eva shrugged at Gray. She closed the door behind them and fastened the top bolt.

"What about these guys?" Gray asked her, kicking the nearest corpse. "Leave them for Igor to find, or let him think they did a runner?"

Eva considered it. "Leave them. Take their belongings. Wallets, phones, everything. Once Igor sees that Poska is still here, hopefully he'll put it down to a robbery. Worst case scenario, he moves Poska, just to be safe."

Eva and Gray went through the pockets of the dead Russians. She came across a phone and tried to open it. The cell required a fingerprint. She pressed it against the corpse's thumb and the screen woke up. Eva went into settings and removed the security features so that she could open it any time. She did the same with the other Russian's cell phone. On her way to the stairs, she popped into the kitchen and picked up the laptop.

"We're coming up," Eva shouted as they began to climb the stairs. At the top, Rees and Travis were waiting.

"Where is he?" Travis asked.

"He's not coming," Eva told him. As she led them to the exit where the SUV was parked, she explained the situation, then handed Rees one of the cell phones. "Go through the contacts. See if there are any for Viktor Sorotzkin and Maksim Baranov. They are known associates of Cherenkov, and I think they'll be the ones holding Poska's family."

Eva checked the phone she was holding. It had entries for both names. They wouldn't have to wait for Cherenkov to return, which gave them a head start. "Never mind," Eva told Rees. She asked Gray to compose a Shield message for Farooq. "Tell him to give me locations for these two numbers."

She read them off as Gray typed.

"Are you a hundred percent sure these are the people holding the wife and kid?" Travis asked.

"Positive. They're part of Cherenkov's team and have been missing since Poska was kidnapped."

He held up the keys to the SUV. "Then let's go find them."

# Chapter 31

Xi Ling placed her flask of tea on the table and kissed Farooq on the top of his head.

"Are you sure you don't want me to come in?" he asked her.

"No, stay here and help Eva. If you go to work, you won't be able to use your cell phone. She might need updates throughout the day. I'll tell them you're still suffering from food poisoning."

"Okay," he said. "And don't go spooking Heaton. We can't let him know we're on to him."

"Of course I won't!" Xi Ling replied indignantly.

She left the apartment, and Farooq prepared a drink before continuing his research on Robert J. Portman.

They had identified him the night before, following his cell phone signal from the country club back to his home in Virginia. Once they had an address, it didn't take long to figure out who lived there.

Gray had interrupted their work, requesting the locations of two phone numbers. Xi Ling had traced them to the outskirts of a small village in Lithuania, a dozen miles from the border with Belarus. One of Farooq's three screens was dedicated to keeping an eye on the cell phone signals, in case the people holding Sofija and Claire Poska decided to move them. Gray said that would be a distinct possibility, given what they had just done. Gray hadn't gone into any details, but knowing Eva and Gray, it probably would have involved a lot of lethal violence.

Now Farooq was back to ripping Portman's life apart, looking for a thread that he could tug on. He'd spent the morning poring over all of Portman's financial transactions over the years, information he'd gleaned by hacking into the Securities and Exchange Commission's database.

None of the transactions caught his eye. Some were for hundreds of thousands, sometimes tens of millions of dollars, but after a couple of years, he'd divested and put his money in other companies.

Farooq moved on to Portman's banking transactions. It took a little longer to get into the databases of JP Morgan Chase, but Farooq was able to learn that Portman had taken out a loan of one billion dollars almost a decade earlier. He'd used his shares as collateral. That money had been transferred to an account with Bank of America. Farooq printed off all transactions, then broke into the BoA database.

What he saw there piqued Farooq's curiosity. There had been three other similar transfers from other banks, plus another billion-dollar loan from BoA, giving him five billion in cash. That money had then been transferred to the account of TNR.

Farooq looked up TNR and discovered that it was Trans Nevada Rail, a private company whose CEO was Seddon Blake, the world's richest man.

Farooq did a web search for Trans Nevada Rail, expecting to see thousands of articles.

There weren't many, and that felt strange. The financial sector normally trumpeted such large purchases, even for private companies, but there was nothing from CNN

Business News, the *Wall Street Journal*, or any other financial news outlet.

Someone had suppressed it.

Farooq went back into the BoA database and looked for all transactions relating to TNR. There were exactly ninety-nine inward transactions, and every single one was for five billion dollars.

*Curiouser and curiouser.*

He printed off the records, then began a search for everything he could find on TNR, his heart racing with excitement. If Seddon Blake was raising half a trillion dollars for a project that didn't make the news, there had to be a sinister motive.

The company had been formed years earlier with, not surprisingly, a five-billion-dollar initial investment from CEO Seddon Blake. It was set up to build a high-speed link between Vegas and San Francisco. That was the extent of the public information Farooq could find. Unlike publicly traded companies, private operations didn't have to file annual accounts with the SEC.

That wasn't going to stop Farooq. He spent the next hour trying to gain access to TNR's company intranet. As expected from a tech giant like Seddon Blake, the servers were nailed down. Farooq didn't think even Xi Ling could gain access.

Farooq returned to the Bank of America account for TNR. Apart from the multiple deposits years ago, there had been no income. All Farooq saw was an endless list of outgoing payments. He scrolled through them, not recognizing any of the names. Unsurprising, since he had no idea about the underground boring industry. He was about to give up when a name jumped out at him.

Darius Kohn.

Farooq went to the coffee table and picked up the magazine Xi Ling had been reading the night before. He flicked through it and found the article she had shown him, one that featured the country's top name in interior design. Xi Ling said she wanted Kohn to furnish their house when they eventually settled down.

Could it be the same person?

Farooq returned to the computer. Why would a boring company require an interior designer? One that cost… thirty million dollars?!

Perhaps it was just a coincidence, and this Darius Kohn was unrelated to the guy in the article. There was a simple way to find out. Farooq found the Kohn transaction in the Bank of America database and navigated to the account holder. He brought up the address, then opened a web browser and searched for the interior designer's company.

The business address was a match.

Farooq sat back. Something didn't make sense. Actually, none of it made sense. If there was one thing he knew about rich people, it was that they didn't throw money away. Certainly not billions of dollars. He searched the outgoing transactions on the TNR account, but none went to Robert J. Portman. It meant that despite his huge investment years earlier, Portman hadn't received a penny from the company in return. He checked three other investors against payouts, and each time he came up empty.

Farooq was no businessman, but he couldn't see how the investors could expect a return on their money. He did some mental math. If ten thousand people an hour used the train once it was completed, and it ran for twenty-four hours a day, in one year that would be… just over eighty-seven million journeys. To make a dent in the half-trillion initial investment, they would have to charge over five grand a ticket to break even after the first year. If someone could afford that, they could also afford a business class flight and still have money left over. And that didn't take into account the running costs. Staff, energy, maintenance. And that was assuming the system *could* carry ten thousand passengers an hour and run twenty-four-seven.

If someone had approached him and asked for even a $500 investment, Farooq would have looked at the figures and laughed. Yet some of the world's richest people, whose business acumen eclipsed anything Farooq could ever dream of, had seen it as worthwhile.

Why?

It wasn't something he was going to figure out on his own. When Xi Ling returned home later that evening, he would get her take on it. In the meantime, he printed off all the TNR transactions from the Bank of America system in the hope that she could make sense of it.

# Chapter 32

When Igor Cherenkov returned to the abandoned factory, he immediately knew something was wrong. Sergei's SUV wasn't there, and his men were under strict instructions not to leave the facility. If Sergei had to leave for an emergency, he would have called to get permission.

Cherenkov pulled up a hundred yards from the building and got out. He took out his Makarov and checked that he had a round in the chamber, then advanced on the decrepit factory, eyes peeled for danger. When he reached the entrance, his adrenaline surged. Sergei was dead, a fly-infested pool of congealed blood forming a dark halo under his head and shoulders. His pockets had been pulled inside out, meaning someone had searched his body and taken his belongings. Phone, wallet, car keys. Was it a robbery? Had he been killed for his vehicle?

The reason jumped into Cherenkov's head.

*Poska!*

Cherenkov sprinted for the basement, no longer caring if danger still lurked. If Poska was gone, his life would be over, anyway.

Cherenkov flew down the stairs and stopped at the bottom. Ruslan was lying outside the kitchen, two bullet wounds in his chest. Aslan was at the end of the hallway, face down and motionless. Again, their pockets were pulled

190

inside out. Cherenkov performed a quick check of the kitchen, then strode to the room holding Poska.

The door was sealed, which Cherenkov found strange. If someone had come for Poska, why lock the door when they left? He pulled the bolt aside, pushed the door open, and rushed into the room, gun raised.

Andrius Poska jumped from his chair.

"Please don't shoot! I'm almost finished!"

Cherenkov lowered his weapon. "What happened here?"

Poska looked at him quizzically. "What do you mean?"

Cherenkov grabbed him by the shirt and dragged him out of the room. He stopped over Aslan's body. "I mean *that!*"

Poska began to shake. "I have no idea. A loud bang woke me up a few hours ago, but I didn't know what it was or where it came from. I heard nothing else, so I got back to work."

Cherenkov wasn't sure he believed him, but what was the alternative? Someone came to rescue Poska, and having killed everyone who stood in their way, they decided to leave him? That didn't make any sense. That left robbery as a motive, and Cherenkov wasn't swallowing it. There were easier people to rob than GRU officers. Someone would first have to know that they were in the building, and if they knew that, they would know who they were facing. Whoever killed his men, they were no mere street criminals. These were professionals.

He struck Poska in the face, a fierce open-handed slap. "Tell me what really happened here!"

Poska recoiled and held his cheek. "I told you. I was woken by a noise, and then everything went silent. I don't know what else I can say."

Frustrated, Cherenkov pushed Poska back into the room. "Finish it. You have until midday tomorrow." He slammed the door and locked it, then took out his satellite phone and called the General to report the situation. Turgenev wouldn't be happy, but then he never was.

The call went to voicemail.

Cherenkov cursed. He was probably showering. It was, after all, just past seven in the morning. Not having the general's home phone number, Cherenkov called Turgenev's aide, Lieutenant Colonel Pavel Duric.

"Get hold of the General," Cherenkov said as soon as the call was answered. "Tell him my men are dead, killed during the night. Tell him the—"

"Colonel, General Turgenev is missing," Duric interrupted. "His car was ambushed yesterday and three of his men were killed. It appears people posing as police officers were behind the kidnapping."

First Turgenev is snatched, and then his men are slaughtered. This was no coincidence.

"Why am I only hearing about this now?!" Cherenkov barked.

"Sir, our efforts have been focused on finding the General."

"And have you?"

Cherenkov heard Duric gulp. "Not yet, Sir."

There was little point berating Duric further. The Lieutenant Colonel was no doubt facing enormous pressure from Turgenev's superiors. The same was true of Cherenkov. He'd promised Turgenev that Juggernaut would be completed by Sunday. Turgenev's boss, Admiral Yevgeny Komarov, would expect him to stick to that schedule, regardless of the circumstances.

Cherenkov had two options. He could move Poska to another location, but that would cause the deadline to slip. The alternative was to stay where they were and bring in more men to defend the facility until Poska's work was complete. Given the time restraints, he opted for the latter.

"Inform Admiral Komarov that my men were murdered earlier this morning and that I need another ten... no, make it twenty men to protect the prisoner," Cherenkov said to Duric. "I need them here immediately. Assure the Admiral that the deadline will be met. And keep me informed about General Turgenev."

Cherenkov hung up before Duric could respond. He went to the kitchen to get a drink and noticed something amiss.

His laptop was gone.

Cherenkov dashed back to Poska's room and was about to barge in when something made him pause.

If he mentioned the missing laptop, Poska would know that he was free to write whatever code he wished without oversight. If Poska was telling the truth, that he had no idea what had happened, then it was better to say nothing. Let him continue working in the hope of seeing his wife and daughter again.

*Speaking of which...*

Cherenkov called Maksim Baranov. It answered on the second ring.

"Any problems?"

"No, everything's fine," Baranov replied.

"Well, something happened here." Cherenkov gave him a brief rundown of events, including Turgenev's disappearance.

"Do you think the attack and the General's disappearance are linked?"

"It's possible," Cherenkov told him. "Can you move the wife and daughter, just in case?"

"We can, but it'll take time to find somewhere suitable."

Cherenkov agreed. It had taken them three days to find the house they were currently using to hold Poska's family. Perhaps he was just being overly cautious. "Okay, stay put. This will be over tomorrow, anyway. In the meantime, stay alert. The people who attacked us were professionals. If they decide to pay you a visit, you'd better be ready."

The chances of Baranov being hit by the same people were slim, but with all the crazy shit going on, it couldn't be ruled out.

Baranov promised to be on his guard, and Cherenkov hung up.

He went to Poska's cell to get an update on progress.

# Chapter 33

Eva's backside was numb.

They'd driven the SUV from the abandoned factory to Moscow, where they'd picked up the bikes. The four of them had then ridden to the Latvian border crossing that they'd used on their way into Russia. From there, they rode to the Lithuanian border and once again went off-road. With stops for gas and food, it had taken them fourteen hours. They had taken turns as pillions, but she still felt stiff when they reached a point a mile from the location Farooq had given them.

Eva sent a message to Farooq, asking for an update, then began a series of stretching exercises to limber up. Farooq replied to say the two phones he was monitoring hadn't moved.

"We're a go," she told the others.

They wheeled the bikes into a small wood and checked their weapons. Eva brought up an overhead view of the property on her map app. They were on the outskirts of a small village of no more than fifteen properties. The one where Sofija and Claire Poska were being held was a single-story affair, with an outhouse at the bottom of the garden.

"Two go in the front and two in the back?" Gray suggested.

"Sounds good to me," Eva said. "Let's see when we get there. The image is a couple of years old, so there may have been some modifications to the building."

They jogged down the country lane at a steady pace, covering the distance in a shade over six minutes. They stopped a hundred yards from the gate leading to the property to catch their breath, then inched closer to get eyes on the house.

The owners weren't into renovations, it seemed. Nor basic maintenance. It was a wooden construction, with a corrugated roof that could have been asbestos or tin; it was difficult to tell due to its age. The building had to be at least eighty years old. The garden was equally unkempt, grass and weeds knee-high.

The dilapidated condition gave Eva an idea. She shared it with the others, and they liked her proposal.

"You and Rees go around the back," Eva told Gray. "I'll go in the front with Travis."

"Give us fifteen minutes," Gray replied. He and Rees backtracked to take the long way around the property, and Eva told Travis to set a silent timer on his phone.

She kept an eye on the property. Darkness had fallen a couple of hours earlier, and she saw subdued light coming from one of the front rooms. There was no movement of any kind.

As the jump-off point approached, Eva led Travis stealthily down the overgrown garden path and to the front door. Up close, it looked as frail as she'd hoped.

Travis had dimmed the screen on his phone. He showed her the countdown. Fifty seconds remaining. They crouched either side of the door, watching the numbers tick down.

When it hit zero, Eva started banging on the door.

\* \* \*

After having navigated through the surrounding woods, Gray and Travis approached the house from the rear. The building seemed desolate, except for a faint glow coming from one window. A Range Rover was parked next to the house.

With three minutes to go, they edged their way to the back door. Once there, Gray put his hand on the door handle. Rees backed up a step and aimed at the lock. If Gray was unable to open it, Rees would blow it out.

Gray checked his watch. Seconds to go. He looked at Rees, gave a nod, then focused on the door once more.

The moment he heard banging from deep inside the house, Gray pulled the handle down and pushed the door. It flew inward, and Gray was first through. The ruse had worked perfectly. Two male occupants stood facing the front door, weapons raised and ready to fire. When the back door crashed against the wall, they turned quickly.

Gray and Rees were quicker. Both fired double-taps, and the targets jerked before crashing to the floor. Gray advanced, checking for other threats, but the kitchen and living room were empty.

"I'm coming out!" Gray shouted, and opened the front door.

Eva and Travis entered.

"Check the attic," Gray told them. "We'll clear the ground floor."

There was a short hallway leading to three rooms. Gray went into the first of them. He kicked the door open, and when no one fired on him, he stepped inside to ensure the room was empty. He did the same with the second. As the third door crashed inward, he could see that it led to a basement. A stun grenade would have come in handy to disorientate anyone lurking in the shadows, but sometimes you had to play the hand you'd been dealt. He flicked on the light, and a single bulb illuminated below.

"Sofija?" Gray called.

He heard scrambling and aimed toward the sound. Moments later, a woman gingerly came into view, clutching a young girl to her chest.

"Is there anyone else down there?" Gray asked her.

Sofija shook her head.

"Okay. Come on, we're here to take you home." He lowered his gun as she climbed the stairs. "How many men were watching you?"

"Two," Sofija said. She pulled her daughter tighter when Gray reached out for her. He noticed a crude, bloodied bandage wrapped around the little girl's hand. The smell emanating from it was concerning.

"No problem," he said, backing off, and gestured down the hall to the living room.

When they reached the bodies of her captors, Gray expected her to recoil. Instead, she spat at the closest one and rattled off a stream of invective. She then went to the second corpse and kicked him so hard in the ribs, Gray was sure the dead man's ancestors would have felt it.

Eva and Travis came downstairs. "Clear," Eva said, and took in Sofija and Claire. She put her arm around the woman and daughter and guided them to the front door. "You're safe now. Come."

Gray went through the pockets of the dead. He collected wallets, phones and the keys to the Range Rover. He also picked up their weapons. Travis, the last man out, turned off the lamp and closed the door behind him.

"Rees, Travis, can you two take Sofija and Claire round to the car?" Gray asked. "We'll be there in a minute."

"Sure thing."

When they were alone, Gray asked Eva what to do with Poska's wife and daughter.

"We could take them to the American Embassy in Vilnius. Tell them to contact Greg Sharpe and arrange travel home."

"You think that's wise?" Gray asked her. "Have Xi Ling and Farooq identified the mole yet? What if it's Sharpe?"

Eva grimaced. "I didn't think of that." She rubbed her head as if to clear it.

"You're tired," Gray said. "We all are."

"Yeah, well, we're not getting any sleep until Poska is out. Speaking of which, give me your phone."

Gray handed it over, and Eva went to the Range Rover. She took a picture of Sofija and Claire, then jogged back to Gray.

"Poska's going to want proof that they're safe," she explained. "Anyway, what to do with them?"

"Claire needs medical care, as soon as possible. If we take them to the local police, do you think they'll be safe?"

"I don't think anyone would try to snatch them again," Eva said, "but if word gets back to Cherenkov, we'll never get Poska out alive. Whether it's the police or the embassy, we run that risk."

Gray only saw one option. He ran to the car and opened the rear passenger door.

"Sofija, do you speak Russian?"

"Yes," she said. "Like a native."

Gray stepped back to see that Eva had joined them.

"How about taking her to hospital and giving a false name?" he suggested. "She could claim to be a Russian fleeing an abusive husband. If they demand ID, she can just say she ran away on the spur of the moment, taking nothing, not even clothes. I'm pretty sure the hospital won't turn Claire away."

Eva considered it for a few seconds, then nodded. "Get in. I'll explain it to her on the way."

Gray took one of the rear seats, Eva the other, while Claire sat on Sofija's lap.

"Travis, drop us off at the bikes," Gray said. "We're going back for Andrius."

# Chapter 34

Xi Ling walked into the apartment and dropped her bag on the sofa. "Looks like they're getting ready to send a second team in to look for Poska."

"It was to be expected," Farooq replied. "They haven't heard from her for days, so they have to assume she failed in her mission. I trust you didn't tell them she's located the wife and daughter."

"Don't be an ass. Of course I didn't tell them. It makes no difference, anyway. By the time they pick the right people to replace Eva, she'll be back with the Poskas and we can call it a day."

"Good. Now, come and take a look at this."

Farooq had reams of paper spread out around the apartment. For the next five hours they went through it painstakingly.

The picture it formed suggested Trans Nevada Rail wasn't the project it claimed to be.

They looked into every single company that had been paid by TNR, either for goods received or services rendered. Many were construction companies, which was to be expected, but billions had been spent on items that had little to do with tunneling under the desert. They placed each transaction into one of three piles: expected, shady, and downright wrong.

The expected pile contained building materials such as steel, concrete panels, things that would normally be associated with a construction project of that size. The shady pile was for dubious transactions. Half a million solar panels, interior designers (which could conceivably be for the trains), thirty elevators, things that *could* be part of the project, but they were stretching credibility.

The downright wrong pile was the largest by far. What did a railroad company need with forty-five thousand bunk beds? Thirty million worth of marble tiles? Twenty commercial kitchens? Two might be needed to feed the workers on site, but twenty? A fully functioning industrial laundry? Two thousand electric cars? Two Boeing 777 Dreamliners? The list went on and on.

"If you ask me, they're not building a tunnel, they're building a city," Xi Ling said, and yawned. It was three in the morning, way past her bedtime.

"Sure looks like it," Farooq agreed.

His cell phone pinged, signifying an incoming Shield message.

"It's from Tom," he told her. "They rescued Sofija and Claire, now they're going back for Poska."

"That's great news. Let's just hope they get there in time."

"Agreed," Farooq said. "Should we tell them what we've found?"

"No, they've got enough to worry about. Besides, all we have are assumptions. Plus, there could be a totally innocent explanation. When I said they were building a city, it could be that he's doing just that. A city for the construction workers. It's in the middle of the desert, after all. It can't be easy to get in and out each day."

"That actually makes sense," Farooq conceded. He picked up the tally sheet from the downright wrong pile. "Would he really spend a hundred and seventy billion on it, though? Seems excessive."

"Then maybe it's not just for the workers. He could be building a destination resort. A mini Vegas, if you like."

"There's one way to find out," Farooq smiled.

"Hack into NORAD and commandeer one of their satellites?"

"That's a stretch, even for me. No, I was thinking of going to Nevada to see what they're up to."

"You think they're just gonna let you walk in and have a look around?" Xi Ling asked.

When she said it like that, Farooq had to agree that it wasn't going to be easy. Even working for NID didn't give him the authority to demand access to a private company's property.

He suddenly realized what would. The Occupational Safety and Health Administration.

"Could you get into OSHA while I look something up?" he asked.

"Duh. In, like, five seconds."

"Okay. See if you can get me an ID."

While Xi Ling got to work on that task, Farooq looked up OSHA's powers. Specifically, the power to show up unannounced to perform an inspection. Apparently, they could.

In the time it took to ascertain that information, Xi Ling had worked her magic.

"Who do you want to be?" she asked.

"Danesh Patel will do. Use my passport photo."

"Job role?"

Farooq thought about it. "Mid-level inspector. Not too much knowledge or power, but not too little. If they ask questions, I want to be able to say it's above my pay grade."

"Done," Xi Ling declared. She printed off the ID, then cut it out and stuck it over her old library card. The final step was to laminate it.

Farooq examined it. "That should pass even a close inspection. Thanks."

"You're welcome. And leave your real ID at home. If you get stopped with two identities, the cops won't like it."

"Will do," Farooq told her.

"Now, clear out. I need to grab a couple of hours before I head back to work."

Farooq kissed her on the forehead. "I'll print out a work order, then I'll go."

Xi Ling headed to the bedroom, and Farooq got back to work.

# Chapter 35

Lieutenant Colonel Pavel Duric woke with a start. He checked his watch and saw that he'd only managed forty minutes. It felt like it. He rubbed his temples, trying to shake off the fatigue he'd felt for the last twenty hours. Since General Turgenev's disappearance, he'd been working non-stop to find him. Co-ordinating with various agencies, including the FSB and local police, chasing up ballistics reports on the weapons used and forensics on the police car, organizing search parties…

He rested his head on his desk and closed his eyes once more, hoping to snatch another quick snooze before having to deal with the next pressing assignment.

It wasn't to be.

His cell phone blared next to his ear, and he jerked upright and checked the caller ID.

Cherenkov.

*Fuck!*

Their last conversation had come during a hectic period, and Duric had completely forgotten about Cherenkov's request. He snatched up the phone.

"Duric."

"*Where are my men?*" Cherenkov screamed.

Duric pulled the cell phone away from his ear. He had to think fast.

*Think…*

*Think!*

"Colonel, I passed your request onto Admiral Komarov's aide yesterday, but I'm afraid it isn't my place to monitor my superiors' actions. I can speak to the aide once more and request an update, but beyond that, my hands are tied." He heard nothing but heavy breathing. "Or perhaps you'd like to ask the Admiral yourself…"

There was a brief pause, then Cherenkov erupted once more.

*"Just get me my men!"*

The phone went dead.

*Didn't think so, you spineless fool.*

Duric immediately called the admiral's aide and passed on Cherenkov's request.

\* \* \*

Igor Cherenkov stabbed at the End Call icon and thrust the phone in his pocket. After one last look around the area to ensure they wouldn't come under immediate attack, he marched back down to the basement. He burst into Poska's cell and found the Lithuanian hard at work.

"How much longer?" Cherenkov barked.

Poska flinched. "I… I don't know. Soon."

"Will it be finished by tomorrow?"

"Yes," Poska nodded vigorously. "Definitely by tomorrow."

Cherenkov left the cell, slamming the door behind him. After securing the bolt, he returned to the surface and stared out of one of the many broken windows.

Thirty-six hours at most. The question was, would he survive that long? There had been no attack since he'd returned, but that didn't mean another one wasn't coming. If he had the reinforcements he'd asked for, he'd feel more comfortable, but for some strange reason Admiral Komarov hadn't seen it as a priority.

Should he wait for them to arrive, or move Poska to another location? That was the question that had been circulating in his head for the last few hours. Both propositions had their downside. If he stayed, he could come under attack again before reinforcements arrived. That was unlikely if the motive for the original incursion was robbery, as Poska would have him believe. However, if Poska was lying… it meant he knew about the attack. But why stay? If he had a chance to escape, he would surely take it.

He whipped out his phone and called Maksim Baranov.

It went straight to voicemail.

Cherenkov tried Viktor Sorotzkin with the same result.

They'd never failed to answer within three rings.

Heart racing, Cherenkov ran down to the basement and into Poska's cell. He slammed the laptop shut and picked it up.

"What are you doing?" Poska asked. "I'm almost—"

"Grab the power cord. We're going."

"Going? Going where?"

Cherenkov pulled his gun out and pointed it at Poska's face. He hoped the intimidating tactic worked, because there was no way he could pull the trigger. If he killed Poska, he was signing his own death warrant.

Thankfully, Poska took the hint. He unplugged the power cord and waited for further instructions.

Cherenkov gestured with his gun toward the door, then a thought struck him. If Poska told his rescuers that he wasn't going without his wife and daughter, they might have given him something to defend himself with. One of the guard's guns, perhaps.

"Strip," Cherenkov barked.

Poska turned. "What? Why?"

"*Strip!*"

Poska dropped the cord and began removing his clothes like a virgin on his honeymoon. When he removed his underpants, Cherenkov could see that Poska wasn't concealing anything. He picked up the clothes Poska had been wearing since his capture and felt the linings.

Nothing.

"Okay, put them back on."

Poska dressed. Cherenkov picked up the laptop cord and told Poska to go.

Upstairs, they ran to Cherenkov's car.

"You drive," Cherenkov told Poska.

Poska took the proffered key and got behind the wheel, then looked at Cherenkov.

"This is a stick shift."

"So?"

"I don't know how to drive a stick."

Cherenkov realized he hadn't thought this through. Now he would be forced to both drive and keep an eye on Poska. He ordered the prisoner out of the car and they swapped seats. Once behind the wheel, Cherenkov stowed his gun between his legs.

He drove away from the old factory, wondering where to take the prisoner. Something wasn't right, and he needed time to figure it out. Until he had things straight in his mind, about what was going on and who he could trust, he would drive into the Russian interior and disappear.

"Open the laptop and get to work," Cherenkov snarled. "And if you make one wrong move, you're dead."

# Chapter 36

Eva pulled up at the pump and stepped off the bike. It was their second gas stop, and she was grateful for the chance to stretch her legs. What she really needed was ten hours in a comfortable bed, but that would have to wait. They were just a couple of hours from the building where Poska was being held. Once they got there, they would wait for night to fall before going in. That would give them time to grab at least a couple of hours' sleep.

She stuck the nozzle in her gas tank and started pumping. Gray was on the pump opposite, looking as weary as she felt.

Their tanks filled, Gray went inside to pay with the money they'd taken from the dead Russians. He returned minutes later with two bottles of chilled water.

"Check on Poska," Eva said.

Gray took his cell phone from his pocket and opened the tracking app. His face told Eva something wasn't right.

"He's moving," Gray said.

Any chance of sleeping soon was gone. "Where are they headed?" she asked.

"East. Away from us. Looks like about a hundred and fifty miles away."

"Then let's get moving. We'll stop in an hour and see where they went."

* * *

Eva pulled over on the tree-lined M7 freeway and waited for Gray to stop alongside her. They'd covered around sixty miles and had just skirted Moscow.

"Did they stop?" she asked him.

Gray checked. "No, they're… a hundred and sixty miles that way." He pointed down the road. "And if they don't stop soon, I'm gonna fall off this thing. My head's fuzzy and my arms feel like lead."

Eva knew exactly how he felt. She was in the same situation. If they carried on like this, by the time they caught up with Poska, they'd be too tired to do anything but screw up.

"I need to sleep," she said.

"Agreed. Let's grab a couple of hours in there."

Gray gestured toward the trees. It wouldn't be the most comfortable rest they'd ever had, but both had been through worse.

Eva made sure there were no cops around, then rode into the woods. Twenty yards in, she stopped, checked that they couldn't be seen from the road, then dismounted.

"Set an alarm," Eva told Gray. She used her jacket as a pillow and was asleep within seconds.

# Chapter 37

Igor Cherenkov tried to make sense of what had happened over the last couple of days, but it was like trying to complete a jigsaw with just a handful of pieces. General Turgenev, missing. The men guarding Poska, dead. Viktor and Maksim, incommunicado. They had to be connected in some way.

He looked over at Poska, who, to his credit, was working feverishly on Juggernaut. He saw the Lithuanian steal a glance in the side mirror as he typed.

Cherenkov still wasn't convinced that Poska was unaware that the facility had been attacked. No one would kill his men just to steal the contents of their pockets, a laptop and a car. They would have checked every room to see if there was anything else worth taking, and would certainly have come across Poska. So why hadn't he left with them, or after they'd gone? Why would they lock him back in his room?

It had to be because the people who attacked the abandoned factory were the same ones who killed Viktor and Maksim. They had to be dead, otherwise they would have answered their phones. That meant Poska's wife and kid…

The truth hit him like a brick. Poska had refused to leave because his wife and daughter would die if he did. That's why he stayed. And now Viktor and Maksim weren't answering their phones, so they were probably dead.

Cherenkov glanced at Poska, who was once again looking in the side mirror.

He wanted nothing more than to smash Poska's head into the dashboard until his face was crushed, but that would be counterproductive. He needed him alive to complete Juggernaut.

*Think, Igor.*

He didn't know how the Americans—and it had to be them—had found Poska. He and his men had been ultra-careful. They'd used burner cells instead of their own phones, and the rest of his team had been moved out of the city for the duration. The only people who knew where Poska was being held were his team and… General Turgenev! That's why he was missing. He'd been kidnapped by the Americans, who had extracted the information from him. That must be it.

Poska coughed. Cherenkov looked over at him just as Poska's eyes flitted to the side mirror once more.

"What are you looking for?" Cherenkov asked.

Poska's eyes snapped back to the screen. "Nothing."

It wasn't nothing, Cherenkov was sure of it.

He was expecting someone.

And if he was expecting them, they must be tracking him. But that wasn't possible. He'd made Poska strip before leaving his cell. Unless they had attached a tracking device to the laptop somehow. No. If it was a physical tracker, he would have seen it when he picked up the sleek laptop, and any software installed wouldn't work unless the machine was connected to a network.

Or they weren't tracking Poska at all.

They were tracking *him*.

His satellite phone.

Cherenkov made an immediate decision. He opened his window and tossed his phone onto the freeway.

Poska looked at him with… what? Was it surprise? That was it. Poska must have known the Americans had his phone number and would be tracking him. Well, the joke was on them.

The questions kept coming. Who had given the Americans his phone number? Could they have extracted it from Turgenev, or got it from his phone? That was the most likely answer.

Still, he wasn't sure he could trust anyone until he knew the truth. Until then, he would keep driving. It had been a day and a half since he'd discovered his men dead at the factory, so the Americans had to be traveling by road. Otherwise, if they had aircraft, they would have been back for Poska well before now. If he stayed on the road, he could maintain his distance from them until Poska had completed his task. If he had to stop… well, so would they. And if it was the same small team that had gone from the factory to Lithuania and back, they would have to stop for sleep. He could carry on for at least the next ten hours. That should be plenty of time for Poska to finish Juggernaut.

On top of all that, they could no longer track him.

Knowing that he had the advantage, Cherenkov managed to smile for the first time in weeks.

# Chapter 38

After stopping off at a hardware store to buy a hi-viz jacket and a clipboard, Farooq took the first flight to Las Vegas. When he arrived, he picked up his pre-booked rental car and entered the town of Beatty into the Satnav. That would take him to within a few miles of the TNR site.

It was almost a two-hour drive through the desert, so Farooq had sprung for a convertible. He connected his phone to the car's onboard entertainment and played his Spotify playlist on shuffle.

What he thought would be a pleasant cruise down the desert highway was anything but. The whole of I95 was awash with eighteen-wheelers. It seemed that every half mile he was forced to overtake a big rig. When he reached a bend in the road, he saw dozens of them ahead, stretching into the distance.

He hadn't known that Las Vegas was such a major exporter of goods. But then, all he'd ever seen of Vegas was the blackjack tables and a couple of shows.

He eventually reached Beatty, a small town comprising RV parks and not a lot more. He spotted a diner and decided to make a pit stop.

The place looked to have been built in the fifties and remained untouched since. Even the old Wurlitzer jukebox looked original. He ordered a coffee and asked where the bathroom was. When he returned to the counter, his drink was waiting.

"Just passing through?" the server asked with a warm smile.

He was in his fifties, and had the demeanor of a man content with his lot in life. His name badge said his name was Joey.

"That's right," Farooq told him. He chose not to elaborate.

A truck passed the diner, and Farooq's coffee danced in the cup.

"Goddamn trucks," Joey said, his smile instantly gone. "They're gonna shake this place to the ground."

"They a regular thing?" Farooq asked, looking at the ceiling to see if it was in danger of falling on him.

"Only this past week," Joey said. "Used to be three or four a day, but now they're coming every ten minutes."

"Why's that? Are road closures diverting them through here?"

"No, it's that Trans Nevada Bullshit Rail. They're gearing up for something."

"How do you know?" Farooq asked.

Joey eyed him quizzically. "You one of them?"

"One of them what?"

"TNR. You work for them?"

"No." Farooq took out his OSHA ID and handed it over. "I'm actually going up there to take a look around. We got a report about unsafe working conditions."

Joey relaxed after inspecting the badge. "Not gonna do you much good. They won't let you in."

"They have to," Farooq said, putting his ID back in his wallet. "It's the law."

Joey chuckled. "That don't mean nothing to them. I remember a few weeks back, the Sheriff wanted to speak to some of their workers about a bar fight here in town. Five guys beat up a local. The Sheriff rolled down there to speak to whoever's in charge and got stopped at the gate by half a dozen armed men. Minutes later he got a call from Homeland Security, telling him to back off. You go there showing that badge of yours, they're gonna laugh you out of the state."

Farooq frowned. "And that doesn't seem strange to you?"

Joey leaned in closer. "Everything about that place is strange." He looked around the diner, but there were only three other patrons and none of them were interested in the conversation. "Six months ago, Danny Barnett and his brother Clyde got drunk and decided to drive out there for a look-see. They're just a couple of high school dropouts with nothing better to do. They heard the rumors, just like the rest of us, and they were curious. So they drove out there one night and parked by the fence. And it's a big fence. Runs four miles in all directions. They had bolt cutters and made a hole, then all shit broke loose. Drones appeared from nowhere and warned them to back off or get shot. Then the armed men appeared. Danny said they just rose out of the ground."

"What did they do?" Farooq asked.

"Hightailed it outta there, of course! That's some strange shit for a construction company to pull."

Farooq thought so, too. Most places had a minimum-wage security guard or two. TNR had drones and armed security. It bore out his initial suspicion that there was more to TNR than Seddon Blake wanted people to believe. It also

217

made him more curious. If what Joey had said was true, then brandishing his OSHA ID was going to get him nowhere.

Time for a different approach.

"Is there a hunting store around here?" Farooq asked.

"Millers. Two blocks that way. You can't miss it."

* * *

Armed with a state-of-the-art rifle scope and two bottles of water, Farooq followed the latest truck heading to the TNR construction site. Looking at the map app, he identified a series of desert roads that skirted the valley where TNR was situated. They appeared to be nothing more than dirt tracks, but one of them would take him to an elevated position in the hills where he would be able to get a good view of the area.

When the truck he was tailing turned onto what was supposed to be a dirt track, Farooq was surprised to see brand-new asphalt. It must have been constructed especially for and by TNR. Two miles on, Farooq exited the road and began the steady climb into the hills.

It wasn't long before he saw the scale of the TNR operation. The fence was as vast as Joey had said, stretching out of sight. Beyond it, he could see nothing.

Yet.

After twenty minutes, he reached the highest point accessible by road. He parked and walked another half hour in the baking sun before he reached the summit. He sat on a rock and looked out. He could barely make out the fence from this distance, and beyond that there was little to see with the naked eye. He took out his scope for a better view.

At maximum magnification, the landscape below became much clearer. He was now able to see the line of trucks in the distance, snaking to a solitary building. Farooq could also see a helicopter landing pad, but that was all. As TNR was a boring company, he'd expected to see a huge hole in the ground. He was no engineer, but how else would the enormous drilling machines be able to get underground? And where were the trucks to remove the excavated dirt?

What really stood out was the lack of any other buildings. He and Xi Ling had come to the conclusion that Blake might be building a company town, but that clearly wasn't the case. There was one building that looked like a warehouse, and that was it.

Unless everything was underground.

But why do that? It would cost ten times more to build an underground city than one on the surface.

Farooq panned the scope around and saw lines of metal poles in the ground. He counted over forty lines, each one stretching almost from fence to fence, the poles a couple of yards apart. What could they be for?

Farooq wasn't going to get any answers sitting atop a hill. He needed a closer look.

# Chapter 39

Igor Cherenkov's eyes grew heavy a lot earlier than expected. They'd been on the road for over ten hours, with just two breaks for gas and food. Beside him, Poska looked equally weary.

"How much longer?" Cherenkov demanded.

"I don't know. A couple of hours, maybe more, maybe less."

"You said that an hour ago."

"And I'll keep saying it until it's finished!" Poska barked.

Cherenkov picked up his pistol and jabbed it into Poska's temple. "Don't speak to me like that."

"Why? What are you going to do? Shoot me? You can't. Not until I'm done. So put that thing away and let me work."

Cherenkov desperately wanted to pull the trigger and end the insolent prick's life, but Poska was right. He was powerless to do anything until Juggernaut was completed. He put his gun back between his legs.

"How long has the world got left?" Poska suddenly asked.

Cherenkov guessed there was no harm in being truthful. "Five days. It will be deployed on Thursday."

"And it doesn't bother you that almost everyone in the US is likely to be dead within a year?"

"People die every day. You, me, everyone, we will all die at some point. So, no, it doesn't bother me. Now, did you make all the changes I asked for?"

General Turgenev had actually been the one to come up with a list of modifications, but there was no need to tell Poska that.

"Yes," Poska sighed. "You can upload a spreadsheet with the names of the targets, and the AI will do the rest. There are also three levels of attack. Number one, you can set a duration. Two, it will simply shut down a system until instructed to turn it back on, or three, it will shut down the system and then wipe the target hard drives. The default is one. If you want any of the other options, just add it to the spreadsheet in the second column."

"Good."

*Not long to go*, Cherenkov told himself. Once Poska was finished, he'd test it before… before nothing. He couldn't test it, because he'd tossed his satellite phone hundreds of miles back. He slammed his hand on the wheel in frustration, causing Poska to jump.

"What?"

"Nothing," Cherenkov growled.

In order to test Juggernaut, Cherenkov would need an internet connection. He knew the infrastructure in rural towns was worse than rubbish, so he would have to wait until he got to a larger city. The next one on the M7 was Kazan, at least three hours down the road. That would be perfect. Poska would be finished by the time they got there.

# Chapter 40

Fortune favors the bold, as the saying goes. Or was it fortune favored the brave? Farooq couldn't remember, and it didn't really matter. If he wanted to know what was really going on inside Trans Nevada Rail, he had to pull on his big-boy pants.

He retraced his route until he came to the newly constructed road. It was late in the afternoon, yet the number of trucks hadn't diminished. Joey was right; they were gearing up for something. It didn't take much to figure out what that was.

Juggernaut.

The line from Paul Heaton in NID to Robert J Portman and ultimately to TNR suggested it couldn't be anything else.

Farooq was curious as to what they'd built underground. It had to be subterranean, because there was no way the cargo on so many trucks could fit into that single warehouse. It also had to be enormous. They had purchased enough bunk beds to sleep ninety thousand people. That had to take up a substantial amount of space. Then they had to be fed. And have recreation space. Plus room to store and even grow food. It was off any scale Farooq could imagine.

Five miles later, Farooq arrived at the gate. The truck in front was waved through, then Farooq eased his rental forward as the barrier came down. An armed guard wearing army fatigues approached him, while another held his rifle ready for use.

"Name?" the soldier asked.

Farooq produced his fake OSHA ID. "Danesh Patel. I'm here to do an inspection."

The soldier looked at the badge, then walked back to his hut. Farooq could see him making a phone call. There was a long, nervous wait, but at least he hadn't simply been told to leave.

The soldier returned and handed Farooq the ID. "About a mile down the road you'll come to a sign. Someone will meet you there."

Farooq thanked him, surprised that his ruse had worked. It seemed OSHA had more power than the local sheriff.

As he drove down the road, Farooq called Xi Ling.

"Hi," she said. "Give me a second."

Farooq heard a car door close.

"Sorry about that," Xi Ling continued. "Just heading home."

"So early? I was going to leave a voicemail," Farooq said. "I didn't expect you to finish work for another hour."

"Same, but Greg Sharpe got it into his head that Eva failed, and as we're only there to support her, he didn't need us anymore. He revoked our security clearances. We're done at NID."

"That's no surprise. He never wanted us there in the first place."

"Yeah. It's their loss. Anyway, what did you find?"

"Not what I expected," Farooq said. "There's nothing here but one big building, and there doesn't appear to be any construction machinery at all. Plus, I've seen dozens of trucks heading to TNR. I stopped at a diner and spoke to a guy called Joey. He said the trucks used to come through three or four times a day, now it's every ten minutes. I think that whatever they built, it's underground, because there's simply nowhere to store all the goods coming in. I'm about to go and check it out."

"Be careful," Xi Ling warned.

"Don't worry. I already got past the armed guards at the front gate. Just showed them my OSHA credentials and they let me in. I'll call you in a couple of hours and let you know what I discovered."

They said their goodbyes, and Farooq put his phone away.

As mentioned, a sign bearing the name Trans Nevada Rail appeared a couple of minutes later. Sitting next to it was an open-topped car, something akin to a golf cart. One man sat behind the wheel while another stood next to it. Farooq grabbed his hi-viz jacket and clipboard, and got out.

The guy standing approached him.

"Danesh Patel?"

"That's me," Farooq said.

The man whipped out a pistol and stuck its nose against Farooq's forehead. With his other hands, he produced handcuffs. "Turn around."

This wasn't the welcome Farooq had expected. He turned and felt the gun against the back of his head.

"Hands behind your back."

Farooq complied and felt the cuffs go on. Rough hands dug into his pockets, taking out his wallet, phone and car keys.

"Move."

Farooq was shoved toward the car. He got in the back, and the armed man got in beside him.

"Is this how you treat all government employees?"

Farooq's captor didn't reply. Farooq faced forward and saw the large building approach. A truck was driving in one end while another left from the other end. The driver pulled up near the entrance.

Farooq was helped out of the cart and the soldier kept hold of his arm, taking him through a side door into the huge room.

There were three trucks inside, all being offloaded by men on forklift trucks. The goods removed from the vehicles were stacked to one side, and another team was taking them to the largest elevator Farooq had ever seen. One was loaded with paletts full of food, everything from crates of champagne to A1 steak sauce.

Farooq's escort took him to a more conventional elevator next to it. Inside, the soldier hit the button for the fourth floor.

Farooq counted ten in all. That went some way to explaining why it had cost half a trillion dollars. He hoped he was going to get the full tour to appreciate the scale of the project, but the handcuffs digging into his wrists suggested otherwise.

When the door opened, Farooq was led into a grand foyer. A man in a suit greeted them.

"Is this Patel?"

The soldier nodded.

"I'll take it from here," the suit said.

Farooq was taken to a glass door, which swished open as he neared it. The suit ushered him inside and told him to take a seat.

The shuttle was swift and smooth.

"Maglev?" Farooq asked his new escort.

"What?"

"Maglev. Magnetic levitation?"

"No idea."

*Another great conversationalist*, Farooq thought.

The ride was short, less than half a minute. When the doors opened, Farooq was stunned by what he saw. Two huge black doors, like they'd come from King Kong's island. They were set in a marble wall and stood twenty feet high. He'd expected nothing like this.

The escort flashed his wrist across a reader at the side of the door and they began to open inward, so silent and smooth that Farooq marveled at the engineering that had gone into them.

He was taken down a hallway the likes of which he'd never seen. Winding staircases ran up the walls either side of him, and a magnificent chandelier hung from the ceiling. It looked to have been cut from real diamonds. Soft classical music came from up ahead, and Farooq was led into an expansive drawing room, with three sofas nestled around a gigantic oak coffee table.

Sitting on the sofa was a man Farooq instantly recognized.

"Danesh Patel," the escort said, and left.

"Sit," Seddon Blake said, gesturing to the next sofa.

Farooq sank into it, the leather squeaking as his hi-viz jacket rubbed against it.

"What's your name?" Blake asked him.

"Danesh Patel."

"No, it isn't. I know it isn't, because when you left that diner, Joey called and told us that someone from OSHA was sniffing around."

Farooq couldn't believe he'd been betrayed by the server. It must have shown on his face.

"Yes, we have an arrangement with the good folk of Beatty. They warn us about strangers enquiring about TNR, and we give them a thousand-dollar bonus. It allows us to get ahead of the game. In this case, when Joey told us about you, I placed a call to my good friend, the Secretary of Labor, and asked her why she was snooping around in my project. Within minutes, she was able to confirm that there were no employees in OSHA by the name of Danesh Patel, and no active investigations into Trans Nevada Rail. So, I ask again, what is your name?"

"My name isn't important," Farooq replied, trying to sound nonchalant. "Now either call the police and have me arrested for whatever charge you want to concoct, or take these cuffs off and let me go."

Blake took a small silver case from his pocket and opened it. He moved some things around with his finger, then took out a pill and placed it under his tongue. He sat back with his eyes closed for a moment, then abruptly sat upright and grinned, reminding Farooq of a serpent about to devour a rodent.

"I don't think so. We're too close."

That didn't sound good. "Too close for what?"

"Oh, wouldn't you like to know. What are you? An investigative reporter?"

Farooq wondered what to tell him. Nothing came to mind.

"Cat got your tongue?" Blake asked, head tilting to one side. "I can get my men to loosen it, if you like?"

None of this was going the way Farooq had envisaged it. He needed to keep Blake talking so that he had time to figure out a plan. One thing he knew about the man was his enormous ego. He decided to pander to it.

"This must be one of the most magnificent engineering projects in the world. Care to tell me about it?"

To Farooq's surprise, Blake jumped to his feet.

"Better than that! I'll give you the guided tour!"

Farooq was stunned. It was more than he'd ever expected. He was also cautious. Maybe Blake's idea of a guided tour meant a dark room and a bullet in the brain.

"Jake!"

At Blake's command, the man who had escorted Farooq into the room appeared.

"Take his cuffs off," Blake said. "We're going to check the place out."

Jake immediately carried out Blake's order.

Farooq, still unsure what was about to happen, followed Blake into the next room. It was small, with just a couple of side tables adorned with flowers, and a single door set in the far wall. Blake flashed his hand over a scanner and the door clicked open.

"After you," Blake said, gesturing theatrically.

Farooq wondered what it was that Blake had taken. He'd gone from Bond villain to Willy Wonka at the swallow of a pill.

Farooq entered and found himself at the top of a spiral staircase. He couldn't help but wonder if he was about to walk to his death.

"Hurry up, down you go."

At Blake's urging, Farooq descended the stairs. At the bottom was another door, which opened when Blake pressed his palm against a reader.

"Precautions," Blake smiled.

Beyond that door was another.

"We have to close this one before we open that one," Blake explained, closing the first door. "And trust me, you don't want to get caught in here. That would really ruin your day."

When the next door opened, Farooq felt like he'd been transported to a NASA flight control room. Dozens of operatives were sitting at three banks of long, arced desks, while on the wall facing them there was a multitude of screens.

"This is my control center," Blake announced proudly. "From here I can control everything in Heliopolis."

"Heliopolis?" Farooq asked.

"Yeah. There's a story behind that. Maybe I'll get to tell you it. For now, let me show you around. Charles, show me the transport deck, if you please."

One of the operatives brought up a video feed on the largest screen on the wall. Farooq looked at it, then walked closer, unable to believe what he was seeing. Was that really a jumbo jet? Underground? And if so, just how large was that... hangar? Only, it wasn't just a hangar. There were other planes, too, but also... tanks? And cars on shelves! This was unbelievable.

He turned to Blake. "I've never seen anything like this."

"Few have. Less than ten thousand people, to be accurate."

"You built all this for just ten thousand people?" Farooq asked. That seemed overkill.

"Bless you. No, we've got ten thousand at the moment. The other ninety or so thousand will start arriving in the next few hours."

That explained all the bunk beds, but it didn't answer one crucial question. Why build it at all?

"I hope you don't mind me asking," Farooq said, "but what's its purpose? And if you're going to build something so magnificent, the likes of which have never been seen anywhere in history, why hide it? Why claim you're building an underground railway? It doesn't make sense."

"Why does anyone build a bunker?" Blake countered.

"To protect themselves from the end of the world," Farooq said.

"Exactly!"

"And you think it's going to end soon."

"Very soon," Blake confirmed. "By the end of the week, to be exact."

"And what's going to cause this… this… end of mankind?"

"Now, that, I can't tell you," Blake said.

*No need, asshole. I already know.*

"And what if we get to Sunday and it hasn't happened? What then? 'Sorry, guys. Let's try again next month'?"

"Actually," Blake said, "it would be a couple of years. In fact, that was the original plan. Fortunately, Heliopolis was months ahead of schedule and an opportunity fell into my hands. Call it serendipity. It seemed a shame to let it go to waste."

Blake came over and put his arm around Farooq's shoulder. "I've been open with you. How about you show me the same courtesy. What's your real name, and what are you doing here."

There was no way Farooq could tell him the truth. Then again, a lie wasn't going to do him much good, either. He'd seen Blake's creation; there was no way he was getting out alive to tell the world about it.

Blake had a damn fine reason to have Farooq killed. His only hope was to find a way to convince Blake to keep him alive. He had to make himself useful. Indispensable.

"My name's—"

Blake stuck a finger over Farooq's lips to hush him up. "Before you tell me, know this. I not only control my own social media company, but I have the owners of just about every business on speed dial. If you lie to me, it will take all of thirty seconds to find out."

That left Farooq with little choice. He had seconds to either concoct an elaborate story that would probably fall apart immediately, or tell Blake who he really was. It was no contest.

"My name's Farooq Naser, and I'm with NID."

The calm look on Blake's face evaporated. Farooq thought he was going to explode. He had to swing the situation to his advantage.

"It's not what you think," Farooq insisted. "I'm not here to stop you. I'm here to join you."

Blake took his arm and led him out of the room, back up the stairs to the drawing room. Only then did Blake speak.

"What does NID know about Heliopolis?"

"Nothing," Farooq said. "I suspect the only other person who knows is Paul Heaton."

He could see that the name was familiar to Blake.

"Heaton is as clumsy as they come," Farooq continued. "Once I discovered that he was feeding information to the Russians about our attempts to stop Juggernaut, I did my own digging. It led me here."

"It was foolish of you to come alone."

"Maybe. But the fact that I didn't turn up with an army tells you that I'm here with good intentions," Farooq said.

"Fair point. But don't think I'm buying your story. Why not be straight with me from the start?"

"You mean send you an email saying, 'Dear Mr. Blake, I understand you're about to destroy the world as we know it. Any chance of a place on your ark?'"

Blake laughed unexpectedly. "Yes, I suppose it is an ark of sorts. Never thought about it that way."

Farooq felt he was winning Blake over, but there was still work to be done. "I had to see it for myself. I mean, it's not as if I can just Google this place and take the virtual tour. My research only told me so much. I wanted to be sure it was the real thing, and if I just turned up and asked for a look around, you would have laughed in my face."

Blake considered Farooq's words, then sat down on a sofa. "You're right, I would have. Actually, one of my men would have. So, having wormed your way in here, what do you have to offer?"

"Offer?" Farooq asked.

"Yes, offer. You think this is first come, first served? No. You need a damn good reason to be part of Heliopolis. What's yours?"

*Good question.*

"Well, when the world starts over, you're going to need smart people."

Blake scoffed. "Oh, please. I've got smart people coming out the wazzoo. What else have you got?"

"Are they really that smart, or are they book smart? Let me ask you, when you started your social media platform, was it because you read about it in a book? No, you had a vision. That's a different kind of smart. *I'm* a different kind of smart."

Blake laid his arms along the back of the sofa. "And if I still say no?"

Farooq shrugged, trying to remain as nonchalant as possible. "That's your choice. If I had to choose between a bullet in the head now or face trying to survive in a post-Juggernaut world, I guess I'd prefer the quick option. That said, it would be foolish not to take advantage of my abilities, and you never struck me as a fool."

Blake gave him a blank look, leaving Farooq unable to tell if his flattery had gotten through. If it hadn't, he'd soon find out the hard way.

"What do you know about AI?" Blake finally asked.

"Plenty. I'm teaching myself."

"Robotics?"

"Very little," Farooq admitted, "but I guarantee you that if I were to study up on it, I would be able to replace your top guy within a month. Anything else to do with computers, you won't find many better."

"And who else have you told about Heliopolis?"

"My girlfriend. She works with me at NID. That's it."

"And I suppose you're going to ask to bring her, too."

"That's up to you," Farooq said. "She's the only person I know who's smarter than me—present company excepted, of course. She'd be an asset. However, if you say no, then I guess she has to take her chances."

"Damn, that's cold!"

*I know*, Farooq thought. *I can't believe I said it.*

Blake's watch beeped. He checked it, then stood.

"I must say, it's been an interesting chat. I have a matter to attend to right now, but I'll make my decision by the end of the day. In the meantime, my man will take care of you."

Jake appeared as if he'd been hovering by the entrance all along.

"Take Farooq to the holding cell on the second level," Blake said, and walked out of the room without another word.

Jake and Farooq took the shuttle back to the grand foyer and an elevator to the second level. When the door opened, so did Farooq's mouth. He'd never seen anything so jaw-droppingly magnificent. The cavern seemed to stretch into infinity and rose at least a hundred feet above Farooq's head. Shelves were stacked floor to ceiling with boxes and paletts of goods, while automated forklifts stacked and picked items.

"In there," Jake said.

Farooq turned to see a doorway marked JAIL. He stepped through it and into an antechamber. Another door clicked open and Farooq saw a dozen empty cells constructed solely of steel bars. Jake told a rotund guard in his fifties to open the first one and Farooq walked in. The door was pushed shut, and Farooq took a seat on one of the two beds.

He had to admit, coming here alone wasn't the smartest idea, but at least Xi Ling knew where he was. When he didn't check in with her, she would know something was up. Not that she could do much about it. His only hope was for Tom, Eva and the others to find Andrius Poska, destroy Juggernaut, and then come to his rescue.

When he thought about it like that, it sounded straightforward.

Farooq knew it would be anything but.

# Chapter 41

*Where the hell is this guy going?*

Eva had purchased a cell phone holder during their last stop for gas, and she was able to keep an eye on Poska's location without stopping every half-hour. Annoyingly, she and Tom didn't seem to be making any progress. Following their short rest break, they found themselves over two hundred and fifty miles from their target, and despite breaking the speed limit, they hadn't managed to significantly close the gap. They were still two hundred miles back, and Cherenkov showed no sign of stopping.

The city of Kazan was the next stop on the M7, and Eva prayed that he stopped there for the night. At least for food. Anything, as long as it gave them a chance to catch up.

Thirty minutes later, her prayers were answered. Instead of remaining on the freeway and skirting Kazan, the marker turned off and headed toward the city. Eva did a mental calculation. If they stuck to a constant seventy, they would reach Kazan in three hours.

Eva opened the throttle a little more, determined to get there sooner.

\* \* \*

Andrius Poska sighed, then hit the Enter key. "It's done."

Cherenkov looked over at him. "Finished?"

"Finished," Poska confirmed.

"That's great."

Cherenkov seemed genuinely pleased. Poska hoped his anus prolapsed.

"Great for you, a death sentence for me and my family."

"We all die at some point," Cherenkov said. "You do realize what you've built, don't you? Do you really think you could survive in the world that's coming? I'll be doing you a favor."

"Yeah, well maybe don't do us any favors. I mean, you know what this is going to do. Why can't you just let me go and be with my family? You got what you wanted."

"Have I?" Cherenkov asked him. "I can't be sure until I've tested it."

"And how are you going to do that? You threw your phone away."

"That's why we're going to Kazan. I'll find a café, a bar, something with Wi-Fi."

They'd already turned off the M7, heading into the city. That didn't give Poska long to convince Cherenkov to let him and his family live. The trouble was, he could think of nothing. Pleading for his life wasn't something he'd ever had to do before.

As they neared the city center, Poska gave it one last go. "If you're worried that I'll tell anyone, you could take me to a police station and tell them to hold me in a cell without a phone call until you launch Juggernaut. After that, they can let me go. Let us all go."

Cherenkov looked at him for a moment, then returned his eyes to the road. "I'll think about it."

That was all Poska could hope for, yet something about Cherenkov's tone said he couldn't be trusted.

He had to have a back-up plan. If he knew for certain that his wife and daughter were safe, he could run, or even fight. No. Violence wasn't in his DNA. He would flee. Find a way to distract Cherenkov and make a run for it. But only if Sofija and Claire were safe.

There lay the problem. There was no way of knowing if the mysterious couple who had tried to rescue him had succeeded in finding them, let alone getting them out unharmed. Then again, they'd managed to fight their way in to rescue him. Surely they could do the same again. Couldn't they?

If they hadn't, and he fled, what would he be consigning his family to? The most unimaginable horrors, that's what.

Poska closed his eyes and took a deep breath to clear his mind. He was going around in circles. Pick a position and stick to it.

Pick one.

*Pick one!*

* * *

Eva glanced down at the cell phone and noticed that the marker hadn't moved in the last few minutes. It was still in a building off the main street, though she couldn't tell exactly what type of establishment it was. It could have been a hotel, or a restaurant.

Or a police station.

They would soon find out.

* * *

Cherenkov drove around the center of Kazan looking for a store that would be able to sell him a cell phone, but he was fresh out of luck. At this time of night, almost everything was closed. Without a phone, he wouldn't be able to contact Admiral Komarov to report on Juggernaut's success.

Or failure.

He would only know once the test had been carried out. For that, he needed a Wi-Fi connection. It didn't take long to find a café-cum-bar advertising free internet access. He parked outside and took the laptop from Poska.

"Once we're inside, don't do anything stupid," Cherenkov warned him, "or your wife and daughter will suffer."

Cherenkov urged Poska through the door, then searched for a suitable seat. The place was quiet, just a handful of customers. He spotted a table near the back of the room, told Poska to sit, then went to the bar.

"Vodka," Cherenkov said.

The barman produced two glasses and a bottle.

"Just one," Cherenkov said. He put his GRU ID on the counter. "I also need a phone."

"There's a payphone in the back."

"No, I need a cell phone. Either get me something from lost and found, or give me yours."

"I can't give you mine," the barman said, clearly not overly impressed with Cherenkov's status.

"Fine. I'll use the payphone. I'll use it to inform my commander that you're obstructing urgent federal business that's of vital national security, and that they should send someone to interrogate you back in Moscow. How does that sound?"

A cell phone immediately appeared on the counter. Cherenkov snatched it up. "I thought so. Give me a pen and paper, too." He swallowed the contents of the glass, took the bottle from the barman's hand and walked to the table. He returned to the bar to get the pen and paper. When he got back to the table, Poska was silent, staring down at the wooden surface.

Cherenkov sat down and used the phone's browser to look up the number for GRU headquarters in Moscow. Like most people, he never stored numbers in his head. Instead, he relied on a Contacts list. Having found the number, he called.

"This is Colonel Igor Cherenkov," he said to the woman who answered. "Put me through to Lieutenant Colonel Duric."

"May I please have your designation, Colonel."

"Mike, Lima, Five, Five, Two."

"One moment."

Duric came on the line moments later.

"Any luck finding the General?" Cherenkov asked.

"Yes. He was found dead a few hours ago. He was shot three times. It appears someone was trying to extract information from him."

"It will be the same people who attacked my facility. I need to speak to Admiral Komarov."

"He's no longer in the office," Duric said.

"Then give me his cell number. This is urgent."

Duric asked him to wait, then came back on the line and read a number off. Cherenkov wrote it down, then hung up and dialed the Admiral's cell phone.

When the call was answered, Cherenkov introduced himself. "I was designated with completing the task assigned to General Turgenev," he explained.

"Yes, Colonel. I've been awaiting your call. I trust you are not going to disappoint me?"

"No, sir. It was completed in the last hour. I'm calling for the test parameters."

"One moment," the Admiral said, and Cherenkov waited, pen poised. "The targets are in Bismarck, North Dakota," Komarov continued. "Basin Electric Power Cooperative, and Bismarck Municipal Data Center for the telecommunications."

"Understood, sir" Cherenkov said, writing down the last of the details. "General Turgenev mentioned an observer…"

"Yes. Let me give you Pavel's number."

Cherenkov wrote it down, along with the name.

"Call Pavel and let him know the test is about to commence. It is to last for exactly one hour, no longer. Call me back with the result."

The phone went dead. Cherenkov called Pavel. The man who answered sounded American.

"If you're about to ask me about my extended warranty, I'm gonna—"

"Pavel?" Cherenkov interrupted.

The voice switched immediately to Russian. "Are you about to run the test?"

"Yes," Cherenkov said. "For exactly one hour. Have a timer ready."

"Okay."

Pavel ended the call, and Cherenkov opened the laptop. He connected to the café's Wi-Fi, then opened Juggernaut.

He typed in the names of the targets, then set the duration of the attacks to one hour.

*Here goes…*

He hit Enter, and immediately the software went to work. A list of attack protocols cascaded down the screen, and seconds later the status label next to the power station changed to SHUTDOWN IN PROGRESS. The telecommunication label followed soon after.

Delighted, Cherenkov picked up the cell phone and called Pavel back to see if it had indeed worked.

It went straight to voicemail.

He tried again, then realized how stupid he was. Of course he couldn't get hold of Pavel. He'd just shut down the cell phone coverage for the entire city of Bismarck!

The counters next to the two targets on the screen slowly ticked down. Cherenkov wanted nothing more than to get rid of Poska and head home, but he had to have proof that Juggernaut worked. He would have to sit and wait it out.

Cherenkov walked back to the bar and ordered two sandwiches.

"Are you finished with my phone?" the barman asked.

"You can have it back in an hour."

\* \* \*

Eva and Gray rode into the city center and parked twenty yards from the building where Poska had been for the last hour. It looked to be a café.

"How do you want to do this?" Gray asked as he removed his helmet.

"First, identify who he's with. If it's just Cherenkov, we take him. If there's more of them, we come out and reevaluate."

"Sounds like a plan," Gray said. "Want me to go in first?"

"No, we'll go in together. A couple will look less threatening. Just follow my lead."

Eva put her helmet in her left hand so that she could easily reach for the weapon tucked into the back of her pants, then led the way.

The café was quiet, which made it easy to spot Andrius Poska and his sole companion.

Igor Cherenkov.

Eva walked toward the table and it all kicked off.

\* \* \*

Andrius Poska saw the couple enter the bar and immediately recognized them: the man and woman who had tried to rescue him. If they were here, it meant they managed to rescue Sofija and Claire. It was time to act.

He wasn't the only one who saw them enter the café.

Cherenkov glanced at them, then at him. Poska knew his face had given him away, because Cherenkov reached for the pistol tucked into his waistband.

Without thinking, Poska kicked his chair back and pushed Cherenkov's chair sideways, sending him crashing to the floor. He jumped over the Russian and ran to the man and woman.

"Go! Go!"

"The laptop," the woman said, moving toward the table.

Poska grabbed her arm. "Forget it. Go!"

Cherenkov got to his feet and drew his weapon. The woman tossed her helmet at Cherenkov and pulled out her own pistol in the same movement. Cherenkov got a round off and ducked just as the helmet reached him. The woman's two shots missed. Cherenkov flipped the table and dove behind it.

As more gunfire erupted, Poska tore the door open and ran into the cold night air. He turned to see the man rushing out, the woman close behind him.

"This way," the woman said, running toward a pair of motorcycles. She got on one, and Poska climbed on the back, wrapping his arms around her. The bike sped off, followed by the other as Cherenkov appeared at the café door. More shots rang out.

They reached the end of the street when Poska felt a savage punch in the kidney. He arched his back and lost his grip on the woman's waist. He tried to grab hold once more, but his arms refused to obey his commands. They flopped by his side, and Poska felt himself tilting over, unable to stop himself.

The last thing he saw was the road rising up to meet his face.

* * *

Cherenkov ran from the café just as the motorcycles sped away from the curb. He fired at the vehicle carrying Andrius Poska, and his third shot hit the mark. He saw Poska arch his back, then slowly slide off the side of the bike. The riders stopped, and the male reached down and checked Poska. The woman had other ideas. She turned her body and fired at Cherenkov, with one round passing so close to his head that he swore he could hear the bullet.

He ran back inside the café, which was now empty. The barman and customers must have gone out a back way.

It was then that Cherenkov spotted the upturned laptop. *No!*

He picked it up and checked the screen. It was cracked, but Juggernaut was still running. The timer had counted down to less than a minute. Cherenkov checked the floor for the barman's phone and found it under a chair. It, too, was still working. He waited for the telecoms counter to hit zero, then called Pavel.

It went to voicemail, and the realization hit Cherenkov square between the eyes. Poska had screwed him. Juggernaut didn't work, and now Poska was dead in the street, killed by his hand. Not only had he failed, but he had killed the only man capable of delivering the software in the timeframe.

Desperately, he called Pavel back. This time it was picked up on the first ring.

"Lights came on a couple of minutes ago," Pavel said. "I just got cell phone coverage back this second."

Cherenkov breathed deeply, relief washing over him. He thanked Pavel and hung up.

Of course, it would take a minute or two for the systems to come back online after a total shutdown. In his panic, he hadn't thought of that.

Cherenkov put it down to a lack of sleep. He needed rest, but first he had to report his findings to Admiral Komarov. Sirens in the distance told him that would have to wait. His rank in the GRU would insulate him from blame in the shootings, but he would still have to waste precious time dealing with the local police. He took the laptop and the barman's cell phone and left the café.

Poska was gone.

But that was impossible. He'd seen him take the hit, fall off the bike, motionless. He hadn't even tried to cushion his fall.

The two strangers must have taken him.

The first police car into the street screeched to a halt next to Cherenkov, who stood there brandishing his ID.

"GRU," he said to the first cop out of the car.

The officer kept his hand on his weapon as he approached Cherenkov. Once he'd confirmed his identity, he relaxed.

"What happened here?"

"It's a matter of national security," Cherenkov told him. "The suspects are on two motorcycles. Dirt bikes. They will probably have a third riding pillion. I need all units looking for them. Once you find them, inform me immediately."

He gave the officer the barman's cell phone number and allowed him to take his name, rank and unit, then walked to his car.

First a call to the Admiral, then some much-needed sleep.

\* \* \*

Gray was a few yards behind Eva's bike when he saw Poska take the bullet to the back. The unorthodox dismount was painful to watch, as the Lithuanian slipped off sideways and face-planted the concrete. Gray slammed on the brake and leaned over to check on him, even though he was convinced Poska was already dead.

He was wrong. In the harsh street lighting, he could see Poska's chest rising and falling. Not dead, but certainly heading that way.

"Cover me!" Gray shouted.

Eva obliged, sending rounds Cherenkov's way. Gray saw the Russian dash back inside the café and made his move. He picked Poska up, ignoring the man's groans, and placed him on the bike. He was limp, unable to remain upright without help. Not a good sign. Gray climbed on behind him and let Poska flop against his chest.

Riding as pillion was not the easiest thing Gray had done. He could barely reach the gear lever or the clutch, and he knew he couldn't do this for an extended period. Thankfully, Eva had another plan. She raced ahead and then abruptly stopped next to a ten-year-old BMW. She had the door open in seconds, and while Gray helped Poska into the back, Eva hot-wired the car. It roared into life, and Eva performed a U-turn in the street, heading for the freeway.

"Stay with us, Andrius," Gray said, slapping Poska's face gently.

"How is he?" Eva asked from the driver's seat.

"Not good. He's not responsive and he's bleeding out."

Gray pulled Poska's shirt off and pressed it into the wound, then turned him over. It looked like the bullet had gone straight through, but had hit something vital in the process.

Gray continued to apply pressure. "Pass me the phone. We've got to get him to a doctor."

Eva handed him the cell phone and he looked up private doctors in Kazan. He noted the name of a side street as they passed it and asked for one nearby.

"Take the third left," Gray told Eva. "There's a twenty-four hour doctor." He hoped it was equipped for their needs.

Eva skidded to a halt, and Gray looked at the building in disappointment. It appeared to be a residential area. If the doctor didn't have a clinic on site, Poska wasn't going to make it.

Gray told Eva the house number. While she got out and rang the doorbell, Gray helped Poska to a sitting position with his legs dangling out of the car. Eva returned to help carry him.

They got to the front door just as it opened. A rotund, elderly man with a forest growing out of his nose and ears took one look at Poska and started to wave his hands in dismissal.

Eva wasn't taking no for an answer. She took out her pistol and pointed it at the man's face, at the same time helping Poska across the threshold.

"Speak English?" she asked.

"A little," the doctor said.

Gray closed the door behind them. "He's got a gunshot wound. In and out. He's bleeding heavily and non-responsive. Save his life or you join him."

The doctor didn't have to think twice about the offer. He gestured to a door off the hallway, and Eva and Tom carried Poska through it.

Gray was delighted to see a fully functioning surgery. Not hospital OR standard, but good enough to help Poska.

"What's your name?" Eva asked the doctor.

"Constantin."

"Thanks for helping us, Constantin."

"Did I have a choice?" he asked. "Put him on the table."

As they did so, Constantin asked for Poska's blood type.

"No idea," Gray said, "but I'm O-negative. Take some of mine if you need it."

The doctor waved him away. "I have plenty."

They laid Poska on the table and the doctor handed Eva some scissors. "Cut his trousers off."

She did so while Constantin examined the wound. His face told them it wasn't going to be an easy fix.

Constantin brought over a drip stand and went to a small refrigerator which contained packets of blood and plasma. He brought out one of each and inserted two cannulas, one in each arm. He then checked Poska's eyes.

"What happened to his face?"

"He came off a motorcycle and hit the road hard," Gray said.

"Head-first?" Constantin pressed.

"Yeah."

Constantin went to a cabinet and took out a vial of liquid. He got a syringe from a drawer underneath.

"I have to put him into a medically induced coma. He has papilledema, a swelling of the optic nerve. That suggests intercranial pressure."

"For how long?" Gray asked him.

"We need him responsive," Eva added. "He has information we need."

"I'm afraid I can't tell you. It could be a couple of days, it could be weeks. To be honest, his only chance of survival is to move him to a hospital after I stabilize him. I can patch him up, but I can't offer the long-term care he needs."

Eva took Gray to the other side of the room. "What do we do?" she asked quietly. "We need to know if he finished Juggernaut."

"You heard the doc. We won't be able to speak to him until he's fully healed." Taking Poska to a local hospital was out of the question, and crossing the border with him on a motorcycle was also out. They couldn't make it into Latvia or Finland by conventional border crossing because the Russians would be watching for them.

"We could tell NID that we've found Poska and get the CIA to take care of him. They must have a setup for situations like this."

"Again, we don't know who inside NID is the mole," Eva pointed out. "Farooq says it was Heaton, but was Heaton working with anyone else?"

"Fair point." That left them back at square one.

"I think there's only one person we can take this to," Eva said. "Give me the phone."

Gray handed it over and saw Eva open a browser. She did a quick search, then made a call. Gray stood close so he could hear both sides of the conversation.

"White House switchboard, how may I direct your call?"

"Nolene Daniels to speak to President Robson. Tell him it's about Juggernaut."

"Hold please."

They waited. Gray wasn't sure the call would be put through, but the next voice on the line was familiar from the TV.

"How do I know this is Nolene Daniels?"

"When I joined NID," Eva replied, "I asked for my people to be brought on board and provided a little test. That was to get the social security number of a court clerk for a random case from two thousand and four."

"Sorry to doubt you, Miss Daniels, but I was told you were no longer with us."

"Slight exaggeration," Eva said. "I have Andrius Poska, but he's badly hurt. He's getting medical attention right now, but he needs a hospital. We're in Kazan, east of Moscow. I need an exfil."

"I'll contact Greg Sharpe now and—"

"No, Mr. President, don't do that. When I arrived in Riga, someone was waiting for me. Paul Heaton told the Russians to expect me. I don't know who else is working with him, but for now, don't trust anyone in NID."

"But Greg is my National Security Advisor. He wouldn't be involved."

"Maybe, maybe not, but for now, trust no one in NID. You need to speak to the director of the CIA directly and have them call me on this number. If you involve anyone else, we could lose Poska."

"About him. Did he complete Juggernaut for them?" Robson asked.

"Unknown. He was shot before I was able to ask him. We'll only know once you help get us out of here."

"Or if the lights start to go out," Robson added. "Did you know that about ninety minutes ago, the power and telecommunications in Bismarck, North Dakota went out for an hour. The IT teams were unable to get into the systems, and then suddenly they came back on. Was that Juggernaut?"

"There's no way of telling until we're able to speak to Poska, and at this moment he's being put into a medically induced coma. It could be days or weeks before he's well enough to talk, but you said yourself, he's probably the only person who could come up with something to counteract Juggernaut. We need him alive."

"Okay, I'll get on to Dan Haskins immediately. Expect his call in the next few minutes. Godspeed, Miss Daniels."

"Mr. President, before you go, please don't take any action against Paul Heaton. If he's arrested, he'll probably plead the fifth and we won't know who he was working with. Leave that to me. And as far as anyone in NID is concerned, I'm dead. Don't give them a reason to think otherwise, or they'll come after Poska."

"Understood. Goodbye, Miss Daniels."

The call ended.

"Wow. Must be nice to have the President of the United States at your beck and call," Gray said.

"It does help," Eva smiled.

They walked back over to the patient. Constantin had placed a mask over Poska's face, and it was attached to a large cannister. "He's under," the doctor said. "I need to make an incision to see the extent of his internal injuries."

"Do what you have to," Eva said. "Just don't lose him."

# Chapter 42

Xi Ling tried Farooq's phone for the umpteenth time, and it still went to voicemail.

Something was wrong. Farooq had never failed to answer her calls. It had now been twelve hours since he'd told her that he'd been granted access to Trans Nevada Rail, and not a peep from him since.

She wanted to report him missing, but who would she call? First, she would have to explain what she and Farooq had found, and also how they'd found it. *Yeah, we hacked into several major banks and had a nosey around.* That would go down well with just about any law enforcement agency she could think of. Even NID was out of the question, as she'd have to explain that she knew about Paul Heaton being a traitor but hadn't told anyone.

It seemed the only person who could help Farooq was Eva. Xi Ling hadn't wanted to bother her, such was the importance of Eva's mission, but she would want to know that Farooq was missing, probably in danger.

She called Eva's number, but that, too, went straight to voicemail, which was understandable. Eva was in the field, and sometimes she would have to turn her phone off or at least set it to Do Not Disturb.

Xi Ling tried Gray, expecting the same result. If she got his voicemail, she would leave a message. She heard the ring tone, then it picked up.

"Hey," Eva said.

"Hi. I tried calling you a few times."

"The GRU took my phone," Eva said. "But it doesn't matter. We'll be on our way home soon."

"You got Poska?" Xi Ling asked.

"Yeah. I'll tell you about it when I get there. I'm waiting for a call right now."

"Oh. Okay. Well, I just called to let you know that Farooq has been missing for the last twelve hours. He went to check out something called Trans Nevada Rail and I haven't heard from him since."

"What's that?" Eva asked.

"We think it's linked to Juggernaut somehow. I'll send you all the details on Shield. Get back to me if you have any questions."

Xi Ling ended the call and opened Shield. She sent a series of messages outlining their findings. From identifying Paul Heaton as the NID mole, to his talking to Robert J. Portman, to Portman's investment in TNR. The last thing she added was Farooq's last message to her. Once done, she asked Eva when she would be back in the country.

Farooq was counting on her.

* * *

Eva read through the incoming Shield messages and shared the details with Gray.

"The timing tells me it's tied to Juggernaut," Gray said. "If they've gone from a handful of deliveries a day to over a hundred, it means they plan to use it soon."

"Agreed. We should let Haskins know when he calls."

"And tell him what?" Gray asked her. "Even if he's cleared to know about Juggernaut, the CIA doesn't operate domestically. They would have to involve other agencies, like the FBI, and they're not going to investigate without a warrant. Even the President is going to want concrete proof that TNR is involved with Juggernaut before he commits to going in. All we have is some billionaires investing in a private company and some coincidental timing."

"And Farooq disappearing after he was granted access," Eva pointed out.

"That could be anything. He could have crashed his car on the way home, or hooked up with another woman, or got sidetracked in Las Vegas. My point is, the President is unlikely to go pissing off the richest man in the world unless he is a hundred percent sure there's fire, not just smoke."

Eva couldn't fault Gray's logic. While Farooq's and Xi Ling's discovery might be enough to sway her and Gray, convincing the President to act required a higher threshold. Proof beyond a reasonable doubt, which they didn't have.

"Looks like it's up to us," she said.

Gray didn't look happy, but he nodded his agreement.

The cell phone rang, and Eva answered.

"Nolene Daniels?" the voice asked.

"Speaking."

"This is Director Haskins. The President said I should offer you any assistance. What do you need?"

"Emergency hospital treatment for a gunshot victim and an exfil for two. Did he tell you where we are?"

"Kazan," Haskins said. "I have a team on the way there now. I'm going to text you the number for Gus. He's the team lead. Let him know your exact location. In the meantime, I'll arrange for the State Department to organize a plane out of there."

"Thanks," Eva said.

"Good luck."

Shortly after Haskins hung up, Eva received the text with just a cell phone number. She prepared a message for Gus and handed the phone to Constantin.

"Enter your address," she told the doctor.

Once he'd done so, Eva sent the message.

"How's he doing?" she asked.

Constantin shrugged. "I've done my best. I managed to stop the bleed, but it's a temporary measure. He really needs a hospital."

"We've got help coming. And thank you. Do you hold any cryptocurrency?"

The doctor looked unsure how to answer. "Why?"

"I want to send you some. For your trouble."

"Okay. I guess." He took out his cell phone and signed into his wallet. "Here's the address."

Eva signed into her own account and scanned the QR code for Constantin's account. She sent him the equivalent of thirty grand.

"Thanks. That's for saving our friend. And your silence, for the next twenty-four hours, at least."

"Trust me, if I mention this to anyone, it would be more trouble than it's worth."

* * *

Two hours later, Eva, Gray and Poska were in a box van on their way to Kazan International Airport. Poska was on the deck, his drips resting on the same shelf where one of Gus's men was working feverishly on his laptop.

"We'll prepare diplomatic passports on the way," Gus told them. He was mid-thirties, Eva guessed. Blond hair and striking features. "We'll take passport photos, and Mike here will photoshop them to change your clothing. If you're wearing the same clothes as the photo, it'll raise alarm bells."

"But how will we get Andrius through customs and security?"

"We skip the normal lines," Gus told him. "We have a private plane, so we'll use a separate gate and avoid the terminal completely."

So it proved. They reached the gate half an hour later, and after a quick scan of the documents, the guard waved them through. They drove to a hangar where a Dassault Falcon 900 waited. When Eva climbed aboard, she saw two men removing seats. A single mattress was leaning against the wall, ready to be placed in the space they were creating.

"How long will it take to get home?" Eva asked Gus when he joined her in the cabin.

"We have to make a couple of stops," he told her. "A short hop to Helsinki, where Andrius will be taken to hospital, then refuel in London. We should reach Dulles in about fourteen hours."

"We have to go to Las Vegas," Eva said.

"Okay, I'll let the pilot know. He'll have to instruct Langley to file another flight plan from DC. We'll have to refuel there and change crew anyway. This thing doesn't have the greatest range."

With the stop in DC, they wouldn't get to Vegas for another twenty hours or so, which would make it mid-morning local time. Enough time to get to Trans Nevada

Rail, scope the place out from distance, and come up with a plan for a night incursion.

It would also give her and Gray plenty of time to catch up on their sleep.

# Chapter 43

Seddon Blake sat in his study, going through the latest stock audit. Eighty percent of the food orders had arrived, and he had ETAs for the remainder. There were also a dozen or so red flags indicating that items in other sections were past their expected delivery dates. He pinged off messages to the warehouse executive to chase these up. None were critical, but he didn't want anything throwing his schedule off.

His phone rang and he checked the caller ID.

Leonid.

Blake smiled and answered. "Mr. President. How are you?"

"Disappointed," the Russian President said. "I was expecting a call from you."

"And I was going to call you in… let me check my calendar… eleven minutes. I thought it best to wait until you were finished in the gym."

Pertsov chuckled. "You have access to my daily schedule?"

*Jeez. How'd this guy get to run a country when he can't remember what he said three days ago?* "No, you told me on Friday, when we last spoke. Remember?"

"Of course," Pertsov said. "It must have slipped my mind."

*Liar. You're just senile.* "So, I understand from the recent events in North Dakota that you had a successful test."

"We did," Pertsov agreed. "Our operative will deliver the software to us later today, and we will prepare for the launch on Thursday. I just wanted to make sure everything was in place."

*You mean you want to know if you still have a place in Heliopolis*, Blake thought. The original plan, concocted eight years ago, was for the apocalypse to take place in 2026, two years from now. Juggernaut had brought it forward, but not everyone had been ready. Pertsov was still a year away from completing his own—albeit much smaller—personal bunker, so it had been decided that he would be granted a mansion within Heliopolis. Nothing as grand as Blake's place, obviously. It was supposed to be used by Efram Hamilton, one of the original investors who had died in the last six months. Hamilton, apparently, had insisted that he didn't bring any of his family with him, so it was unlikely that they knew of his plans.

Their loss, Pertsov's gain.

"Everything is set and just awaiting your arrival," Blake told him. "What time is your flight scheduled to land? I'll make sure I'm there to greet you personally."

"Nine o'clock on Tuesday evening," the Russian president told him.

"And it's still just yourself and your lovely wife?"

"Yes, just the two of us."

Blake knew of the rift between Pertsov and his only son. The boy had revealed his true sexuality a year earlier, just after turning eighteen. It was the last time the two had spoken.

"No problem," Blake said. "I'll have a bottle of Billionaire vodka chilling."

The vodka cost almost four million dollars a bottle—mostly for the jewel-encrusted bottle—but it seemed an appropriate purchase. Blake had ordered a crate of twelve. Heliopolis had come in under budget, so why not splash out a little.

"That's very kind of you," Pertsov said. "And back to business. Do you have the list of targets?"

"All set to go," Blake assured him.

That had been a challenge. He'd had to schedule the attacks so that one didn't interfere with another. If the power went out in Los Angeles before the water had been cut off, he wouldn't be able to go into the water utility plants and delete their software. If someone miraculously managed to get the power back on, the water would also start flowing again. No, it had to be done in a set sequence, and not only for the United States. The destruction would affect every country in the world. It had taken the world's most powerful AI days to determine the right order, and all the details were now in a spreadsheet awaiting the arrival of Juggernaut. Pertsov would bring it with him, and the games would begin.

"I'm glad to hear it. We lost some good men getting this set up. The woman they sent, Nolene Daniels, was almost successful in stopping us. My only regret is that she managed to escape."

"Don't worry, Leonid. In a few days, she'll have plenty of time to look back on her failure."

"I hope so," Pertsov said. "I'll see you on Tuesday."

Blake put his phone away and returned to the schedule, but was soon interrupted again.

"Sir, your artwork has arrived," Jake said from the doorway. "Would you like me to oversee the installation?"

"Yes. Make sure the Picasso goes in the hallway instead of the Rembrandt. I'll have that in here."

"Very good, sir. Also, what would you like to do about the prisoner?"

"Prisoner?" Blake asked.

"Farooq, Sir."

"Ah, yes. Completely forgot about him."

Farooq was an interesting guy. Clever enough to discover Heliopolis, yet so stupid, he came alone. But what to do with him?

"At the moment I've got too much to do," Blake told Jake. "I'll make a decision later. Until then, make sure he's fed. Maybe give him a book or two, but no electronics."

"Yes, sir."

# Chapter 44

Eva bounced off the plane feeling totally revived. A proper hot meal followed by ten hours of sleep and a reinvigorating shower had her ready for action.

Gray followed her down the stairs looking equally refreshed.

Their first stop had been in Helsinki, where Andrius Poska had been transferred to a local hospital and, with the permission of the Finnish authorities, registered as a John Doe. Once he was settled in their ICU, Eva had called Travis Burke. Claire had seen a surgeon and had her wound treated. Sofija had been looked over but given a clean bill of health. The pair were ready to leave, and Travis wanted to know where to take them. Eva used her phone to transfer funds to Travis's bank account, and on her instructions he purchased two tickets to Helsinki for the Poskas, as well as hotel accommodation for three weeks, just to be on the safe side. Eva would pay for an extension, if needed. There was also enough left over to get Travis and Rees back to the States. Eva promised to catch up and thank them properly when she returned.

With Andrius Poska and his family safe, they had taken the next leg to London. This time they didn't leave the plane as it was refueled, then flew over the Atlantic to Dulles for another pit stop. It was ten in the morning when they finally touched down in Las Vegas. Their rental car was waiting for them, and Eva had already mapped out the route to Beatty.

Before they left Sin City, they drove to an exhibition hall for a gun expo. A loophole in the law allowed people to buy guns from private sellers without undergoing background checks. Eva was able to pay cash for two pistols in excellent condition. She also purchased cleaning kits as well as extra rounds and magazines.

Gray started cleaning the weapons as they left the city limits.

"When we get an overview of the place, we should really have some bins," he said as he stripped the first Glock. "I looked up Beatty on the flight over, and there's a hunting shop. We should be able to get some there."

"Sounds good to me. And once we see what the people there are wearing, we can buy something similar and try to blend in."

That was the entirety of their plan. They would decide on the next steps once they had taken a look at what they faced.

Even before they reached Beatty they noticed the huge buildup of traffic, mostly trucks.

"Farooq wasn't kidding," Gray noted. "He said they were ramping things up. There must be enough trucks here to stock a dozen supermarkets."

"Makes you wonder how big this place is," Eva said.

"It has to be huge. Xi Ling said they had over forty thousand bunk beds. Imagine the space needed for all those people."

"And all their supplies. I mean, when I do a weekly shop for Sonny and me, it fills the refrigerator. Imagine how much food you would need for tens of thousands of people."

"They'll need some big-ass fridges," Gray agreed.

Eva slapped his thigh and smiled. "You're becoming more American every day."

Traffic grew even worse the closer they got to Beatty. Trucks were now nose-to-tail and crawling along at walking pace. Every now and again, one would pass in the opposite direction. Eva pulled the rental out of the line at the hunting shop.

Inside they saw every conceivable type of hunting rifle. This had to be one of the biggest stores in town.

"Can I help?"

The man had a cherubic face and black hair in a side parting. He reminded Eva of a young Jimmy Osmond.

"We're looking for binoculars," she said.

He winced. "You're the second person this week. We got some on order, but they won't be here until Friday. Can I interest you in anything else?"

"You know where else we could get some?" Eva asked him.

"He shook his head slowly. "Around here? Sorry."

"We'll take a scope," Gray said, looking at samples hung on a wall. "Best magnification you got."

Young Jimmy walked around the counter and picked one off the wall. "This is the best we have. Top of the line. Cheap at only three hundred bucks."

Gray took it from him and walked to the window. He focused on a distant mountain top and adjusted the focus until the image was crystal clear.

"We'll take it. Honey, pay the man."

Back in the car, they had to wait for a trucker kind enough to let them reverse out into the line of traffic, then they puttered along until they reached the turnoff for the hills.

Eva followed the road until they reached a dirt track that led to higher ground. Once that petered out, they walked the rest of the way.

"Should have brought water," Gray said.

"Bit late now."

Eva sat on a rock and looked out over the valley below. In the distance, she could see a snaking line through the heat haze. She asked Gray for the scope and focused on it. It was the line of trucks. She played the scope along the length of the queue until she saw the sentry at a gate. She adjusted the magnification to get a better idea of the scale of the property and saw that it extended for miles in all directions. Returning to the line of trucks, she followed it until she saw the lead vehicle enter what looked like a warehouse through a large door at one end. Eva watched a man in a dark uniform walk the line of trucks. He climbed the side steps and took what was probably the bill of lading from the driver before walking back inside the warehouse. Panning out again, Eva saw that this was the only building for miles.

She handed the scope to Gray. "I see one building and a helipad. That fence goes on forever."

Gray had a look. She saw him make a few adjustments to the magnification and focus. He was turning his head slowly when he suddenly froze. "Who's that?"

Eva took the scope from him and looked at where Gray was pointing. She could just make out the faint cloud of dirt. She looked through the scope and saw a pickup truck driving at speed along the outside of the fence. It bounced over the uneven ground, but the driver never once let up on the gas. The truck suddenly stopped and two men got out. On closer inspection, they looked like teenagers. Both held bottles that were probably beer.

"Just a couple of kids," she told Gray.

She was about to return her focus to the building when something flashed across her line of sight. She zoomed out on the boys and saw it again. It looked like a commercial drone, only this one was the size of a suitcase. It flew faster than any drone she'd ever seen. Another joined it, and both of them seemed to line up on a boy each.

The kids looked petrified.

Eva soon saw why. Gunfire erupted from both drones simultaneously, chewing up the ground at the feet of the kids. She swore she could hear their screams, even from a mile away.

The gunfire stopped and the boys froze in place for a moment. Then, in unison, they jumped back into the truck, made a three-point turn, and roared away.

"They've got sophisticated weaponry down there," Eva said, and explained what she'd seen. "I didn't see where it came from or where it went."

"That limits our options," Gray said. "Going through the fence could get us shot. Trying to bluff our way in through the front gate will probably get us detained, like Farooq."

Eva peered through the scope once more.

"Then we get creative."

\* \* \*

Eva and Gray returned to Beatty and parked on the edge of town to avoid the traffic. Their first stop was a clothing store, where they purchased the darkest clothes they could find. Eva also had another purchase in mind. Gray had picked out black jeans and long-sleeved T-shirt, and saw Eva admiring some leather belts.

"I don't think that's gonna fit you," Gray told her. The one she was holding looked to be about ten sizes too big.

"The bigger, the better," she said. After trying it around her own waist, she picked another three from the rack and put them on top of the pile of clothes she'd chosen.

"I'll explain later," Eva said, noting Gray's curious look.

After completing their purchases, Eva and Gray decided to eat. They found a quiet diner, the lunch rush clearly over. They sat opposite each other in a booth, and the moment they took their seats, a man appeared with a pot of coffee and two mugs.

"Can I get you started?"

They both accepted his offer. As he poured, Eva noticed his name badge. Joey.

"You guys just passing through?" Joey asked.

"Yeah," Eva said. "Just had a week in Vegas. Wasn't until we left that we realized we hadn't eaten the whole time we were there."

"We ate some," Gray said, adding to the story. "Just not recently."

"Just wanted to fill up before the long drive back to Reno," Eva said.

Joey looked confused. "You drove all the way from Reno to go to Vegas?"

"No, we're originally from Seattle," Eva told him. "We flew into Reno for a couple of days, then got a rental and drove to Vegas. Our flight back home is from Reno-Tahoe."

Joey produced two menus. "Then I can highly recommend the everything burger. That'll fill any hole."

"Sounds good," Eva said. "We'll take two."

Joey wrote the order down and walked back to the counter.

"What was that all about?" Gray asked quietly when Joey was out of earshot.

"Just don't want anyone knowing our business," Eva said. "He seemed keen to know why we were here."

"I think it's called being polite."

"Maybe, but Farooq told Xi Ling that he bumped into a server named Joey in a diner, a Joey who asked a lot of questions. Farooq tells him he's going to TNR, and the next thing you know, Farooq's missing."

Gray shrugged. "Coincidence. Or not. Who knows. I'll bow to your greater knowledge. You're better at the spy shit than I am."

"And don't you forget it," Eva smiled.

"Speaking of which," Gray said, lowering his voice, "what's your plan?"

Eva glanced up at Joey to make sure he couldn't hear them. He was on his phone, but suddenly he looked right back at her. He could have just been checking to see if she needed anything, but Eva had a feeling there was more to it.

"We're gonna sneak in under a truck," she told Gray. "That's what the belts are for. It's going to take a couple of hours to get into TNR, and we can't hang on for that long. So, we wait by the traffic lights. When we get a red, we get under a truck and rig two belts each to the chassis. One under our chest, the other under our legs."

She saw Gray struggle with the picture she was painting. "Lie on your back and thread the belt through a gap in the metal frame, then fasten the belt. It will loop down. Do the same about three feet along the chassis, then climb into the loops."

"Ah, got you."

"Once you're in position, tighten the loops as necessary."

"Loops?" Joey asked.

He'd appeared from nowhere and was standing at Eva's shoulder. He placed two full plates on the table and fished cutlery from a pocket in his apron.

"Loops, you were saying?"

"I'm a dressmaker," Eva said, sticking a couple of fries in her mouth.

"Right, right. So, you're from Seattle? My wife and I were there about ten years ago. We stayed at… what's the name of that big hotel opposite the Space Needle?"

"No idea," Eva said. "We only moved there a couple of weeks ago, but we had this trip planned for months. We both work from home, so we haven't really been out yet. You know how it is. Boxes to unpack, redecorating, work. Doesn't leave much time for sightseeing."

Joey looked disappointed. "Yeah, lots to do, I guess."

He wandered off, and Gray leaned in close. "Looks like you're right. He's definitely fishing."

"Yeah. If he comes back over, raise your voice and accuse me of having an affair. That should make him back off."

Thankfully, that wasn't necessary. Joey left them alone, though Eva caught him staring in their direction more than once. When they finished their burgers, Eva and Gray declined dessert and asked for the bill. They left a twenty percent tip.

\* \* \*

Joey watched the couple leave, still undecided. He was sure as shit that they were there to check out Trans Nevada, but he had no proof. Their story was believable. It was just… something wasn't right about them. He stared out the window, watching them carry their shopping bags to a car. His old eyes couldn't make out the plate, but that didn't matter. There'd be no bonus this time.

Or would there?

He took out his cell phone and stared at it as he tried to come up with a plan. What was he going to say? He had no names, and couldn't tell the make of their car or the license plate. Would TNR give him another grand for details of some vague interaction with a couple from out of town? Hell, no. He'd just be wasting a phone call.

Unless…

He found the number in his recent calls list and heard the ringing tone.

"Hello, Joey."

*How the hell did they know my name?* he wondered. Then he remembered he'd called two days earlier.

"Hi. I may have something for you."

"May have?" the voice asked.

"Well, I'm pretty sure they're here to check you guys out," Joey said.

"Okay, let's hear it."

"Okay, so, this couple just came in. From out of town. Said they were from Seattle, but when I quizzed them, they didn't know anything about the city they're supposed to live in." He conveniently left out their explanation. "Also, said they're driving from Reno to Las Vegas and back. Who does that?"

"Is that it?"

"Well, I guess," Joey said, deflated. It had sounded so much more convincing in his head.

"What are their names. We'll keep an eye out for them."

Joey needed to regain the advantage. "They refused to give them," he said. *That would make them seem suspicious.* "And they'd covered their license plates with mud, you know, so no one could read them."

He waited for a response, and it took a while to arrive.

"Thanks, Joey. If it pans out, we'll be in touch."

The line went dead. Joey put his phone away and wondered if he'd done enough to get his second reward of the week. If he had, he might just treat himself to a trip to Vegas.

\* \* \*

Rick Bonham, head of security for Heliopolis, read the latest alert from what he liked to call the snitch team. A mysterious man and woman from out of town. Jeez. How many of these quack calls were they going to get? He'd made it clear to Blake that offering cash for information was a bad idea. All it did was incentivize people to call the hotline and report anything even slightly out of the ordinary. Sure, there were some good tips, like the guy pretending to be from OSHA, but ninety-nine percent of the tips were just a drain on his resources.

Still, he had to follow up on every call. Every single one. And with the big day approaching, the calls were growing in both frequency and absurdity. A truck driver with an ill-fitting uniform. A truck with Maine plates. A family in an RV park who were openly critical of Seddon Blake's social media platform. The tips ranged from the bizarre to the ridiculous.

And they all had to be investigated. After twenty years in law enforcement and ten running his own private security firm, Bonham was all about the details. Skip one thing and a job could turn to crap quicker than you could say "contract terminated."

Bonham got on the radio. "Foxtrot Papa Three, come in."

"Foxtrot Papa Three, go ahead."

"Just got a call from Joey," Bonham said. "He works at the diner on the corner of South Second Street and Main. Something about a strange couple. Check it out."

"Roger that."

It was probably nothing, but Rick Bonham wasn't about to jeopardize his place in Heliopolis.

\* \* \*

Eva and Gray returned to the rental car to change into their dark clothes. Gray let Eva go first and stood guard outside in case anyone took an interest in what Eva was doing. There were few people around and the occasional vehicle passed them on Main Street. On South Second, the procession of trucks continued unabated.

A man emerged from the diner and took an immediate interest in Gray. The stranger took out a phone and held it up. It was clear he was about to take a photo. Gray turned his body away and tapped surreptitiously on the side window. Eva lowered it a little.

"Looks like we've got a new friend," he said. "Guy across the street taking photos of us. Want me to have a word with him?"

"No, let's just get out of here," Eva said, pulling the black jumper over her head. "We'll head back into the hills and see if we can find the best place to sneak aboard a truck. Too many people are taking an interest in us to do it here."

272

Gray took the wheel and drove back to their observation point above the Trans Nevada Rail facility. When they reached their vantage point, Eva went first with the scope. This time her focus was on the gate. Depending on where they made their move, they could be stuck under a truck for many hours, perhaps even into the morning.

"The trucks are literally crawling along," she told Gray.

"Then we should, too," he said.

"What do you mean?"

"I mean, instead of hanging from the underside of a truck, we should crawl along underneath them. It's not the most efficient way of moving, but no one should see us. As long as traffic doesn't start moving too fast, we should be okay. If it does pick up speed, we just cling on until it slows down again."

Eva liked the idea. As long as the vehicles remained in close formation, they would remain invisible. When they got close to the gate, they could revert to her plan and strap themselves to the underside of a truck. "Let's give it a go," she said. She raised the scope back to her eye and looked for a suitable place to infiltrate the convoy.

* * *

"Hornets' Nest, this is Foxtrot Papa Three."

"Go ahead, Foxtrot Papa Three," Bonham replied. He was in his control room on the fourth floor, separate from the gaudy command center that Blake liked to pop into unannounced. Bonham would never stand for that bullshit. Security was his domain, and his alone. No one got entry without his say-so, not even the man who was paying his salary. The last thing he wanted was amateurs impinging on his operation.

"Yeah, I just checked with Joey. He said he couldn't get the plate number because it was covered in mud, but then he pointed me to their car. He's full of shit. Plate's clear as day. I'm sending it to you now."

That seemed to confirm Bonham's suspicions that it was a waste of time.

"Also," Foxtrot Papa Three continued, "the guy next to the car didn't seem happy with me taking his picture. Turned his back on me as soon as I raised my phone."

Others might call that coincidence, but Bonham never believed in that idea. Things happen for a reason. "Where are they now?" he asked.

"Took off down I95, heading west," Foxtrot Papa Three told him.

That road skirted Heliopolis. Sure, it eventually led to Reno, but it first passed the facility he was tasked with securing.

His phone chirped with an incoming text message. It was the license number for the mysterious car.

"Weathers, I want you to run a plate," Bonham said to one of the four men sitting at desks in front of a plethora of screens.

Weathers got to work.

While Bonham was waiting for the results, his cell phone rang. The caller ID said it was Seddon Blake. Bonham cursed. He'd worked for some needy customers in the past, but Blake was by far the worst. If it wasn't for the opportunity to avoid the upcoming global devastation, Bonham would have told him where to shove his contract long before now.

"Yes, sir," he said after answering the call.

"Where are you? We need to talk."

"I'm in the security control room. Where are you?"

"Level six," Blake said, and hung up.

*I guess I'll come to you*, Bonham thought sarcastically.

"Call me when you've got a name," Bonham told Weathers, then walked out of the room and to the elevator.

When the door slid open on the sixth level, Blake was waiting, hands on his hips.

"Care to explain what that is?" Blake asked, pointing to the park area.

Bonham looked but couldn't see what Blake was getting so worked up about.

"What am I looking at?"

"Him!" Blake shouted.

Bonham saw someone walking along a path, looking up at the trees.

"I know every VIP and their guests," Blake said, "and he isn't one of them. I'd like to know how he got past your security measures and into the VIP recreation area."

Bonham checked his tablet. "That's Greg Baker, sir. He's the head of park services. Once we're in lockdown, he'll only have access between ten at night and six in the morning, but until then, we wanted everything looking great for our guests."

"Oh," Blake said, looking sheepish. "My mistake."

Bonham chose discretion. "No problem, sir. Better safe than sorry."

His tablet vibrated, then played the jingle for the video app. He saw that Weathers was calling him. Bonham answered.

"The car is a rental," Weathers said. "The driver's name is Nolene Daniels. When I added that to the incident ticket, I saw that she claimed to have driven from Reno to Vegas and was heading back. How'd she do that if they rented the car in Vegas?"

Bonham felt Blake's hand grip his arm. "Did he just say Nolene Daniels?"

"He did," Bonham confirmed, and watched the blood drain from Blake's face. "You know her?"

"Not personally, but this woman just waltzed into Russia and started killing their best people to prevent us launching on Thursday. If she's here, it's for one reason. I want this place locked down tight."

"It's already locked down tight," Bonham assured him.

"Then lock it down tighter!"

# Chapter 45

General Franklin Sinclair took the front passenger seat in the Humvee and told the driver to move out.

This was it. No turning back.

The exercise, aptly named Operation Phoenix, had been announced seven hours ago, and now he and four thousand of his troops were heading off base and into a new era.

"You ready for this, Dooley?" Sinclair asked the colonel behind the wheel.

"Born ready, sir."

Sinclair looked for signs of doubt, of reticence. He saw none. Dooley was one hundred percent with the program. The colonel would follow his orders to the letter, Sinclair was certain. They'd discussed it the previous evening and come to the agreement that what they were about to do was for the greater good. Things could not continue the way they were, and what they were about to do was for the betterment of the country. People would die, some of them at Sinclair's own hand. He had come to terms with that.

"Sir, Camps Baker, Harland and Harper all report that they're underway," said the combat signaler who was manning the radio.

"Good, good."

That left four camps, and Sinclair was sure they would soon report in. The men had been expecting the movement orders and would have been prepared. He checked his watch. ETA at Heliopolis was oh-three hundred. What was normally an eight-hour drive would take much longer thanks to the equipment they were bringing along. They'd ruled out tanks, but had included a couple of self-propelled artillery units, plus some M3 Bradley cavalry fighting vehicles. Being tracked vehicles, they were unsuited to making the journey under their own steam, so would be transported to Heliopolis on flatbeds.

Sinclair's phone rang. It was Xavier.

"I'm sending you some co-ordinates," he said. "We're a little behind on deliveries, so we're gonna have you hold outside the fence."

"For how long?" Sinclair asked.

"Unknown. Could be two hours, could be twenty. We just don't want you rolling up and giving the truckers something to talk about."

That made sense to Sinclair.

"I'll send a driver to pick you up. The others will have to remain with their vehicles, I'm afraid."

"They've been through worse," Sinclair assured him, and hung up.

The co-ordinates arrived by text message. There were also instructions on which roads to take, as some were just dirt roads that didn't appear on any map. Sinclair fed the details into the driver's GPS, then instructed the signaler to pass the information to the other drivers.

It was truly no hardship for his men to wait it out in the desert. The majority were being transported in buses, so at least they had something to sleep in or under if need be. They all had a day's worth of MREs—meals, ready to eat—too, so they wouldn't starve.

Another text message arrived, this time from his wife. She had reached Heliopolis and was about to be shown to their quarters. He responded with his ETA.

"Sir, the remaining camps are en route."

Sinclair acknowledged the signaler.

Thirty thousand men, all heading to the Nevada desert for what the news would report as a training exercise.

For General Franklin Sinclair, it would be the most remarkable military operation in history.

# Chapter 46

The closest Eva and Gray could get to the convoy without being seen was just short of a mile from the gate to the Trans Nevada Rail facility. As darkness fell, they drove back to I95 and took the road back to Beatty. Two miles from the small town, they turned off into the desert, ensuring they stayed well away from the perimeter fence. When they could see the convoy a mile or so in the distance, they stopped the car and got out. By this time, the sun had completely sunk below the horizon.

Eva had the scope to her eye, panning left to right slowly. She lowered it.

"There," she pointed.

Earlier, she'd spotted the hulk of a burned-out car on the righthand side of the road. Leading to it was a small depression about a hundred yards long that would give them a little cover until they reached it.

They jogged the first half of the way, then slowed and crouch-walked to the mouth of the depression. They were approaching the vehicles from the passenger side, which would make them harder to spot. Eva hoped the drivers were all focused on the vehicle in front.

When they reached the car, Eva was glad to see that the convoy was now at a complete stop. Whoever unloading was clearly struggling to deal with the volume of cargo. That would work to their advantage.

The truck directly in front of Eva was in the perfect position, and the one behind it was so close to its tail that she couldn't see the driver. That meant he couldn't see her. Time to make her move.

Eva dashed out from behind the car and threw herself under the truck, then lay on her stomach and waited. If anyone had seen her, they would surely get out of their vehicle to investigate. After a couple of minutes, she beckoned for Gray to join her. He copied her move, coming to rest next to her. Again they waited to see if they had been spotted, but when no one jumped down from their cab, Eva signaled for Gray to go ahead.

Gray crawled on his knees and elbows. Eva copied his movements, and every twenty yards or so she checked behind to see if anyone was taking an interest in them. No one did.

For the next hour, they crawled from vehicle to vehicle until they came across a couple of drivers who had left their cabs and were smoking and chatting, mostly about the time they were wasting. Gray edged over to the side of the truck so he couldn't be seen, and again Eva mirrored his actions.

It took three hours to reach the point where they could see the gate. When Gray stopped for a rest, Eva tapped his ankle and held out her belt. He nodded and removed both of his belts from around his waist.

Eva turned onto her back and threaded the first of her belts through a space in the chassis. She then shuffled backward a few feet and repeated the process. Once both belts were attached, she slipped her legs into the first loop and tightened it, fastening the belt on the last available hole. Getting into the second loop was more difficult. She'd misjudged the positioning by a few inches, and once she got her upper body inside it was closer to her neck than her armpits. There was no other place to secure the belt, so she would have to make do.

By the time she made herself comfortable, Gray was already secured to the underside of the truck. All they could do now was wait for it to get to the warehouse. At that point, it would be a crap shoot.

* * *

Bonham stood looking at the screens in front of him. The majority were covering the sixteen miles of perimeter fence.

"All I can find on Nolene Daniels is a news clip from a couple of weeks ago," Weathers said. "Apparently she parachuted onto a cruise ship and took out a shitload of hijackers. Apart from that, nothing. It's like she only popped into life in the last year."

*Who the hell is this woman?* Bonham wondered. One minute she's tackling terrorists on the high seas, the next she's taking on the Russians in their own back yard.

*And now she's nosing around Heliopolis.*

"Get a couple of drones up," Bonham told a second operative. "Have them fly the perimeter."

"Drones up," the man confirmed.

Bonham walked over to the corner of the screen array and looked at the guards on the gate. He'd sent an extra four men to check every driver and every vehicle entering the facility. Bonham saw one of them standing next to a driver, checking his paperwork. Another was at the back of the truck, inspecting the seal on the container. A third checked inside the cab for stowaways.

The fourth was standing by the gate, chatting to one of the armed personnel. Outraged, Bonham snatched up a nearby radio. "Johnson, what the fuck are you playing at? Check the goddamn truck!"

"There's three of them already checking it," Johnson replied. "What am I supposed to do?"

"Check underneath and on top!" Bonham growled.

Finally, Johnson began doing what he was paid to do. Bonham watched him climb the side of the rig and peer across the top of the container, then jump down and check underneath.

\* \* \*

Eva held her breath as the truck finally started moving. When she'd scoped the place out, she'd seen a couple of guards checking deliveries against a list on a clipboard. Now, there were more checks taking place. Drivers were being asked to step down while two others checked the vehicles over. Thankfully they hadn't checked the underside of the truck she was strapped to. As it moved away, Eva craned her neck to look back at the next vehicle in line. It had stopped next to the barrier, and she saw the legs of the driver when he got out. One guard climbed inside the cab while another went around the back. A fourth member of the team appeared, and she saw him scale the side of the truck, then jump down and lie on his stomach to shine a flashlight below it.

She was relieved to have sneaked through the gate before the guard started checking underneath, and hoped it was a sign that luck was on their side tonight.

They would find out in the next hour or so. That was how long Eva expected it to take them to reach the warehouse.

It turned out to be an hour and a half, by which time Eva had come up with the next step in the infiltration plan. She checked that no one was within earshot, then half-shouted to Gray and told him what she wanted to do. She got a thumbs up in return.

Once they passed the threshold from darkness to strip lighting, Eva unfastened the belt around her torso and clung to the chassis while she slipped her feet out of the other loop. She watched Gray do the same.

From her vantage point, she could see the truck to their left already being unloaded. Forklift trucks hauled pallets of goods from the rear and piled them in a row, where a man with a tablet scanned each consignment. Another crew then took these pallets and dumped them in a freight elevator the size of two buses stacked on top of each other. The car quickly filled, and a gate slid down before it began to descend. Next to it, another gate slid open, revealing an empty elevator car. The warehouse team quickly began to fill it.

Eva dropped to the ground and crawled behind the big rig's forward wheels. She waited until the forklift driver collected the first pallet from the back of the truck, and as he swung away to stack it for collection, she rolled out and ran at a crouch to the next truck. Once underneath, she waited for the opportune moment and signaled for Gray to follow. When he joined her, Eva pointed to the stacks of goods waiting to be loaded into the elevator. Gray went first this time, sneaking in between two pallets of cooking oil. Eva had to wait for the chance to sprint across the gap, but eventually she spotted an opening.

This was the tricky part. Forklifts were constantly in and out of the freight elevator, so there was no way they would be able to sneak inside. They couldn't just sit where they were, either. They would soon be discovered.

It was time to get ballsy.

Eva tapped Gray on the shoulder and motioned for him to stand. He looked confused, but when Eva got to her feet, he did the same.

"And I told him that the—"

"Hey! You!"

Eva turned to see the guy with the clipboard raging toward them.

"Who the hell are you, and what are you doing here?"

"There you are. Seddon wants to know what's taking so long. That queue of trucks can be seen for miles. We're supposed to be a secret facility, but because of your incompetence we might as well take out an ad in the *New York Post* announcing our existence."

At the mention of Seddon Blake's name, the man fell apart. "I… well… it's…"

"Look, Seddon likes straight talkers. He doesn't appreciate deflection, and he hates those who show no accountability. Tell me what the issue is, and I'll see if we can resolve it."

"S… staff… staffing," the man eventually managed.

"Staffing?" Eva asked him. "That's it?"

"I… I tried mentioning it before, but…"

"But nothing. I'll have half a dozen men sent up in the next half hour. After that, I expect—no, Seddon expects—this backlog to start disappearing."

"It will," the man said, relief dripping from every pore.

"Okay," Eva responded. To Gray she said, "Let's check how things are going downstairs."

They walked into the freight elevator and stood aside to allow more goods to be loaded. Once it was full, the gate came down and the car slowly descended.

"That took some guts," Gray said.

"We were fresh out of options," Eva replied, "but all we did was buy ourselves an hour or two."

# Chapter 47

When the gate slid open, Eva took in the sight, then slowly turned to Gray. He stood in the freight elevator with his jaw on his chest.

"Holy shit."

Eva felt the same. She'd expected a large underground storage area, but nothing of this magnitude. She was looking down one aisle of what appeared to be hundreds, and it seemed to stretch into infinity. There were many men and women in view, but most seemed to be monitoring the automated loaders, which took pallets the forklifts had dropped off and placed them on shelves high above them.

The moment was broken by a forklift driver who deftly picked up the nearest pallet from the elevator and pirouetted away to the drop-off point, where the automated loaders were waiting. He was immediately replaced by the next driver.

Eva and Gray stepped out into the warehouse. Only then could they get a true sense of the scale of the place.

Eva noticed that she and Gray were getting some attention.

"We need to blend in," she told him. "Follow my lead."

Eva walked over to the nearest woman who was holding a tablet. "We were sent up to help," Eva said.

The woman looked put out. "Sent from where?"

"Reassigned from Catering," Eva explained. "Our boss told us to come up here, get some uniforms and report to…" she looked at Gray "…was it James?"

"Could be," Gray said. "I wasn't really listening."

The woman stopped a passing forklift, scanned the load, then waved the driver on. "Down there," she pointed vaguely. "Aisle eighty-seven, section three-four-two."

She moved on to the next forklift, and Eva and Gray left her to it.

Numbers were attached to the end of each aisle. They found the one they needed and began searching for the correct section, sticking to a marked path punctuated with white drawings of walking figures. The first section was numbered one-one-three. A hundred yards later they came to a crossroads, and after ensuring they weren't going to be crushed by an automated order picker, they crossed into the next section.

One-one-four.

"This is going to take us months," Gray said. "I know a better way to get uniforms."

Eva suspected she knew what he had in mind. After ten minutes of wandering among the shelves, she discovered that she was right.

A man with the ubiquitous tablet appeared at the end of the aisle and walked toward them.

"Why aren't you in uniform?" he demanded.

Eva repeated her story about being reassigned, but this time he wasn't buying it.

"Goddamn it, Carl," he mumbled to himself. "Why the hell would I need two dishwashers screwing up my inventory?" He took out his phone.

Eva wasn't about to let him make a call. She prepared to strike, but Gray beat her to it. He got the man in a choke hold and eased him to his knees, then squeezed until the lights went out.

Eva kept a lookout, but there was no one around. Only the robots going about their duties.

Gray quickly stripped the coveralls from the unconscious worker and rolled his body underneath the nearest shelf. He then dressed in his dark gray uniform and stuck the man's cap on his head. It was a little tight, but it would have to do. She noticed that the employee had a wristband, and it didn't appear to be a decorative accessory. She unclipped it and handed it to Gray, who fastened it to his wrist.

"He won't stay asleep forever," Gray reminded Eva. "We have to find out where Farooq might be held."

Eva agreed. Time was running out. If the supervisor on the ground level didn't get suspicious when his extra staff didn't show, then the man currently asleep under the shelf would certainly raise the alarm.

Time to be more direct.

Eva doubled back to the nearest crossroad and took a right, Gray on her heels. Eva checked down each aisle until she saw a lone worker. She approached him and guessed they were the same height. He would do.

The man held up a hand, then tapped on his screen for a few moments. When he was done, he looked up at Eva and Gray. "What?"

"Where are the prisoners held?" she demanded.

The man looked confused. "Prisoners?"

"Yeah, prisoners. Bad guys. People who need to be locked up. You understand the concept?"

"I understand," he said, clearly not appreciating her tone. He puffed his chest out, trying to appear officious. "Why do you need to know?"

Eva pulled the Glock from her waistband and stuck it in the man's face. "Let's just say I'm the curious type."

His bravado instantly evaporated. He swallowed, eyes wide as the color drained from his face.

"One last time," Eva said. "Where do they keep the prisoners?"

He raised his arm slowly and pointed. "The jail. By the elevators."

"That's the way we came in," Gray said. "I didn't see a jail."

"It's a small door, off to the right," he said, eyes crossed as he focused on the gun millimeters from his face. "It's easy to miss."

Gray walked behind the man, drew his own weapon and clubbed him on the back of the neck.

"No sleeper hold?" Eva asked as she began to strip the man. He also had a wristband. She took that, too, along with his tablet computer.

"He was a dick. Let him wake up with a headache."

Eva couldn't argue with that. She dressed quickly while Gray hid the man under a shelf.

Walking back to the elevators, Gray asked how they were going to spring Farooq. "It won't be as easy as knocking and asking if we can see our friend."

"It might," Eva said. "We'll soon find out."

They strolled back to the elevators, Eva stopping occasionally to glance up and tap on the tablet's screen to make it look as if they belonged there. Just two more workers getting through the day.

When they reached the freight elevator, Eva and Gray turned right and saw the door they were looking for. Sure enough, the JAIL sign was small and easily missed. The door was solid, so they had no idea what was behind it. It could be a sprawling incarceration center, or two cells and an overweight guard.

As they stood there planning their next move, an elevator pinged and a woman strode out pushing a cart. On it were two trays of food. The woman was heading to the jail, and Eva saw her opportunity. She told Gray to stay where he was, then ran after the woman with the cart.

"Hi," Eva said when she caught up. "Feeding time at the zoo?"

"Tell me about it. This guy eats enough for a soccer team."

That sure sounded like Farooq. "All that food for one man?"

"Nah, some of it's for Mike."

Eva suspected that Mike was the guard. She would soon find out.

They reached the door. The woman waved her wristband over it and the door clicked open. She pushed it open. When Eva tried to follow her in, she held up her hand. "Sorry, authorized personnel only."

"No problem." Eva retrieved her weapon. "Here's my authorization."

The woman froze. Eva turned her around and stuck the gun against her lower spine. "Nice and calm. If you try to warn Mike, you die. Understood?"

The head bobbed feverishly.

"Good."

They were in a chamber, with another solid door facing them. In the corner, near the ceiling, was a camera.

"Who's your friend, Alice?"

"I'm new to the night shift," Eva said. "Alice is showing me the ropes."

The door buzzed open. Eva let Alice walk through first and kept the gun against her back.

The jail was small, just a dozen cells along one wall. On the other side of the aisle, a plump guard sat at a table. He closed his book as Alice pushed the cart toward him.

Eva was more concerned with the cells. Only one was in use, and the occupant leapt to his feet when he saw her.

Eva pushed Alice to the floor and pointed her weapon at the guard. "Mike, is it?"

He nodded.

"Take it out nice and slowly," Eva told him. "Finger and thumb only."

Mike removed his pistol from its holster.

"Toss it down there," Eva said, and he threw the gun behind him.

"You're making a big mistake."

"Yeah, I do that a lot," Eva said. "Empty your pockets."

Mike complied, tossing keys, phone and wallet on the table.

Eva walked toward him, gesturing for Mike to back up. He did, and Eva took the keys from the table. She retraced her steps, keeping the gun on the guard, until she was at Farooq's cell. Only one of the keys was big enough to fit the cell lock. She tried it, and the door clicked open.

"I knew you'd come," Farooq said, throwing his arms around Eva.

Mike saw an opportunity and took it. He dived for his weapon and fired from a supine position. His bullets went wide, but Eva got the message. She pushed Farooq through the entry door and slammed it shut.

"Pray this works," she said, and waved her wristband over the scanner. She got a green light and a click.

The moment they were back in the warehouse, sirens blared and red lights flashed on every wall.

"That's not good," Farooq noted.

"You think?"

Eva dragged him to the freight elevator, and Gray ran to join them.

Farooq planted his feet. "Where are we going?"

"We're getting out of here. Up to the ground level."

"Unless you've got a chopper waiting, we can't go up there. They've got killer drones and armed guards everywhere. We won't last two minutes."

"Then what's the plan?" Gray asked.

"Well, believe it or not, I've had a while to think of one. Our only option is to take someone prisoner, a hostage, and leave with them. Once we're far enough away, we let them go."

"It would have to be someone important," Gray said.

"And I know just the person."

Farooq ran to a small elevator. He looked for a button, then turned to Gray. "We need a wristband."

Eva stepped forward. She scanned her band and a light above the door showed that a car was on its way.

"Where are we going?" she asked.

"Fourth level. That's where Seddon Blake stays."

"We're gonna take the world's richest man hostage?" Gray asked. "With all these sirens and lights, you think he's just gonna sit and wait for us to come? No guards, nothing?"

"Of course not, but if anyone can get to him, it's you two. He has a palace—and I mean an actual palace—on the fourth level."

The elevator arrived and they got in. Eva went to press the button for the fourth floor, but it was grayed out. She tried anyway, but nothing happened.

Farooq grabbed her wrist. "These bands must have different security clearances," he said. "Let's go to three and see if we can find stairs down to four."

"What's on level three?" Eva asked.

"No idea."

She pulled him out of the elevator. "We'll find stairs on this level," she said. "If we show up on level three, it could be the security floor. There could be hundreds of people waiting for us."

Farooq looked shocked at the prospect. "Okay, we'll do it your way."

The door to the jail burst open and Mike emerged. He saw the trio and fired three quick shots. All went high or wide, but Gray's response didn't. Mike staggered backward and ended up in a sitting position against the wall, the gun falling from his dead hand.

Eva grabbed Farooq's arm. "We gotta go."

# Chapter 48

They drove at the speed of the slowest vehicle, those being the flatbeds carrying the Bradleys. General Franklin Sinclair stayed with them for the first couple of hours, then instructed his driver to put his foot down and get to Heliopolis as soon as he could. A colonel was left in command of the rest of the convoy.

Sinclair had things to do, preparations to make, before his men arrived. For one, he wanted to see the schematics for Heliopolis. Xavier had explained that it would be Sinclair's job to protect the facility once they went into lockdown, so asking to see the blueprints shouldn't be too much of an ask.

Sinclair stared out of the side window. *So this is what the richest country in the world looks like.* Having passed through Fresno, they came into a small town. The housing was low quality, the commercial buildings had seen better days, and the only growth industry appeared to be graffiti. Places like this didn't stand a chance, and few of the residents would ever amount to much. Most would never leave the town they were born in. They would grow up, work low-paying jobs to barely scrape by, have kids of their own, and the cycle would continue.

Sinclair hoped to change all that. In fact, what he was about to do would change everything. Norms would be discarded like soiled tissues. The entire world order would be turned on its head.

Sinclair was still deep in thought about the state of society and how he would fix it when Dooley broke in.

"Should be there in twenty minutes, sir."

\* \* \*

Rick Bonham strode into the security command center and demanded to know what was going on.

"Mike in the jail raised the alarm," Weathers said. "Says a woman broke the prisoner free."

*A woman. It has to be Nolene Daniels.*

"Give me cameras in and around the jail."

The screens changed from the perimeter fence to the second floor just in time for Bonham to witness Mike being blasted in the chest. He watched the guard stagger backward and collapse against the wall.

"Holy fuck," Weathers exclaimed.

Bonham was thinking the same thing. If it was Nolene Daniels, she wasn't working alone. The shooter was male. "Get me a closeup of the woman with the prisoner," he barked.

The face appeared, filling the largest screen.

"Weathers, is that Nolene Daniels?"

"Give me a second," Weathers said. Bonham watched him check online for Daniels, and a clip of her being placed into a government vehicle after her exploits on the *Pearl of the Orient* cruise ship appeared on the main screen. It confirmed that it was the same woman.

This was disastrous. Not only for operational security, but for Bonham personally. Once Seddon Blake found out that he'd allowed Nolene Daniels into the facility, Bonham would be out on his ass. He had to rectify matters immediately.

"I want all personnel converging on the second floor immediately." His use of the word *all* was ironic. Aside from the men in the room with him, Bonham had twenty men working alternating shifts at his disposal, against a woman who was prepared to take on the Russians in their own back yard. Four of his team were at the main gate checking the incoming trucks. It seemed they were no longer needed there. "Tell Johnson and the others to get their asses in here. And order the day shift back on station."

A second operative confirmed that the other six security officers were heading to the scene and that the off-duty men had been informed.

Bonham wasn't geared up for something like this. The job description was for someone to maintain security within the facility, dealing with the occasional drunk or fights between workers. He also had to repel casual observers and troublemakers, like the kids in the truck who liked to buzz the perimeter once in a while. The real defense would be provided by the army, but they wouldn't arrive for another few hours. Until then, Bonham would have to make do with the few men he had.

"Warn them that the intruders are armed and extremely dangerous," Bonham said.

His phone rang, and Bonham checked the caller ID.

Seddon Blake.

That was all he needed.

\* \* \*

Eva saw the universal sign for stairs and pulled Farooq toward it. She yanked the door open and stepped into the landing.

"Clear."

Farooq followed her into the stairwell, with Gray not far behind. Eva led the way down, but after three steps she stopped.

"Someone's coming," she said. In fact, it sounded like at least four people, and they were in a hurry.

"Back up," she told the others.

On her way back to the landing, she noticed the signs posted to the right of the doorway. A down arrow pointed to Accommodation. The up arrow said Transport.

"First floor," she told Gray. "They might have a car we can borrow."

"They've got more than that," Farooq said.

When they reached the first-level landing, Eva checked through the window in the door. Nobody appeared to be waiting for them. She pushed through and stopped dead. Eva was used to the scale of the facility, but not the sheer variety of vehicles on show. Commercial airliners, two battle tanks from a bygone era, helicopters, cars, trucks, the list seemed endless. And it wasn't just the variety. The number was mind-boggling. There had to be thousands of craft of all descriptions. There was only one thing Eva couldn't see: a way out.

The three of them ran between electric cars on one side and a number of what appeared to be drones on the other, only they were as large as family sedans and had a passenger pod in the middle. Eva considered taking one, but they only held two people.

"Look for an exit," she said. "There has to be a ramp leading to the surface."

The least she expected was signs pointing the way, but there was nothing to suggest any way for the vehicles to get out. It was as if the planes and automobiles had just appeared underground. Perhaps they'd been put in place before the ceiling had been added, but that made no sense. They'd have to get them out somehow.

The answer came with the groan of giant hydraulics from behind them. Eva turned to see a large section of concrete slowly descending. Sitting atop it was a military Humvee, and standing next to it were four soldiers.

Eva raced for the nearest electric car and hid behind it, taking in the view through the car's windows. Gray and Farooq appeared either side of her.

"Looks like we found the way out," Gray said.

"It's not that easy," Eva reminded him. "Even if we get one of these started and drive onto the platform, we still need someone to raise it."

"And then battle our way past the killer drones," Farooq added.

"And as the army have just arrived, them, too," Gray said.

Their situation was getting worse by the minute. It appeared the only way they were going to get out was with a valuable hostage, but Seddon Blake was no doubt locked down in a secure room, waiting for the alert to end.

A loudspeaker burst into life.

*"Attention all crew, attention all crew. Be on the lookout for three intruders. Two males, one female. They were last seen entering deck one, transport. If you see them, report their location to your supervisor immediately. Do not engage, I repeat, do not engage."*

"That's not good," Farooq noted.

Eva had to agree. It appeared they were stuck inside with no way out. Even if they reached the surface unseen, there were still the automated killer drones to contend with. Their only hope was to get to Seddon Blake.

"I say we split up." Gray said. "They're looking for three people. If we pretend to be looking for the intruders, we might get away with it."

"And in a place this big, we'll never find each other again," Eva countered. "No, I suggest we find a large enough vehicle and hide inside until the commotion dies down."

"Yeah, I like that idea," Farooq said. "What about one of the jumbo jets? We could hide in one of the lower levels, like the baggage hold."

Eva looked over at the two commercial liners and immediately ruled them out. "They're too open. We'd easily be spotted as we approached." She looked around for better alternatives. Nothing caught her eye. "Let's just keep moving away from the stairs. We're sure to find something."

\* \* \*

General Sinclair stood next to the Humvee as the entire landing pad began to descend into the ground. The action was smooth, if a little noisy. It could be heard even over the sound of the PA system that was coming to the end of an announcement. Something about "do not engage."

"It's like we're heading into a Bond villain's lair," Colonel Dooley noted.

Sinclair couldn't agree more. That's exactly what they were doing, though there would be no suave, invincible British agent to come to the rescue.

When the platform dipped below the surface, Sinclair got his first glimpse of the inside of Heliopolis. It was breathtaking. Like nothing he'd ever imagined. He was still admiring the sight when the platform came to rest, and two men jogged over to the Humvee. One wore a suit, the other dark gray coveralls.

"General Sinclair, I'm Rick Bonham, head of security," the suit said, extending his hand.

Sinclair shook it. "Are my schematics ready?"

Bonham looked hurt by the brusque response, but Sinclair wasn't there to massage the man's ego. He had a single job to do.

"They are, but at the moment we have a security issue. I've been asked to take you to your quarters immediately."

"What kind of security issue?" Sinclair demanded.

"Three intruders. One was a prisoner here and the other two came to rescue him. They've already killed one of my men."

"Then it's all the more imperative that I see the schematics. Let's go."

"Sir, I was under strict orders—"

"When the shit starts flying, Marines don't hide in their bunks. They head toward the gunfire. I hope I don't have to repeat myself."

"No, sir," Bonham said, coming to some semblance of attention.

"Good. Lead the way." Sinclair turned to Dooley. "How long until the men arrive?"

The Colonel checked his watch. "Roughly eight hours, sir."

That would give him ample time to identify every single entry point to the facility, plus all the critical infrastructure that was open to sabotage.

"I take it the facility's designers are here?" Sinclair said to Bonham.

"Yes, sir."

"I want to speak to them. Arrange a meeting in three hours."

# Chapter 49

Eva woke with a start. Her dream had been a collection of disparate incidents that culminated in an explosion of violence. She hoped it wasn't a portent of things to come.

"I'd offer you breakfast, but we're fresh out of coffee," Farooq deadpanned.

Eva sat up and rubbed her eyes. "What time is it?"

"Just after ten in the morning. I'm gonna grab some shuteye."

She'd slept for nine hours, which surprised her. She'd had a good sleep on the plane over, but her body obviously needed more. Eva stretched, then paused as she spotted movement in the corner of her eye. At least a dozen soldiers, dressed ready for close quarter combat, were going from vehicle to vehicle. Eva reckoned they had about ten minutes before they reached the bus they were hiding in.

She pulled Farooq down, away from the window. "That might have to wait. Looks like they're searching all the vehicles."

Eva kicked Gray's foot, rousing him from his slumber. He was instantly awake.

"What is it?" he asked.

"We've got company," Eva said. "They're doing a methodical search of every vehicle. We have to move."

Gray stuck his head up and took a look for himself. He sat back down. "Maybe now's the time to split up?" he suggested. "They'll still be looking for the three of us."

Eva had to agree. "Okay, but first we need to get a uniform for Farooq."

"Leave it to me," Gray said. He crawled to the door and forced it open at the bottom, squeezing through the gap. Eva watched him slink away.

"I don't feel happy going out there alone," Farooq said.

"I know, but Tom's right. If we stick together, we'll attract too much attention."

"So, we just find our own way out?" Farooq asked her.

"No. We'll all scout around for a way out. There must be one that takes us out of the range of those drones. See what you can find, and we'll meet up by that white 747 in five hours."

Gray returned within ten minutes, carrying a set of coveralls similar to what he and Eva were wearing.

"Closest fit I could find," Gray said, tossing the uniform to Farooq. "What's the plan?" he asked Eva.

"As you said, we split up, look for an out, and meet at that white jumbo jet at fifteen-thirty."

"And if we haven't found anything?" Gray asked her.

"Then we go looking again."

* * *

General Franklin Sinclair had been awake for over thirty hours, and he was beginning to feel it.

He'd spent the first three hours poring over the floor plans for Heliopolis. The place was immense, as he'd already seen, but there was much more hidden from view than he'd imagined. For one, they weren't reliant on electricity for access. The hydraulic lift that took craft to and from the transport level, and the elevators that fed the ground level unloading dock, were not the only ways in and out. He identified a series of stairwells that led from ground level all the way down to the tenth floor. These were spaced four hundred yards apart and ran along each wall. However, it was the ones in the middle of the transport level that most intrigued Sinclair. They didn't lead straight to the surface, but instead ran along tunnels just below it. Bonham had been using these to guard the fence, guiding his men to wherever an intruder was spotted. The network of tunnels covered a vast area, meaning a security detail could suddenly appear at the fence line at almost a hundred different points, using high-powered electric shuttles to get to the correct spot in the shortest time possible.

That was a lot of exits to cover. Fortunately, manpower was something Sinclair was blessed with. Several thousand men were already at Heliopolis, and the remainder would arrive in the next six hours.

News of intruders wasn't welcome, not with the big moment approaching. Sinclair had stationed six men on each stairwell landing with orders to identify anyone moving from floor to floor. If their bracelet didn't match their Heliopolis profile, they would have some explaining to do. In particular, Sinclair's men were looking for two names, those of the employees who had been attacked and stripped of their uniforms by the intruders.

Intruders who were on the transport level.

Sinclair had told Bonham to review CCTV footage from every single stairwell on that floor, and the trio they were looking for hadn't shown their faces. They'd been seen to enter level one after killing the jailer, but they hadn't left. That made Sinclair's task a lot easier.

He assigned groups of men to search every craft in the inventory, starting at one end and moving slowly to the other. It would take time, but eventually they would find the woman and two men.

And when they did, Sinclair wanted to speak to them. He wanted to know who else knew about Heliopolis.

Sinclair's next task had been to speak to the engineers who had built the place. He'd asked about the vital life support systems that would keep Heliopolis running for a year. Everything from fresh water to electricity and air management were located on the tenth level. Most of the residents only knew about floors one to nine, because like passengers on a cruise ship, they weren't privy to what made the vessel tick.

Level ten was the heart of the facility. Waste water was recycled and used for the animals and plants on the level above. An intricate system pulled fresh air in from above ground and pumped stale air, heavy in carbon dioxide, to the nurseries where the food was grown.

The most important system was the electricity generator. Without it, nothing else worked. The occupants of Heliopolis would be forced to flee above ground if the electric grid went down.

Sinclair had been given a guided tour. He demanded to be shown any vulnerabilities in the network, as well as backups and redundancies. The engineers had proudly proclaimed the system to be so robust that backups were not needed. Sinclair thought that foolish. Everything had a weakness. You just had to apply enough pressure.

He told the engineers that twenty armed guards would be posted within the power station, day and night. There were no objections. In fact, Sinclair got the impression that the engineers were humoring him. They could think what they liked; Sinclair had a job to do, and he would do it.

But for now, he needed rest.

"I'm gonna hit my bunk," he told Colonel Dooley. "Wake me if there are any major updates."

\* \* \*

Eva walked confidently along the rows of vehicles, occasionally stopping by a license plate and tapping on the tablet screen to make it appear that she was busy doing her job. In fact, she was searching for an exit. She soon spotted one, a doorway with a green EXIT sign above it. She walked over to check it out, but as she neared, the door opened. A woman walked through, clearly not happy.

"This is getting ridiculous," the woman huffed.

"What is?" Eva asked.

"The bracelet checks. I just walked up from the accommodation level and they're checking them on every single floor. It's bad enough that the elevators don't go to this floor anymore, but now you waste half your break just queueing up to prove who you are. It's madness."

"Sure is," Eva agreed, but inside felt it was a sensible move.

The woman was holding the door open for Eva. "Are you going down or not?"

"Not," Eva said. She patted her thigh pocket, where she'd stowed her pistol. "I was just gonna eat my chocolate bar.

Might as well do that up here if it's going to be so much hassle."

The woman let the door swing closed. "I don't blame you."

She walked away, leaving Eva to assess the situation.

It was bad.

With the elevators out of action and guards in every stairwell, there was nowhere to go. They were trapped.

Things suddenly got a lot worse.

*"Attention all crew, attention all crew. Evacuate transport level one, I repeat, evacuate transport level one. All personnel on transport level one are to make their way to the accommodation level immediately."*

The announcement was repeated over the loudspeakers, but Eva had already heard enough. With all exits covered, the net was closing in. She had to get to the meeting place and discuss options with Gray and Farooq.

She jogged toward the jumbo jet, but didn't get far.

"Hey!" A soldier stepped out from between two trucks. "Exits are that way."

"I left something at my station," Eva said, trying to get around him.

"Doesn't matter. Head for the stairs right now."

"But it's important," Eva pleaded.

He raised his rifle. "I don't care. Orders are orders."

Sensing that he wasn't going to back down, Eva turned and retraced her steps. She looked back and saw that the soldier was watching her.

"Wilson! Give me a hand over here!"

The soldier responded to the shout, running to where another Marine was trying to deal with half a dozen unruly employees.

Eva saw her chance and dived to her left, between a pickup and a speedboat on a trailer. She worked her way deeper within the cluster of vehicles until she was sure she was out of sight.

What to do?

Gray and Farooq were sure to be having similar issues, but she couldn't worry about them now. She had to concentrate on reaching the rendezvous point. If they didn't join her soon, she would figure something out.

Eva got down on her belly and looked for booted feet. Seeing none around, she crawled beneath vehicles toward the Boeing 747. Every now and then she had to stop as soldiers passed her location, but she soon got to within spitting distance of the plane.

That's when she heard the whistle. It came from above her, and Eva looked up hoping to see Gray or Farooq. Instead, she was looking down the barrel of a rifle. The soldier carrying it stood on top of an electric sedan, and the sound of pounding feet intensified as more marines came over to answer his call.

"Get up nice and slowly."

Eva had no choice. There was no way she could crawl fast enough to outrun a bullet. She stood and placed her hands behind her head. She was immediately slammed into the side of a van and her legs were kicked apart. Rough hands pulled her hands down behind her and applied plasticuffs.

"Let's see who you are," one said, and held a scanner against the bracelet Eva was wearing. The sound of high-fives soon followed. Two soldiers grabbed an arm each and marched Eva out into one of the main aisles.

"That's all three of them," one said over a radio.

Eva's heart sank. Her only hope had been that Gray might come to her rescue, but that was now out of the question. Actually, that wasn't true. While she was alive, there was always hope.

\* \* \*

"Sir, we captured the intruders."

Sinclair was awake after the first word, and he sat up in his bed. The clock said he'd been asleep for three hours. It would have to do.

"Where are they?"

"In the brig," Dooley told him.

"Okay, keep them separated. I'll be there to speak to them soon."

Before that, he had other matters to attend to. Today was Tuesday, when the last of the VIPs were due to arrive. Most would arrive by air, so it was good that the security threat was over and the transport level could get back to normal. That was one less thing to worry about.

Sinclair went to the head and brushed his teeth, then splashed water on his face. His close-cropped hair needed no attention.

"Going out already?"

Sinclair turned to see his wife, Diana, standing in the doorway. "I told you I'd be busy from the moment I arrived. Just a little while longer and this will all be over."

Diana folded her arms. "You're going through with it?" she asked, concerned.

"We've already discussed this. It's something I have to do," Sinclair said. He kissed her on the forehead and stepped out of the bathroom.

He had two hours before his meeting with Seddon Blake, so he used his wristband to travel down to the recreation level for a quick five-mile run to blow away any remaining cobwebs.

It was going to be a busy day.

* * *

"General, so good to finally meet you."

Seddon Blake extended his hand and Sinclair shook it. "The pleasure's all mine, sir."

They were standing in the middle of the park on the recreation level. The ceiling was a gigantic LED display which currently showed a blue sky dotted with small cirrocumulus clouds and a bright sun. Blake spread his arms. "What do you think?"

"It's… big." Sinclair said.

It irked Blake that people focused on the size of Heliopolis while disregarding the thought that had gone into it. The innovation. The attention to detail. Why could they never give him the credit he deserved? He forced a laugh. "Oh, General, you can do better than that. Try… spectacular. Or magnificent. Or… or… breathtaking."

"It's certainly all of those," Sinclair agreed. "I haven't had time to take it all in just yet. Once I get my duties out of the way, I'll be able to bathe in its splendor."

Blake wasn't sure whether the General was mocking him, but he let it slide. "Sure thing. What else do you need to do?"

"I have to assign personal security to each of the Phoenix members. I'll need a list of their names and where they are staying."

Blake turned to his assistant, Jake. "Get that to the general in the next ten minutes."

Jake disappeared without a word.

"And thank you for finding the terrorists," Blake said. "They could have delayed our launch, and I hate to miss a deadline."

"Terrorists?" Sinclair asked.

"Of course, terrorists. Why else would they be here?"

"That's a very good question," the soldier said. "I plan to find out later today when I speak to them."

Blake didn't see the point. "Just get rid of them. What their motives are doesn't matter now. In two days, we'll be safe in here while their world burns."

"It matters if they're an advance team ahead of a larger force," Sinclair said. "In order to defend this facility, I need to know if anyone else is coming, and in what strength."

Blake hadn't considered that. "I guess that's why you're the general and I'm not," he said. "Okay, talk to them. Let me know what they say. Do you need anything else?"

"Just one. How long before your deliveries are completed?" Sinclair asked. "I have thousands of men waiting out in the desert. I'd like to get them inside, and bussing them in fifty at a time is slowing me down."

Blake brought up his tablet and checked the schedule. "Looks like we have another… thirty-seven trucks coming. Should be done within three hours. You can move your men after that."

"Understood," Sinclair said. "And what time is the last guest scheduled to arrive?"

Blake again referred to his tablet. "Most of them are already here. Three more will be arriving by road in the next four hours, and one flight landing at nine this evening."

"So after that, anyone approaching the facility can be considered hostile?"

Blake considered who else might be coming, but could think of no one.

Jake returned at that point and handed Sinclair a tablet. Blake asked him if he knew of anyone arriving after nine.

"No one is scheduled, sir."

"Then sure," Blake said to Sinclair. "Consider anyone else hostile."

"Roger that. Now if you'll excuse me, I'm going to speak to                          our                          prisoners."

\* \* \*

Eva sat staring out of the cell. She'd already tried the bars and they were solid. She wasn't forcing her way out of this one. Three cells down, Gray was sleeping on his cot. Farooq, a further three cells away, had his head in his hands.

As situations went, this was dire. The only person who knew where they were was Xi Ling, and there was no way she was going to mount a rescue mission. Sonny was too hurt to be of any use, either. With the amount of soldiers she'd seen, fighting their way out was going to be nigh-on impossible.

For once in her life, Eva Driscoll was out of ideas.

The door to the jail opened and two soldiers walked in. One had the look of a fighting man, with a chiseled jaw and sleek movement. The other was about ten years younger, maybe early forties, and stockier.

They walked past all the cells, before returning to Eva's. The elder one told the new jailer to open it and then walked inside. He stood over Eva.

"My name is General Franklin Sinclair," he said. "Who are you?"

"If I told you, you wouldn't believe me."

"Try me," Sinclair said.

"President Robson's personal assassin," Eva said.

Sinclair considered her reply for the briefest moment. "You're right, I don't believe you."

"I don't blame you. So, you here to witness the end of the world?"

Sinclair took a seat on the opposite cot. "What do you know about that?"

"Enough," Eva said. "Juggernaut, the Russians, do I need to go on?"

Sinclair shook his head.

His approach wasn't what Eva had expected when she'd first seen him. She imagined a man like this, a general according to his army insignia, would be in her face, demanding answers, yet Sinclair was… conversational, as if he was conducting a job interview.

"You have a name?"

"You can call me Nolene."

"Thanks. Why are you here, Nolene?"

It was a pretty dumb question. "I came to tell you that your extended warranty has expired. Why the hell do you think I'm here? To stop you killing millions of innocent people, obviously."

"Just the three of you?"

"Yeah. The rest couldn't get the day off."

Sinclair sighed. "Who else knows about this place, Nolene?"

The only other person was Xi Ling, but Eva wasn't going to tell him that. "Everyone from the President down. They'll be here any minute now."

"Please, I want the truth."

His tone was disarming. She expected anger, threats, but Sinclair remained calm. In any other situation, she might have warmed to him.

He abruptly stood. "Think about your answer," he said.

"Why?" Eva asked. "Why do you need to know? You're going to unleash Juggernaut soon. What does it matter who knows about it?"

He thought for a moment, then said, "I have my reasons."

The jailer unlocked the cell, then locked it again after Sinclair left.

He didn't look back.

Eva tried to figure out why he needed the information. If someone in power knew what was going on here, they would have acted by now. Even if Eva escaped and blew the whistle, could anything really be done before civilization started to collapse? She doubted it. Sure, sending in the rest of the armed forces, those who hadn't sided with Sinclair, could lead to this place being captured, but that wouldn't stop the Russians launching Juggernaut. And he didn't seem to care who knew about Juggernaut. He was more concerned with who knew about this facility. Perhaps it was because he was tasked with securing it, but Eva suspected it was something more.

# Chapter 50

"Sir, President Pertsov is ten minutes out."

Seddon Blake thanked Jake and finished fixing his hair. The big moment was here. The Russian was the last of the Phoenix members to arrive, and then preparations could really begin. Years of planning and building were about to pay off. All that remained was to put the solar panels in place and then lock down the entire facility before letting Juggernaut off the leash.

Blake wished he could be up there to see it, but that was far too dangerous. Instead, he would have to rely on the occasional scouting mission once the power went out and television stopped working. Most of the stations would have backup generators, but they wouldn't last forever. By the time broadcasts ceased, the full extent of the chaos would be evident. Four months after that, General Sinclair would begin sending his men out in force, checking with the nearest big cities to understand the scale of devastation. Only once it was clear that ninety percent of the population were gone would they think about emerging.

*Rising from the flames.*

That was to come, but tonight was a celebration in its own right. Every Phoenix member, all one hundred and one, would dine together in the largest of the restaurants. Blake had prepared a speech, riddled with false praise for his donors whose only redeeming qualities were the size of their

316

bank accounts and their lack of empathy toward their fellow man.

Qualities Blake both shared and admired.

He took the private elevator to the transport level, his trusty assistant at his side.

"He's landed," Jake said as they stepped out of the car.

"Okay. Call the kitchen, make sure everything's on course for tonight's meal."

There was no need to check, but Blake hated standing around doing nothing. It would be a few minutes before Pertsov's plane was on the platform and ready to enter Heliopolis.

Jake spoke on the phone briefly, then hung up. "All set. Food is prepped, drinks on ice."

"And the extra table?" Blake asked.

"I spoke to the chef earlier. He assured me that it would be set up."

Though not Phoenix members, some of the staff warranted special attention on a night like this. General Sinclair and his wife, who would be providing security for the next twelve months. Secretary of Defense Donald Killman and his mistress, without whom they wouldn't have had access to so many men. There were also a couple of governors without whom Blake wouldn't have got his permits to build Heliopolis in the first place and avoid scrutiny once spades were in the ground.

The hydraulic columns hummed as they began to descend. It took Blake a moment to see exactly which aircraft the Russian President had chosen to bring. His official government transport, or one of his toys?

It turned out to be the latter. An Airbus A330neo, a quarter of a billion dollars' worth of opulence. And why not? It would just be trashed otherwise.

Stairs were driven to the side of the plane as the door opened. Once secured in place, Pertsov emerged, quickly followed by his wife. Behind them, four men in suits scanned the area for threats. Pertsov had insisted on bringing his own security team, despite Blake's insistence that it wasn't necessary. The entourage was followed by a man in uniform, Admiral Komarov. A last figure descended the stairs. He had a mole on his face and carried an attaché case.

A smile appeared on Blake's face.

Juggernaut.

The means to destroy the world contained in such a small package.

Blake walked over and hugged Pertsov, then kissed his wife's hand.

"Leonid, Nadia, welcome to Heliopolis. I hope you had a pleasant flight."

Pertsov looked back at the plane and smiled. "In this? Always."

Blake laughed. "Come, let me show you to your… slightly less elegant accommodation."

* * *

Eva saw General Sinclair return. He went straight to her cell and ordered the jailer to let him in. This time he sat immediately and leaned in close to her.

"Who else knows about this place?"

318

His voice was low. He clearly didn't want this conversation to be overheard by the jailer, who had returned to his desk.

"Again, why do you need to know?" Eva asked, matching his volume.

She could see him consider his words carefully. "Because I'm about to do something highly illegal, and the fewer people who know about it, the better."

"Well, I think everyone's going to notice in a few days, don't you think?"

Sinclair appeared exasperated. "Okay, forget about that. What's your involvement in Juggernaut?"

Eva saw no reason to lie. The shitstorm was on the horizon and heading their way. Whatever she said now would make no difference. "I was asked by President Robson to go to Russia to find Andrius Poska, the man who designed Juggernaut. My job was to bring him back and prevent it being completed."

"And you failed," Sinclair said, only it didn't sound like an accusation coming from him.

"Only half-failed," Eva corrected him. "I got Poska back, but the Russians got the software."

"I know. It's here, along with the Russian president."

Eva hadn't expected that. "What's he doing here?"

"He's about to light the blue touch paper," Sinclair said. He stood. "Thanks for letting me know what your intentions are."

The jailer unlocked the cell and Sinclair left.

# Chapter 51

Seddon Blake sat on his sofa opposite Leonid Pertsov. The two richest men in the world, worth close to a trillion dollars between them, sipping Billionaire vodka. Igor Cherenkov sat in a chair off to the side, having to make do with Stolichnaya. He hadn't left Pertsov's side since they boarded the plane. The four members of the Russian security detail stood near each corner of the room, which unnerved Blake. He was used to being master of his own house.

"Are you going to keep the same name, or pick something new?" Blake asked Pertsov.

"What do you mean?"

"Russia," Blake clarified. "Is it still going to be called Russia?"

"Of course. Why wouldn't it be?"

"I don't know. I'm thinking of changing America to something else. Maybe... Blakeland. Or Blaketopia."

"Are you serious?" Pertsov asked.

"Why not? It's the start of a new world. A new beginning. Why cling to the old names?"

Pertsov looked pensive. "You have a point, my friend. Maybe I will change the name. Pertsovia. Yes, I think that has a ring to it."

"Sir," Jake announced from the doorway, "dinner will commence in thirty minutes."

Blake waved him away. "That's fine. On an occasion like this, it won't hurt to be fashionably late. No point fighting for a shuttle, after all. Let everyone else get seated, then we'll make a move."

"I'll inform the chef," Jake said, and disappeared.

Blake poured two more glasses of vodka and handed one to Pertsov. "You know, I think I'm going to miss the old ways."

"What's to miss?" Pertsov replied. "Regulators telling you what your companies can or cannot do? Courts fining you for your employment practices?"

"You know what I mean. The thrill of the chase. Making that first billion, then the first ten billion, the first hundred billion. Once this is over, we'll have everything. Every building will be ours. Every road, every park, every blade of grass. There'll be nothing to aim for."

"That's a sad way to view being the ruler of half the planet," Pertsov said. "Think of the freedom to innovate. Didn't you have plans to implant microchips in offenders?"

"The behavioral inhibitors? Yes, but the FDA—"

"Will no longer be around to stop you," Pertsov finished.

Blake downed his vodka. "You make a good point. Come, let's eat."

\* \* \*

Eva wasn't expecting to see Sinclair again so soon. Was that good news, or bad? She wasn't sure, but she'd made up her mind that when the opportunity arose, she would pounce on him and rescue the others. They might not make it out, but better to die trying.

When the jailer opened the cell gate, Sinclair remained outside and gestured for her to join him. She watched the guard open Gray's cell, then move on to Farooq's.

"Where are we going?" Eva asked the general. "Time for our firing squad?"

"No," he said, walking out of the jail. "You risked your life to stop Juggernaut. I thought you might want a front row seat for tonight's performance."

"You're going to activate it now?" Eva asked. Her thoughts turned immediately to Sonny and Melissa. They would be caught in the middle of it.

Sinclair didn't answer her question. "There's someone you'll want to meet. I'll let you introduce yourself."

Eva stopped. "Either tell me what the hell is going on, or shoot me here."

Sinclair weighed up her demand. "Gladly."

\* \* \*

"I can't believe the size of this place," Igor Cherenkov whispered to Oleg, one of President Pertsov's bodyguards. He got no response, nor did he expect one. The four men were trained to focus solely on protecting their principal, despite being in such a safe environment.

The elevator stopped on the fifth level, where the restaurants and bars were situated.

"This way," Blake announced.

Cherenkov followed close behind Pertsov, the case containing his laptop in his left hand. There appeared to be a welcoming party waiting outside the restaurant.

"General Sinclair," Blake said haughtily. "I expected you to be seated by now. And why are you still in uniform?"

Cherenkov saw at least a dozen soldiers in combat gear standing behind the general, their weapons ready. Something wasn't right.

"I'm still in uniform because I am an officer in the United States Marine Corps," Sinclair announced. "And I'm here to shut you down. Hand over Juggernaut."

Blake laughed, the sound of a man unable to believe what he was hearing. "Are you serious? We're this close to reshaping the world and you're having a change of heart?"

"No, I haven't changed my mind. From the moment I signed on to this, my intention was to stop you, not help you. You see, while you identified the problem, you offered the wrong solution. The situation in this country is getting worse each year, that's true, but we both know the reason why."

"Enlighten me," Blake said.

"You," Sinclair said, "and the people inside that restaurant. People with more money than they can ever spend, living every waking moment to make even more. The problem in this country—in the entire world—is greed, pure and simple.

"You're delusional," Blake scoffed.

"No, I'm a patriot. And so is this lady."

Cherenkov watched a woman step out from behind the group of soldiers. "Hi," she waved and smiled. "I'm Nolene Daniels."

Cherenkov immediately recognized her as the woman who had tried to kill him in the café in Kazan. Pertsov seemed to know her, too.

Cherenkov heard the President whisper a command, and his bodyguards sprang into action. They drew their weapons and began firing on the soldiers, taking three down in the first volley. People scattered in all directions as more shots rang out, and Cherenkov knew it was time to make himself scarce.

Clutching the case to his chest, he ran into a restaurant, past empty tables and into the kitchen. As he reached the door, he heard pounding footsteps behind him. It was Pertsov and one of his bodyguards.

"Activate Juggernaut!" the President screamed.

The target list had already been uploaded, so all Cherenkov had to do was set it in motion. Not an easy task while fleeing for his life.

"Get him to hold them off," Cherenkov told his president. The bodyguard did as he was ordered, while Cherenkov put the case on a countertop and opened it. He double-clicked the Juggernaut icon and waited for it to load. There was no password to enter, just a green button with START written on it. Cherenkov clicked it and saw the progress bar appear.

"It's running," he told Pertsov, and stuffed the laptop under his arm.

"Make sure it finishes. If they get that laptop, this will all be for nothing."

Cherenkov knew that, too. If the laptop was damaged or someone ended the program, this entire venture would have been a fantastically expensive waste of time. It wouldn't end well for him, either.

A shot missed Cherenkov's head by a millimeter. He ran through a service door and into a corridor that fed all of the venues on the strip. He had to hide the laptop. It would take many hours to complete the target list, and he couldn't run for that long.

Cherenkov barged into one of the side doors. It was another kitchen, also empty, and he spotted his hiding place: a large laundry chute in the wall.

Cherenkov didn't hesitate, diving in headfirst, the laptop stretched out in front of him. It was much steeper than he'd envisaged, almost vertical. He used his knees and feet to slow his fall through the pitch-black tunnel. He felt his ears pop as he dropped farther and farther into the facility, until he saw a glimmer of light ahead. The opening rushed toward him, and he fell out of the chute into a basket filled with used tablecloths.

Cherenkov got his breath back and took stock. He doubted anyone would follow him down that way, but if they'd seen him go in, they would know where he was headed. He needed to hide the laptop somewhere, anywhere, to let it complete its work, and he didn't have much time.

The laundry room was in full swing, with scores of workers filling and emptying giant machines while others ironed, folded and stacked.

Cherenkov ran past them and through a door that led into another hallway. The first door he entered appeared to be a kitchenette, and he saw where to leave Juggernaut. Pulling a stool over, he climbed up and placed the laptop on top of a wall cabinet. When he jumped down, he was sure no one would be able to see it from ground level. By the time anyone discovered it, it would be too late.

All he had to do now was get out alive.

* * *

Eva ran through the open door and into the empty kitchen. There was no sign of Cherenkov, but she heard something coming from her right. She edged closer to the laundry chute and heard the squeal of rubber on metal. It had to be him. Eva pulled a trolley over, sat on it and put her feet into the chute. Easing herself in with the rifle she'd taken from a dead soldier clutched to her chest, she let herself fall.

When the descent ended in a pile of linen, Eva found herself in the laundry room. She got to her feet.

"Where did he go?" she shouted.

Many fingers pointed in the direction of the exit, and Eva ran through it.

Straight into Igor Cherenkov.

They both fell sideways, with Eva slamming into a fire extinguisher mounted on the wall. Her shoulder screamed in agony, but she had no time to worry about it. Her rifle had fallen from her grasp and it lay halfway between her and Cherenkov. He was already on his feet and reaching for it. Knowing she wouldn't beat him to it, Eva grabbed the fire extinguisher and threw it at him. He deflected the blow with his forearm, but that gave Eva the second she needed. She dived for the gun and got a couple of fingers on the stock, but Cherenkov kicked the rifle sideways and then aimed a boot at her head. Eva rolled onto her back and the foot flew past her face. She brought her knees up to her chest and launched herself to her feet. The moment she landed, she spun and delivered a roundhouse kick to Cherenkov's sternum. It knocked him backward, but he came back for more, raining blows and kicks that Eva easily blocked. When he attempted a roundhouse punch, Eva slipped underneath it, let the arm fly over her head, then threw all her weight behind a punch to his throat.

Cherenkov spluttered and grasped at the invisible hands choking him. He fell to his knees, trying in vain to get his crushed larynx to work.

Eva heard his last breaths, and he toppled sideways, unseeing eyes wide in death.

Only now did she realize that Cherenkov no longer had the laptop. She'd seen him bent over it in the restaurant, but now it was gone. He must have ditched it somewhere between the fifth floor and here, but where? The corridor she was in stretched for hundreds of yards in both directions. He could have put it anywhere.

Eva ran back into the laundry and asked how to get to the fifth floor. One of the workers pointed her toward an elevator. Eva got a staff member to activate it with their wristband, then rode it to the restaurant level. She entered a random kitchen and walked through to the dining area. From there she could see a gaggle of soldiers standing over kneeling prisoners. Eva walked out and saw a long line of them, all with their arms tied behind their backs with plasticuffs.

"There you are," Sinclair said. "Where's the laptop?"

"That's what I came to tell you. He stowed it somewhere. I need as many men as you can spare to help me find it."

Sinclair told a nearby sergeant to give her a hundred troops and more if she needed them.

"Get the first thirty to meet me in that kitchen," Eva said. "I'll give them their search area, then take the rest downstairs to the laundry."

# Chapter 52

It was seven the following morning when they found the laptop. Over three hundred men and women ended up joining the search, but the eventual discovery was a bittersweet moment. The screen showed that Juggernaut had finished. Its target list was executed. Above their heads, the world was about to change forever.

General Franklin Sinclair ordered Colonel Dooley to have men monitoring the fallout.

"One thing puzzles me," Eva said to the General as they stood in the Heliopolis command center. "You told me how Xavier recruited you, and then helped to pick the four thousand men to join you. How did you convince so many people to change their mind?"

"I didn't," Sinclair told her. "Those men are back at camp, awaiting orders that will never come. The men I brought with me are loyal."

That was a nice move. "So, what now?" she asked. While it was safe inside the facility, she was desperate to get back to Sonny. Gray and Farooq, sitting in operators' chairs and keeping up to date with their loved ones, also had reasons to leave.

"We wait," he said, scanning through personnel files on a tablet. "Blake brought people in who would know how to turn the power back on. Our first task is to have them assemble, ready to go. As power stations fall, we'll go and try to get them back online. Same with water and communications."

"But how long do we wait? We all have people on the outside."

"Appreciated, but I'm not going to make a move until we know the extent of the damage. The first reports should be coming in soon."

Five screens had been repurposed as televisions, each one hosting a different news channel. At the top of the hour, the lead story on each was the mysterious video that had interrupted all stations in the US earlier that morning.

"That's Cherenkov," Eva said.

The clip looked to have been taken by the laptop camera, and along the bottom of the screen a text crawl showed a list of utility companies and a progress counter for each one.

It was two hours later before CNN news reported that an electricity generating station had been taken offline. It was in Kostroma Oblast, three hundred kilometers from Moscow.

"Sir, a water company has reported going offline. Again, in Russia."

"Nothing Stateside?" Sinclair asked.

"Nothing yet, sir."

They watched for another three hours, but the closest they got to a national disaster was a burst water main on Rodeo Drive. In the meantime, the news channels were reporting major outages throughout Russia.

"I don't get it," Eva said to Gray.

"Me neither. Melissa says there's nothing on the news and everything's working properly. Was it set to delay?"

"Could have been. General, any chance you could contact a major power company and ask if they've had any cyber attacks in the last few hours?"

"That wouldn't be a good idea," he said.

Eva thought that strange. "Why not?"

"Because they would ask why I, a Marine officer, was interested. What do I tell them?"

It was a good question. There would be no need for a military officer to request that information.

"Then what do we do?" Eva asked. "Just sit here forever?"

"You told me that you brought Andrius Poska home. Is that right?"

"Sort of. We got him out, but he was in a coma. They took him to Helsinki."

"Then get someone to wake him up and ask what the hell is going on."

# Chapter 53

It was a few hours later when General Sinclair declared the emergency over. Not a single national utility company had been affected by Juggernaut, though reports were coming in of increasing outages inside Russia.

"Hey," Farooq said, showing Eva the tablet he was holding. "Guess who I found in the personnel list?"

"Elvis?"

"No, Paul Heaton. The guy from NID who sold you out."

"Maybe I'll pay him a visit before we leave," Eva said. "Wish him better luck next time."

Eva's phone rang. It was the hospital she'd been calling since noon.

"Hello."

"Is this Nolene?" a woman's voice asked.

"Yes."

"I am Sofija. Sofija Poska."

"Hi," Eva said. "How are you and Claire doing?"

"We're okay. Andrius woke up. He said to tell you, 'only Russia.'"

*Only Russia?*

"Did he say anything else?" Eva asked.

"No. He is sleeping again. He is very weak. I… I want to thank you for all you did for us."

"Don't mention it," Eva said. "Sorry, but I have to go. I'll be in touch as soon as I can."

She ended the call before Sofija could respond.

*Only Russia* fit with what was happening right now. No other country seemed to have been affected by Juggernaut.

She took this thought to Sinclair.

"When we rescued him in Kazan, I tried to grab the laptop. He told me to leave it. Maybe he knew it wouldn't affect us."

"It could be," the General said. "I guess we'll only know when he's been debriefed. In the meantime, I think it's time we pulled out."

"I agree," Eva said. "Who's coming to deal with the occupants? The FBI? Local police?"

"No one," Sinclair said, looking her dead in the eye.

Eva was about to ask if he was going to just let them go, but the truth suddenly hit her. They weren't going anywhere. "You're going to seal them in."

"Exactly. No one outside of my men and your friends know that this place exists. Sure, people will miss them, and investigations will take place, but no relative is going to come out and say 'hey, they're in Heliopolis.'"

"Surely their aircraft will have been traced to here."

"Undoubtedly. But if anyone comes to investigate, all they'll find is a big crater and lots of twisted metal. A tragic accident."

"You're going to destroy it," Eva said slowly.

"That's right. My men are setting charges as we speak. There's a huge reservoir of gasoline down on level ten that'll go up nicely. The blast from that should bring the whole place down on top of itself, but just to be sure, we're setting more at all the structural weak points, such as load-bearing columns, and we're going to cave in every exit so no one gets out before it blows."

"You'll kill everyone," Eva noted, thinking of the laundry staff, the waiters, the cleaners. Had they really done enough to deserve that fate?

"If you're wondering if anyone should be spared, the answer's no. Every single person in this facility was invited in. They had a chance to say no. They knew what they were signing up for and they made their decision. They can't go back just because it didn't work out in their favor. Besides, if we let anyone go, they'll talk. One might be dismissed as a crank, two could still be ignored, but in large enough numbers, someone will start listening. And what will they say? That I was here, and so were my men... and so were you."

It didn't sit well with Eva, but Sinclair was right. Heliopolis had to be destroyed, and those who had been willing to benefit from it deserved the fate they were willing to inflict on others.

"Even Seddon Blake?" Eva asked.

"Especially Seddon Blake. He's already down on level nine along with the other men and women who funded this monstrosity. My men are sending everyone else down there now. Once we detonate, my men and I will cancel our war games and return to base."

Eva couldn't help thinking there were loose ends that needed tying. "What about your men? Are you sure none of them will talk about this?"

"They won't," Sinclair assured her. "The only ones who have been inside are busy setting charges. If they talk, they implicate themselves. Who wants tens of thousands of murder charges hanging over them?"

Eva couldn't fault that logic.

A soldier approached and saluted the General. "Sir, Major Wells reports that the last of the prisoners are on their way down to level nine and the animal evacuation is almost complete."

"Roger that," Sinclair said. He turned to Eva. "I'm about to go and say my goodbyes to Blake. Wanna tag along?"

"Would I ever. But first, I have one request."

"What's that?" Sinclair asked.

"I need Juggernaut. President Robson asked me to bring it home. I'd hate to go back empty-handed."

# Chapter 54

Eva and Sinclair took the elevator down to the ninth floor. The moment the doors opened, Eva was transported back to her youth, when she would drive past farms on her way to school. The smell was exactly the same. Some things may change over time, but not the stench of animal shit.

They stepped out to see scores of soldiers hard at work, loading pigs into the huge freight elevator. Beyond them, thousands of people stood around, armed soldiers watching their every move.

"We're letting these guys go," Sinclair told her. "More precisely, we're taking them to nearby farms. Same with the sheep, cows, chickens, and horses."

Eva thought that a nice touch. The only real animals that deserved to die in this place were Blake and his minions.

The gates to the freight elevator closed and it rose to the surface.

"Seddon Blake!" Sinclair boomed in his commanding voice.

Eva saw Blake emerge from a smaller group of people near the left-hand wall. Even in the end times, the rich stuck together.

Sinclair walked over to Blake, who looked defiant.

"What did you hope to achieve by bringing us all down here, General?"

"Equity," Sinclair said. "Parity. Call it what you will."

"I call it bullshit." He sniffed. "Or maybe pig shit. Hard to tell."

"No, that's the smell of greed," Sinclair said.

The freight elevator arrived. When the gates opened, Eva saw that it was full of people. The soldiers ordered them out one at a time and searched them. Any cell phones were confiscated and thrown into a sack.

Eva saw Paul Heaton, head down and looking miserable. She considered confronting him about his actions, but that seemed petty now. He would soon learn the consequences.

"Greed is normal, General," Blake said. "In fact, it's an asset. It motivates people, spurs them on. Nothing great in this country would have happened without greed. No company innovates simply to make the world a better place. They do it to make more money. Can't you see that? Without greed, we wouldn't have cell phones, flat-screen TVs, electric cars."

"Or poverty," Sinclair countered. "Or homelessness, or people being denied life-saving healthcare to protect the insurance company's bottom line. You're a man of numbers. How long would it take you to spend your half-trillion dollars, assuming you burned through ten million a day?"

Blake appeared to be struggling with the math, so Sinclair helped him out. "A hundred and thirty-six years. And how much do you actually spend a day? Not on yachts or houses. You've got plenty of those. How much does it cost you to live your current lifestyle? A hundred grand a day? A million? If it's a million, then it would take you over seven thousand years to burn through it all. Yet you just want more. Tell me that's just."

Blake looked furious. "I earned that money!"

"I know," Sinclair said, "but at what cost?"

The question seemed to confuse Blake.

"I know veterans, people I served with, who have to rely on food stamps and Medicaid because the corporations won't pay a living wage, even though they announce record profits every year. It's not that they can't, it's that they choose not to. The argument Xavier made to me was that decreasing living standards would eventually lead to a revolution, yet you and all the people behind you are the ones responsible for the current situation."

Blake put his hands on his hips. "And you wait until now, just before we're about to launch, to tell me all this?"

"Of course," Sinclair replied. "It was pointed out to me by your friend Xavier that if I tried to blow the whistle, no one would believe me and my career would be over. That's if I could even find someone who wasn't on the guest list. I figured I'd wait until everyone was here. That way, no one escapes justice."

"Justice?" Blake scoffed. "My lawyers will have a field day with you."

"I know. The system is rigged in your favor. If this went to trial, I wouldn't put it past you to bribe the judge, the jury, or even the prosecutor. You'd probably walk away without so much as a fine."

"Exactly," Blake said, triumphantly, but then Sinclair watched his expression change. The smile faded, replaced by concern. "What do you mean, *if* this went to trial?"

"I mean just that. You see, in my line of work, we evaluate probable outcomes before making decisions. In this case, the outcome of you going before a judge is that you'll most likely walk. Therefore, I'm taking a different approach."

Blake hesitated before asking the obvious question. "Which is?"

"Gather you all in here and bring the roof down on your heads."

There was stunned silence for a brief moment, then Robert J. Portman stepped forward.

"You can't do this! My uncle was the President, and so was my great uncle. We have rights!"

"Yeah, you forfeited those rights when you conspired to kill hundreds of millions of Americans," Eva jumped in. "You and everyone in here knew the cost of launching Juggernaut, but you were willing to do it anyway. Time to pay the price."

Portman ran at her as fast as his old legs would allow, pure rage etched on his face.

It remained there in death.

Sinclair removed his pistol and shot Portman in the forehead. As the old body flopped to the ground, Sinclair turned the gun on Seddon Blake. "We're going now. I'd offer you the crumb of comfort that perhaps someone might come to rescue you, but sadly, no one knows you're down here. Ain't that a shame."

"General, you're about to make the biggest mistake of your life. Think of the money you could have. Half of my fortune! Yes, yes, I'll give you half of it. All you have to do is let me go." He turned and waved at the throng behind him. "Never mind them. Do what you want with them, but you have to save me." He turned back to Sinclair, eyes pleading. "Please!"

Sinclair lowered his weapon. "All of it."

Blake looked stunned. "What?"

"I want all of it," Sinclair said.

Blake considered it, his mind working overtime. He suddenly smiled. "Sure, sure, all of it."

Sinclair produced an envelope from his jacket pocket. From it, he pulled out a few sheets of paper, unfolded and handed them to Blake, along with a pen. "Sign that."

"What's this?" Blake asked.

Sinclair ignored the question and addressed the crowd of VIPs. "Anyone here an attorney?"

A hand went up, and Sinclair beckoned him forward.

"That's a durable power of attorney," Sinclair told Blake. "It gives me complete control of all your assets."

Blake gulped.

"Or were you just lying about giving me everything?" Sinclair said.

Blake appeared torn.

"Five seconds," Sinclair declared. "Your money or your life."

While Blake hesitated, Sinclair began his countdown. When he reached two, Blake grabbed the envelope from Sinclair and snatched the pen from his hand. "You win." He signed the document on the last page, then handed it to the attorney who had appeared at his side.

The man began to read it, but Sinclair pointed the gun at him. "Sign it."

The attorney did so, then backed away.

Sinclair checked the signatures, then refolded the papers and replaced them in the envelope. "Thanks," he said to Blake. "These charities will be most appreciative, I'm sure."

"What?"

"The VAA, Save the Children, Greenpeace, and a host of others," Sinclair smiled. "You just signed everything over to them. You see, not all of us are motivated by greed. The people behind you, though, seem to be motivated by your betrayal. Good luck with that."

Eva and Sinclair watched as the angry mob closed in on Blake.

"Now, wait a minute. I was going to help you, too, obviously…"

Eva couldn't hear the rest of Blake's pleading as raucous cries drowned out his words.

Sinclair backed into the elevator, and Eva followed. The rest of the soldiers formed a defensive line in front of them until the gates closed.

"Sorry you had to witness that," Sinclair said as the car began to rise.

"Are you kidding? If you hadn't been there, I would have done a lot worse."

Sinclair looked at her, his eyebrows furrowed. "Who the hell are you?"

Eva sighed. "Trust me, you don't wanna know."

# Chapter 55

Eva, Gray and Farooq helped themselves to one of the electric cars on the transport level. Eva checked that it had a decent charge, though their journey would be short. They would drive out to the wasteland, pick up the rental car, then return it to the dealership in Las Vegas. From there, they would book a flight to Dulles.

Sinclair met them on the transport level. "You sure you don't want to take anything else?" he asked. "I'd say you earned it."

"We're sure," Eva told him. "It's a shame the artwork has to be destroyed, but if anyone's caught with it or tries to sell it, it would invite too many questions."

"Don't worry about that," Sinclair said. "We're going to go through the place with a fine-toothed comb. Everything of value will be taken and stored in a secure facility. The following day, I'll move it again. I'll anonymously reveal its location in a few years, but just in case I die suddenly, it'll also be in my will. Hopefully, the government will put them in museums for the whole world to share."

"Nice touch," Eva said, offering Sinclair her hand. "And thank you, General. It's reassuring to know there are still good people in the world."

He shook it, and Eva got in the car.

Gray drove them to the landing platform, where a couple of Humvees were waiting. They rose to the surface, just as the first light of the day broke the horizon.

"What time did he say they were going to blow it?" Farooq asked.

"Midday," Gray replied.

"Wanna hang around and watch?"

Gray looked at Eva.

"Sure," they said in unison.

\* \* \*

From their vantage point high on a hill, the trio watched as the last of the military vehicles left the compound through the main gate. It was ten minutes to twelve.

"You know the saddest part about all of this?" Farooq mused.

"What's that?" Eva asked.

"It shows that man is capable of great things, yet such insufferable selfishness at the same time. It's no wonder the world is in turmoil."

"Don't get all philosophical on me," Gray said. "I'm just here for the big bang."

"You get what I mean, though, right?"

"I do," Gray replied, "but the rich and powerful have a vested interest in the status quo, so little is going to change."

"Yeah, but most of the rich and powerful are down there, and in… six minutes they won't be rich or powerful anymore."

"Maybe not," Gray conceded, "but that money will be inherited by others who'll take their place."

"Not all of it," Eva said. She recounted Sinclair's actions on the ninth level. "He got Blake to sign his entire fortune over to a couple of dozen charities. That money will go to worthy causes."

"Ooh, I bet that hurt," Farooq smiled.

"Yeah, Blake didn't seem too pleased."

The ground shook beneath them, and the trio looked out over the valley below as a sound like distant thunder reached their ears. Farooq expected a fountain of fire, but he was disappointed. The ground beneath the solitary building sank, throwing up a cloud of dust.

They waited for it to settle.

All that remained was a crater a hundred yards deep and a thousand yards wide.

"That's it?" Farooq asked, disappointed.

"That's it," Gray confirmed. "No one's getting out of that alive."

"Come on," Eva said, standing. She held up the laptop containing Juggernaut. "I've got to deliver this to the President."

# Epilogue

Eva exited the elevator and strode down the corridor to the private room. As with most US hospitals, the smell of disinfectant hung in the air. She found Room Four easily enough. It was the one with two heavies standing outside it, pretending not to be armed security. Eva showed one of them a pass that had been given to her, and he stepped aside. Eva knocked.

"Come in."

Eva entered and saw Sofija and Claire Poska in chairs next to Andrius's bed. He was sitting up, eating lunch from a plastic tray. His eyes lit up.

"That's her!"

Sofija and her daughter threw themselves at Eva, hugging her tight enough to restrict her breathing.

"Hey, calm down," Eva laughed. They eventually backed off, and saw tears in Sofija's eyes.

"Thank you. For saving us. All of us."

"Don't mention it," Eva said. "I just popped by to make sure you were okay. President Robson told me you were here."

Eva's debrief had been a challenge. Should she tell him the truth about Heliopolis, or let him believe what the news channels were reporting, that it was a tragic accident, an explosion that investigators were trying to get to the bottom of? After discussing it with Sonny and the others, Eva decided to play dumb. Being open would implicate Sinclair and his men, without whom the ending would have been a lot different.

"We're fine," Andrius said. "I should be out of here in a few days."

"And Claire?" Eva asked the little girl. "How are you doing?"

Sofija sat and pulled Claire onto her lap. "She's fine. She lost the finger, obviously, but no other lasting damage."

"You're such a brave girl," Eva said to Claire. She looked at Sofija. "Could I have a word with Andrius…?"

Sofija got the hint. "Sure. Come on, Claire, let's go and see if we can find a vending machine with decent candy."

They left, and one of the security detail walked down the corridor with them.

"I can't thank you enough," Andrius said when they were gone. "They are everything to me."

"I can tell," Eva said. She sat on the side of the bed. "So, what exactly did you do to Juggernaut? The President said you'd been debriefed, but I thought it better to hear it from you."

The fallout had been all over the news for the last few days. She knew what he'd done, but not how.

"Well, when you first tried to rescue me, I knew I had a small window to make some changes to the software without Cherenkov watching over my shoulder. I altered one of the libraries that would disregard all commands entered and instead do what I had pre-programmed."

"Which was?"

"Once a certain date and time was reached, a copy of the software was uploaded to the Camber Blair servers, and it would run from there. That way, if anyone tried to stop it

345

by destroying the laptop, it wouldn't do any good. It would read the list of targets and ignore them if they weren't inside Russia. If none of the targets on the list were Russian, it would attack my own list of key Russian installations. The oil companies, electric power stations, water, gas, communications, everything I could think of. Cherenkov told me it would go live on the Thursday, so I set the check date to two days earlier."

That certainly worked. The only areas to suffer any cyber attacks had been inside Russia. The country had been brought to its knees, but not before the culprit appeared on every television in the world.

"Don't worry, though. I have nothing against the Russian people. The systems will come back online in about four hours. It was only ever a temporary measure."

"And Cherenkov's TV debut?" Eva asked.

"Ah, yes. I wanted the world to know who had done it. I thought it might be Pertsov himself, but that was too much to ask for. I told the software to record the user whenever Juggernaut was activated and stream it live over every TV channel the software could find. It found a lot, apparently."

"It did indeed. Everywhere from Alaska to Australia. Nice touch."

"Thanks. The Russians were sure to say it was the Americans who had crippled their country, but with proof like that, their accusations will fall on deaf ears."

"Hasn't stopped them trying," Eva said. "They're claiming it's an AI deep fake."

"Yes, I saw that this morning. Doesn't make them any less guilty in the world's eyes, though. I notice Pertsov hasn't had anything to say on the matter."

*Nor will he ever*, Eva thought. "Yeah, strange."

"I was told that it was one of your friends who found me. Traced my data packages when I logged onto the work server?"

"Something like that," Eva said. "He's the tech-savvy one, not me."

"Well, please thank him, too. And if he ever needs a job, I'm sure I can get him something at Camber Blair."

Eva smiled. "They couldn't afford him."

## THE END

If you would like to be informed of new releases, simply send an email with "Times" in the subject line to jambalian@outlook.com to be added to the mailing list. Alan only sends emails when a new book is coming out, so you won't be bombarded with spam. You can find all of Alan's books and the reading order at http://www.alanmcdermottbooks.co.uk/.

Printed in Dunstable, United Kingdom